Sipson's Island

Katherine Nora

Cover artwork by Katherine Nora

ISBN 978-0-359-81509-8

Chapter One

Try telling someone that you once had a conversation with an individual who lived a couple hundred years ago, and of course no one will believe you. The kindest will indulge you for a while, ask a few polite questions and hope the conversation swerves to a more manageable topic. No one has yet taken me seriously so I've learned not to bring it up, but it's true, and as time passes I find I can't let such a remarkable story remain untold. I've been persuaded by my friend Theo, who was there, to write about those months on the bay, and so I will try to set it all down here as accurately and coherently as possible.

I'm more of a painter than a writer. I've never kept a journal or even written a passable essay in college but Theo, who is a journalist, told me to start from the beginning and try not to be creative and metaphorical, just say what happened in my own way. Well, my own way *is* creative and metaphorical, but I know what he means.

My name is Elli, short for Ellinor, which is actually my middle name. My first name, the godawful Eugenia, a family name, is only here for the record. I was born in New York, but grew up in Paris. I suppose a good place to start my story is the spring of 1968. I was twenty, an otherwise unremarkable French girl attending Bard college in New York, trying to take my studies seriously and keep my grades up but also manage a social life, which is ultimately what got me into trouble and started this whole adventure.

It was May Day. I was sneaking back across the campus to my dorm after a forbidden overnight in the room of my then boyfriend. The night before he'd taught me the famous ditty about the first of May, and we spent hours joking about where the best spot on campus would be for carrying out the tradition, in between bouts of practicing for it. Bard College is a very good school but I was not yet "living up to potential," as my father had written to me only a month earlier. I don't know how he knew that, but he was right. I spent a lot of my time smoking grass and listening to music with my new American friends. I didn't take attending classes very seriously, because the impression I had of Americans was that they didn't either, and I wanted badly to integrate. They seemed to do everything with unconcerned ease and much laughter, as if all was obtainable and would come to them with only the slightest bit of effort. I had latched onto a group of students who fooled around playing music, and soon began a little affair with a piano player named Don whose sensuous lips rippled like a bivalve filtering seawater, but his chin was covered in thick black stubble. His kisses were painful, literally, so even after a winter of passionate necking we had not progressed much beyond that stage.

On the grounds of Bard there is a little pond which is a perfect ellipse, a shiny black mirror level with the surrounding lawn. That morning, on the way back to my dorm room, I paused to look because the sunrise had turned its surface a luminous orange, arresting against the vivid, chemically-enhanced green. I scolded myself for the wasted precious hours I'd spent fooling around instead of seriously preparing for my future, and I stood there vowing to change my ways. As I murmured a pledge to the divine light on the little pond I became aware of a presence across from me and looked up. It was a boy we called Tonto, who worked in the administration building. He was called that because of his hair which was long and black and held in place with a leather headband across his forehead, like the character from The Lone Ranger. Now that I think of it, it's fitting that he was there at the beginning of this story. It's just the kind of synchronous detail that doesn't seem so random to me anymore.

"A telegram came for you," he said, and walked around the pond to hand it over. He waited for me to rip it open, then hurried away. Maybe he knew. It was from my mother, a message that my father had died, and flight details for the trip home to Paris.

I went back and stayed for three days, moving in a fog of misery wherever someone guided me, from the apartment to the church to the gravesite and back. Throughout the ordeal I kept picturing the ellipse pond. I saw myself standing there again, but I'd direct a different scenario, a boring one which involved nothing more than me walking back to the dorm room to study. I visualized it over and over. I was miserable about my father's death, but

3

my mother was shattered, inconsolable. She sent everyone away after the funeral and went directly to bed. My father had died so suddenly and had been buried so swiftly that I hadn't had time to begin even the first stage of grief. Which one is that, anyway, shock? I just looked it up: denial. I should have guessed. I'm not sure I have progressed much further. At any rate I was left with my mother's grief which turned her into an all-consuming life form, a cocoon with huge eyes that opened now and then to look beseechingly at me before spilling over with tears. My sister Charlotte, who had also been summoned home from school, stayed in her room with a stash of chocolate and other comfort foods and was on the way to adding a few more kilos to her already chubby nineteen year old body. Of course I loved my sister and mother, but neither one seemed to know that my father and I had an exclusive bond, a type of attachment they were not privy to. I was officially alone.

I left Paris abruptly, on impulse, desperate to get away. I didn't even say goodbye. I changed my ticket at the airport and took off back to New York. My mother had bought the ticket so I could fly to Paris, attend my father's funeral and spend some time at home before going back to school, even though at that point there were only five weeks left before summer break. She thought I'd need some time to digest the fact of my father's death and assume my own version of a pupal stage for a while, but I wanted out. Before I left I had enough sense to write myself a check from my father's account, fake his signature, take it to the bank and exchange the francs for dollars. I was ashamed of my duplicitous behavior, but I could live with that. My mother would understand, I told myself.

This was on the 5th of May. The next day thousands of students marched in protest against the government, which

4

led eventually to a complete social revolution in that country and which I would have liked to have been a part of, since I considered myself French. If I had gone to the bank a day later it would have been closed because of the riots. That would have made running away difficult, so I might very well have stayed and been caught up in the events of that time, and I would not be writing this now.

As it happened that wasn't the worst of it. When I got back to school I found a letter pinned to my door. It was from the dean, expelling me and another girl for being discovered after curfew in bed with our boyfriends. Though Don and most of the student body had protested and sided with us against our informers, it was too late. Letters had already been sent to our parents.

I couldn't possibly go back to Paris. I didn't know if the letter from Bard expelling me had even reached there, but my mother's grief and my sister's disconnect were a formidable entity combined, not to mention the painful presence of my father's collections, his smell, his love, and all the memories of my childhood which I had fled on such a self-protective impulse. I thought briefly of getting on a train to join all the freaks streaming toward San Francisco, but something held me back. Perhaps it was the added distance from France, or merely a fear of stepping outside my cosseted life.

I did have a place to go, though, a place which had popped into my mind a few times since moving to America, a house I dreamed I might one day visit under much different circumstances. It was the summer house my father had bought when he and my mother were first married and were both still Americans, before they moved the family to France. There is a small painting of this house in our Paris apartment. It shows a little shingled cottage perched on a

5

bluff overlooking the water in a place called Pleasant Bay on Cape Cod, in Massachusetts. I didn't know much about Cape Cod except that it was north along the coast from New York, that it had beautiful beaches, and that it was where my mother had first learned to paint. My father often said that we would go back there one day.

I took off from Bard with the same suitcase I'd packed for the funeral. I left behind a beautiful cashmere coat and a pair of fur-lined boots which would keep some lucky girl very warm that winter, but I was not thinking of the weather or anything sensible then. I fled, simply kept on traveling. That way I would not have to stop and consider what I was actually doing.

At Penn Station I bought a train ticket which would take me through Connecticut and Rhode Island to New Bedford, Massachusetts, as close as I could get to Cape Cod. The lady at the ticket office told me I'd have to find a bus from there. While I waited in the station I stood in front of a large wall map of southern New England and traced my route. I thought all the place names quite complicated and exotic and I tried to feel adventurous and nonchalant like my friends at Bard. After all, it was America, and I was technically an American. But when the train left the city and began its trek northeast along the coast I felt a little uneasy being away from the city, but I thought about all the times my father had described this trip to me. Remembering his words and imagining him driving his car along this same route to a place called Provincetown at the tip of the Cape Cod peninsula made me feel connected to him, and that made me more certain about my hasty decision.

"It's where God goes for his holidays," he used to say.

My father, Achilles Nikolaos Overton, was one of those larger than life men who easily commanded attention, yet he never took it for granted. He didn't seem to be aware of his considerable charm or the power he radiated solely by existing, and often spoke of others as if their friendship was a favor granted to him, when I could tell it was mostly the other way around. He and my mother both made a living in the world of fine art. My mother is the painter Ria Bang Overton, whom you may have heard of, but my father was more of a behind-the-scenes person. I don't know exactly what he called his profession but it had to do with the buying and selling of valuable *objets d'art* which, for most of my life, filled all the available spaces in our apartment in Rue Fremicourt in an ever-changing display. I would often come home from school to find him sitting at the dining room table polishing some knob of gold or holding his cigarette out of the way while leafing gingerly through an old manuscript that permeated the air with the smell of mildew.

"Careful," he would say as I bent to kiss his cheek. "Don't drool on the page!"

My sister and I usually ate in the kitchen because the dining room table was covered with books, papers, rolled tapestries, carved boxes, gold statuettes and other un-crated marvels. Thickets of packing excelsior covered the floor and piled in little drifts around the table legs. Often there would be someone sitting with my father and we would overhear murmuring praise, the negotiation of a deal in hushed, deferential tones. Though he conducted his business in French we spoke English in our household, and my father with a pronounced Greek accent, he being originally from that part of the world. He used to mumble to himself in Greek when one of us annoyed him, or when my mother got the better of him in an argument. His French was heavily accented, too, but it sounded exotic and enhanced his image as an urbane connoisseur. When we were little we weren't allowed in the dining room, but as we got older and could keep our hands to ourselves he showed us many wondrous things from all over the world. I wish now I had paid more attention to what passed through that room and less to our television screen, but I was a teenager, so how could I have known?

My mother was not around much. She had her studio in the back of the apartment and it was where she spent most of her time. If we wanted something or needed to talk to her we tiptoed down the hall and gingerly pushed the door open a crack. If she was sitting in her chair with a cigarette it was OK to enter and talk with her, but if she was painting, forget it. She worked in a trance of concentration, often for hours at a time while listening to American jazz on scratched LPs. You could stand there and try to get her attention and you might get a "Mm-hmm," but it didn't mean she heard you. It was all right for us girls to stay and watch and I found it spellbinding. To me her paintings looked like giant, smeary messes. In fact, they were often made by using her fingers to move the paint around. In my naive way I saw that she was painting her own sort of alternate reality and that excited me, but wasn't until later in my life that I truly understood what she had accomplished and why she was so famous. While I was growing up she seemed to be selfishly unavailable and I was jealous that her paintings and Charlie Parker got most of her attention. Every once in a while she'd appear at the kitchen table when my sister and I were eating supper which very often was a bowl of chocolate Blédine, a baby cereal we refused to outgrow, accompanied by a piece of ham or some other meat. Our cook was under instructions to always include some vegetables, but since our mother so seldom made an appearance the salad or cooked tomatoes sat untouched. When our mother sat with us she would pick at them, and we'd feel honored by her participation. Now and then she'd be in between works of art and we would get her for a few days. Those were fun. When we were little she would take us to Montmartre to walk around the cemetery, which I found creepy, or to ride the funicular railway. I liked to run down the steps, racing my sister to the bottom. We would ride the metro to Buttes-Chaumont park to stand barefoot in the manmade streams, letting the water rush over our toes. At the end of the day we would meet our father at the Cafe de la Paix where it seemed he had a permanent table. I always sat next to him, and people would gaze at us admiringly as I sipped my *limonade*. When we were older, if it was our cook's day off, we loved to accompany our mother when she shopped at the open-air market, a place where you could see horrible things like a man walking with a skinned and hoofless calf slung over his shoulder, and my mother would point out the marvelous creative beauty in the painstaking displays of dried fruit, flowers, and pastries. Before I was sent to Bard and still attending Université at Nanterre, my mother would now and then meet me at one of the numerous outdoor booksellers to browse the displays while we talked. She loved to look at reproductions protected by tissue paper in moldy old art books. I used the opportunity for serious talk without the presence of my sister. I wasn't very happy at school, and wanted badly to drop out. My father was aware of my feelings and had been hinting around about switching me to Bard College in New York, his alma mater.

He said it was a haven for European intellectuals, and had just expanded its curriculum to include the visual arts, so he was working on getting my mother to agree to send me there. One Saturday she and I were standing at one of the bookstalls flipping through the stacks and discussing this very issue, when she pulled from the pile a fat volume of American poetry. She briefly perused the index before opening the book to a poem by Henry David Thoreau. She read "The Fisher's Boy," to herself, her lips moving slowly. Then she slammed the book shut and said, "You know, I think your father is right. You should go to school where you will be happy." That was it. Months later in the school's library I looked up that poem, and why it changed her mind is still a mystery to me. Maybe she was missing Cape Cod.

I thought a lot about those outings in Paris with my mother as the train sped northeast along the Atlantic. I was only beginning to understand how to exist in the culture of the U.S., and I wondered what the hell I was thinking leaving New York which was at least a civilized place, and going somewhere that looked, from what I remember of the little painting, pretty empty. By the time I got off at New Bedford several hours later I had worked myself into an anxious snit which I was trying to smother with a blanket of guilt. Guilt seemed somehow easier to manage, being more familiar. Guilt told me I'd already screwed up whereas anxiety suggested I was about to. The bus to Hyannis was not due to leave for another three hours, so I went into a little restaurant near the station and ordered a sandwich. I sat there taking deep breaths, giving myself a pep talk and trying to look like I knew what I was doing. I needed to stay strong and alert for what was ahead. I looked around the room. The restaurant's decor was very strange.

A dozen whale's rib bones had been arranged on the walls in a wavy pattern. I had no idea what they were. I was trying to work it out when the waitress put my sandwich in front of me and sat down. I pointed to one of the mammoth white crescents and started to ask when she said, "You guessed it, whales. You'll have a hard time getting away from them in this town."

Now I know that a hundred years before New Bedford had been the largest whaling port in the country. That day I was simply bewildered but glad for the company. The waitress had long red hair and wore a pendant tight to her throat, a gold sun with wide radiating rays. I couldn't help watching to see if she'd be jabbed by their points as she moved her jaw. The sun had a happy, puffy face and merry eyes. She asked where I had come from. "I saw you get off the train."

"New York. On my way to Cape Cod," I said. I took a bite of my sandwich. It was delicious. Soft white bread with egg salad and lettuce. "I'm going to Orleans. Pleasant Bay. On the bus." I said.

"You a camp counselor?"

I didn't know what that was. "No. Only going to my parents' house. I-I've never been there." I don't know why I said that. Maybe I wanted someone to assure me it was the right move. "It's a summer cottage," I added.

"Ah," she nodded. Her necklace squinted at me, laughing. "Are they waiting for you, or are you getting there by yourself? Because once you get to Orleans, you won't find a taxi. There are none."

"So . . .?"

"Tell you what," she said, glancing at the door. "Hang around for a while and you'll see a bunch of guys come in here for coffee. All fishermen, all going home as soon as

11

they get paid. I know at least two from P-town. They'll pass right through Orleans. I'm sure one of them can drop you off right at your door."

"P-town?"

"Provincetown, out at the end. You know." She held her arm up as though making a muscle, and pointed to her fist. Her arm made a map of Cape Cod. "Up here," she said.

Provincetown, right. God's vacation spot.

Four hours later I was riding along beside a man named Ed who smelled like the fish stalls at Les Halles and who talked almost nonstop for the entire trip. He whooped gloriously when we reached the canal separating Cape Cod from the mainland. He told me it had been dug in the early part of the century to save ships from having to go around the isthmus on the way north and south along the coast. Ed held up his arm in the same way the waitress had, and made a slice across his bicep.

"Right through there," he said, as we crossed the bridge.

An hour later we left the highway at Orleans, swinging onto a smaller, tree-shaded road.

"What's the address?" Ed asked, slowing the car.

I stared straight ahead, slowly shaking my head. Of course I hadn't thought about that part, nor about what I was going to do if I got there. But it seemed to me that there were so few houses around that surely everyone must know where it was. And I was right, sort of.

"OK, what's your family's name?" he asked, pulling into a parking space in front of a large, white clapboarded building. A sign hanging over the door said "The Foc'sle."

When I told him he said, "Wait here," then went inside while I sat looking around at the town. It was fairly small, but cute, I supposed. A cross of streets with some more of the white-painted buildings and a stretch of shops joined by a brick facade. None were taller than two stories. I wanted to cry. What had I done?

I forced myself to calm down by staring at the pavement next to the car, where someone had recently spit a wad of chewing gum. It lay there glistening, a pink globule which so far had not been stepped on. I used to beg my parents for gum, something considered a disgusting novelty where I came from. But at Bard my friends chewed it all the time, and so I did, too. I once saw a snippet of film of Bob Dylan. He was busy composing a song, ruminating and strumming his guitar and chewing gum. I associated gum with creativity. The stuff on the sidewalk was a signal to me that I was no longer an obedient daughter, but an independent person, a freethinking, rule-rejecting creator. Of what, I had yet to know, but as I sat there gazing at the gum I knew somehow my life had changed and I was at the beginning of a new era.

I know: gum. It really is disgusting, but right then it meant a lot to me.

Ed came back to the car and started the engine. "OK, I got it," he said, backing up. "You out on Barley Neck?"

That's what it said on the back of the painting, come to think of it, so I nodded. "Yes, that's it! I just forgot. It's been so long." I smiled enthusiastically.

We drove for a few miles along some beautiful country roads. So many trees! The way they hung over the road made me slightly nervous. Ed turned onto a sandy track that plunged us even deeper into the foliage, but after a few minutes it opened up in a clearing and there sat the house in the painting. I could see the bay beyond with a sailboat flitting across. The one story cottage was shingled in wood with white trim boards around the windows and up to the roof peak. Some of the shingles were hanging askew, about to fall off. The windows were covered with sheets of plywood.

"Is this it?" Ed turned to me as we got out. "Looks like no one has been here for a while."

"Yes, this is my parents' house," I said, pretending to fish around for the key in my bag. I didn't really want Ed to accompany me inside. I knew he was dying to get back home to see his kids. He'd talked about them for most of the ride.

"Thank you very much for bringing me, I'll be fine," I said, as I hauled my suitcase out of the back seat. I set it confidently on the doorstep as Ed got back in the car. "OK," he said, waving. "Good luck, and enjoy your stay." He sat there for another several seconds, staring at me. Doubtless he correctly assumed that I had no idea what I was doing, and was debating with himself about helping me further. But eventually he backed the car up, turned it around, and left.

There was no key, of course. I walked around the place in the fading light. In the front, facing the water, was a screened porch. I tried the door, and it opened. Inside were a picnic table, a couple of wicker chairs piled one on the other, and a bicycle. I tried the door to the house. Locked. I walked all around the house looking for a way in, but every window was securely covered. I stood in the front yard looking out over the water, wondering what to do. I could see the shore off to the right, now in dark shadow, and a marsh, and a couple of islands. Out beyond them, a mere strip of blue, was the Atlantic ocean. There were several white-painted stones set along the edge of the bluff. I reckoned they were there to make you remember not to step off. I picked one up, went inside the porch and tossed it against the glass part of the door.

Chapter Two

As soon as I entered I found a candle and matches –
thank god– and I confess I spent the next ten hours clinging
to that tiny bit of company. The absolute quiet terrified me.
I had never been away from the comforting sounds of
thumping neighbors or traffic below on the street or the
occasional siren reminding me that I was protected and
would be rescued if necessary. Even the little town on the
Hudson River where Bard is located had some life going on
after dark. Out on Barley Neck the only thing happening
that night in May was the wind shushing through the pines
and rattling what glass was left in the porch door.

Before the sun went down I had a look at the place,
making the rounds with the candle. Because of the plywood
on the windows it was quite dark inside but some light
leaked in through the transom above the front door. I could

see that the house consisted of a large central room dominated by a stone fireplace, and off that were two bedrooms, a kitchen and a little bathroom. After checking the fridge (what was I thinking?) and the cupboards (empty) I walked around looking at the house's other contents. There were two identifiable Ria Bang Overtons hanging on the walls, little abstract flowers and such, and some framed children's drawings which had to have been done by me. In front of the fireplace I pulled a sheet off a fat brown velvet sofa which looked quite comfortable. A matching chair was angled nearby. The bathroom had a pull chain toilet and a rust-stained tub with a row of toy sailboats perched along the rim. The bedrooms were too dark to investigate fully, but I knew I was not going to sleep in either of them. I was scared stiff just being in the living room. Next to the fireplace was a pile of wood, paper and kindling, enough for a nice warm fire. But having never in my life made one, I was afraid I'd burn the house down so I didn't. I'm glad I was smart enough to make that decision because, two days later when I felt a little bit more confident, I discovered what the brass lever mounted under the mantle was for as I opened the flue, spilling sixteen years' worth of old squirrel nests onto the hearth in a roiling, sooty heap that landed with a giant thump and spread in dusty waves across the room. At the time I barely knew what a squirrel was, much less about its nest. Now I know I was lucky there wasn't one sitting on top.

That first night was long and spooky and cold. I curled up on the sofa with the candle set on a little table nearby, listening to the strange sounds made by the wind. The sofa smelled of my father, of cigarettes and a certain cologne even after all those years. I buried my face in its upholstery and started to cry. Why were his arms not wrapped around me, keeping me safe and warm? Why did he have to die? Why had I so impulsively come to this desolate place? I ought to have had the sense to return to Paris, help my mother and sister through this awful time, get back into Université and learn to go forward with my life *sans* the most important person in it. I was an idiot, a child. I was the little girl breaking in Bob Dylan's '*Just Like a Woman*,' one of my favorite songs back then. I let the opening strains run through my mind, the emphatic harmonica hitting those high, plaintive notes. I spent a lot of time trying to make the lyrics fit my situation and matching my pain to Dylan's before I got cold and had to go in search of a blanket. I got as far as the door to one of the pitch black bedrooms, then backed away and returned to the sofa, shook out the sheet I had flung into the corner, wrapped myself in it, and drifted off.

The next morning I awoke to a cacophony of birdsong. It was so loud I was almost afraid to open the door and go outside. When I did I just started laughing, it was such a rowdy, enthusiastic party. Most of the noise seemed to be coming from a stand of trees near the house, so I wandered closer to see what kind of birds America had flying around. One of them screamed *"Richard! Richard!"* at me several times, then flew off. Another said, *"You too, you too, you too."* I tried to pick out a call I recognized and heard the familiar soft cooing of a pigeon. It made me think immediately of being with my mother in the park, my sister and I tossing breadcrumbs, trying to get close enough to touch a silken feather. As I scanned the underbrush for movement I spotted the corner of another building hidden in the trees. When I got closer I could see it was a little shed grown over with a tangle of vines, fallen branches and other woodsy riffraff. I pulled the stuff away from the door and tried the handle. The door opened a few inches so I stuck my head inside a good-sized room with one large plywood-covered window. Two green upholstered armchairs faced the window, a small table between them. Sunlight hit the floor in dappled stripes. I looked up. Boards had been hammered across four narrow skylights in a long slope of roof. One wall was covered in little slashes of paint, as though someone had run it off the edge of a painting, then taken the painting away. My mother, of course, and this had to be her studio. I liked it. I squeezed myself in and stood leaning against one of the chairs for a while. It felt good in there, safe, even though the trees blew around and tapped against the walls, and the floor breathed with dancing, speckled light. I seemed to be standing in one of my mother's paintings. Maybe I did understand them, after all.

Some time later I had most of the vines pulled away from the door and window, and was ready to take the plywood off if I could find a hammer, but I was seriously thirsty and sat there thinking about how to get some water. Naturally I had assumed the stuff would flow from the tap in the kitchen, not knowing a thing about wells, pumps or pipes. I was also hungry. I thought I might take the bicycle into town to buy some food, but after all those years the tires were both flat. I got up, pulled the twigs out of my hair, got some dollars from my bag and shoved them in my pocket, then started walking. Luckily I have an excellent sense of direction and had paid close attention when Ed drove us out there. There was only one road anyway, and I noticed it ran right past a little store. I'd also spotted a phone booth next to the entrance. I figured it was time to call my mother.

When I arrived back at the house that afternoon, after having walked all the way back into town when I found the little store closed, I saw a man emerging from the hatchway door to the cellar. He was short, muscular, and wore a white shirt with the sleeves rolled up. He had cheerful blue eyes and gray hair slicked to a tiny point in back. Whistling to himself, he held up a large wrench and adjusted the gap.

"Oh, hi," he said. He stuck the wrench in his armpit and gave me his hand. "Micah Newcomb. Everyone calls me Moony, though," he added. "Your mother phoned me." He stepped inside the now unlocked front door and I followed.

"Almost got it," he said, fiddling with the kitchen tap. A gurgling, clanking noise started up under the floor, getting louder and closer until finally, with an earsplitting squeal, a gush of brown liquid squirted from the faucet, spraying the sink, the floor and the man's shirt. He just stood there waiting and getting soaked while the liquid gradually turned clear and the stream became steady. He smiled at me. One of his front teeth had a corner broken off.

"That was easy, considering," he said, then went into the bathroom. My mother must have phoned him immediately after she spoke with me. I guess they'd been paying him well to look after the place, because I had never heard of such swift service. Maybe that's how things are done in small towns, I thought as I stood watching him tinker with the bathroom fixtures.

An hour or so later he had taken off all the plywood window covers, stacked them neatly against the house and was up on the roof of the studio wrenching the boards off the skylights. The electricity was on and the toilet flushed. A temporary piece of cardboard was tacked to the porch door where I had smashed out the glass. My meager food supplies were put away, and I was looking around the kitchen at the equipment. How did one make coffee in this country? I had promised Moony a cup when he finished, but I saw no familiar looking device. In Paris we had a contraption of two stacked glass containers. A small heater burned alcohol, sending the boiling water up a clear tube in the lower half and through the coffee grounds in the top part, then it dripped back down. *Voila!* It looked like something in a science lab, and I loved it. But I never learned to use it because we had a cook, and she made everything we ate, except on her day off, when my parents would take us out to eat. I was standing there holding the can of coffee I'd bought and looking stupid, when Moony came in and went to the sink to wash his hands. When he was done he lifted a metal gadget from a peg on one of the cabinet doors.

"Looking for this?" He handed it over. What was it? It had a crank thing on one side, and a long, two-part handle. I turned it over in my hand, wiggled a metal bit.

"For the coffee," he said.

"Right."

"To open it."

Ah, of course! What an idiot I was in those days. He showed me how to operate the can opener, took the coffee pot from the cupboard and set the thing up on the stove, which he lit with a match. He made me practice lighting the stove several times until we were satisfied.

I don't know what Moony thought of me back then but he was always patient and polite and in fact rescued me from a few similar situations in those first weeks at the cottage. I liked his quiet, determined manner, though on several occasions I found him in mid-task, staring off

21

across the water, lost in a reverie. He told me later that an elementary school teacher had come up with his nickname after having to call his attention away from the window on a daily basis. A few times I did catch him watching me skeptically as I attempted some task, like the time I discovered a fishing pole in the cellar and stood with it out on the lawn, mimicking a cast. I very much wanted to catch a fish, because I wanted to fry one in a pan and eat it.

"If you want to go fishing, I can show you how." He inched closer and took the pole away from me. The hook was flying around our heads.

"Was this my father's?"

"I think your mother used it," he said. "I was sorry to hear about your father. He was quite a character."

I nodded, willing away tears. Moony had not yet mentioned either one of them.

"Did you know them well?"

"No, not really. But they were nice to everyone. I remember you girls, too." After a long pause during which I tried to summon even a scrap of memory of being there, and failed, he added, "There is a boat, if you want."

"A boat?"

"Uh huh. Only a skiff, but it's a good one. I can show you what to do if you want to try catching something."

"Oh. Yes, I think so."

"Then I might as well put in the dock, too." He gestured with his chin toward the water. "Look here."

We stepped to edge of the yard where I'd picked up the white rock. He pointed straight down to the little pebble-strewn sliver of shore, about twenty-five feet below. Two fat wood pilings stood in the sand at the bottom.

"The rest is stored under the house. I can set it up if you like. Good place to tie a boat," he added, no doubt noticing the look of pure incomprehension on my face.

"Oh, right . . . yes," I said. I liked the idea of a skiff, whatever that was. It sounded small and manageable.

He handed me the fishing pole, then took off his cap and raked his fingers through his hair, shaping the point in back. "I'll be back in a couple of days," he said, slapping his hat back in place.

A week later the little dock had been installed as promised, and tied to it was a sweet little *canot,* painted green with a white stripe around the edge. A pair of oars were tucked under the seat. Moony gave me a few rowing lessons and a stern warning to stick to roaming around at low tide only, and to stay close until I knew the water better. I think he got a kick out of my enthusiasm and the fact that a girl could be willing to go out there and do the job. He took me on in a matter-of-fact fashion, giving me a detailed explanation of the types of fish in the bay, where I could find them, and when. I was delighted to find out the water was full of coquille St. Jacque, my absolute favorite, though apparently I had to wait until October to gather them in season, not to mention learn how to get them out of the shell. Moony gave me something called a drop line, which he told me was much better than a fishing pole and was nothing more than four sticks crossed like the symbol for pound, with string wrapped around it and a hook on the end. You wind or unwind as needed, turning the thing hand over hand. The drop line came with some practical instructions. He'd say, for example, "Best bait for flounder is worms, period. Flounder hang around on the bottom. Go out at low tide and look for their tracks, then when the tide's higher go back to the same place. Drag your worm along the bottom and they'll grab on." With his finger in the sand he sketched a few lines to show me what a flounder looked like. He also pointed out the good spots for collecting mussels and clams. A few days after that I found a worm in a puddle. I had to steel my nerves to pick it up. I put it in a bowl in the fridge until I was ready to go out on the water with my drop line, but I panicked when it came time to stab the hook through its head, and accidentally flung it overboard. I figured that was the end of my dream of fried flounder until a few days later, when I spotted a can of shrimp at the store. I brought it home and tried one, and it worked beautifully. So does a plain old kernel of corn, I've since discovered, though I didn't mention those things to Moony.

It took me some time to learn that and a lot more about fishing, and gradually I became good at it, but I knew I would need to find a job at some point to keep my seafood diet supplemented with some store-bought food. I still had more than half of the two hundred from the bank in Paris, though I knew it wouldn't last. As the days passed and I became used to the quiet, I wanted only to stay there on the bluff, or roam around out on the water, and so I made fewer trips to town. When I ran out of something I put off buying more and made do without. I settled nicely into the little cottage. I discovered all kinds of things there to keep me company. The first day I lifted a woven scarf from a long shelf arranged with the sorts of little treasures my father loved: Japanese netsukes, an Egyptian oil lamp, turquoise statuettes and beads, a clay bird whistle from Turkey, carved stones, painted tiles. Other shelves held a wide-ranging selection of books. Mixed together in no particular order were old novels, collections of fairy tales, children's picture books, a pile of National Geographic magazines, books on art history, guides to birds and plants. If I wanted to look at a book I had to first take it outside and whack it against the shingles to get the dust off. There were clothes in the closets which I made use of as the weather warmed. The things I had with me were not really suitable for life in the woods and on the water. My favorite pink linen culottes were needlessly fashionable for Cape Cod, and ridiculous as fishing gear, but my mother's old shorts and blouses fit me well enough. I found a pair of scuffed espadrilles which I hardly ever took off. Her bathing suit was so outmoded I couldn't bring myself even to try it on, so made do with my underwear. My father's shirts were too big but I put them on anyway, tied up with the sleeves rolled. They were my evening wear. I spent a lot of time in a sweet blue terrycloth bathrobe which must have been hanging on the back of the bathroom door for all sixteen years it was so stiff and moth eaten in places, but I washed it in the bathtub and it came back to life, sort of.

The kitchen had a basic collection of pots and tools and a Betty Crocker cookbook with grease spotted pages and slips of paper marking favorite recipes. I found I enjoyed baking, and could live off a pan of cornbread and a pot of pea soup for almost a week, along with the mussels I gathered, the clams I dug, and the few fish I managed to catch.

I no longer slept on the sofa, but in my parents' room. Opposite the bed was a window facing the water, so I could lie there in the mornings and watch the day begin. On the wall beside the window was a large map of Pleasant Bay, an old thing from 1922, with a beautiful compass rose drawn in calligraphic curlicues. Our place was marked with a red star. I often lay in bed, staring at the map and memorizing the names and locations of the islands, ponds and inlets, headlands and points, then identifying those places out the window. The house sat on the southern edge of a fat thumb of land which stuck out into the bay between two wide estuaries, facing south. Town was to the west and the Atlantic to the east over a dune of barrier beach which held half a dozen islands within its long arm. At first I couldn't figure why the place was named Barley Neck until I'd walked to town a few times and realized that the open land on either side of the road could very well have been full of ripening barley at one time. I guess the shape of the land could be called a neck. Where the head was meant to be, I didn't know. Many place names on the map were strange, not English, not any language I'd ever heard or read before, like Pochet, the island on my left. Or Namequoit, another point nearby. Portanimicut, Keskayogansett and Quanset were duly indicated in flowery longhand and I learned them, twisting my lips to fit my best guess at pronunciation. I know now that those are the original, native names given by the Nauset tribe which inhabited the area back in the day.

I promised my mother I would phone her regularly, and so every Monday I rode my bike –another thing Moony fixed– up the road to the phone booth at the little store to put through a collect call to our apartment on Rue Fremicourt. Not surprisingly, my mother seemed fairly blasé about my new state of affairs. She was angry at first about Bard but so preoccupied with her own life and all its complications that she was probably relieved to simply have me somewhere safe and in the care of Moony. Not only was she suffering from the loss of my father and dealing with my sister, who had taken a leave of absence from school and ensconced herself on the sofa in front of the TV, but she was also under pressure to organize a collection of paintings for some show to be mounted in July. When I told her about catching my first fish she didn't seem overly impressed, but sighed dramatically. "How well I remember that beautiful bay," was all she said, then took a big drag on her cigarette. I began to describe the agony of having to whack the poor thing to death with the oar, but she interrupted me, saying, "This is costing a mint, honey. We'll talk about it one day when I'm there." Then we had to hang up.

I depended on the comfort of those Monday phone dates more than my mother knew. I didn't want to mismanage her trust, so I never allowed what fear and anxiety I felt to tint my words. I reminded myself that at least I had her undivided attention which was not something I was used to, and I wanted to make it worth her time to give it to me, so I was consistently cheerful. The truth was I suffered more than I care to admit, and there were times when I wanted to beg her to come and get me.

One thing I missed badly in those early days was my record collection. I had selected ten beloved LPs to bring along to Bard, music I played every day. The Beatles, the Kinks, the Rolling Stones, the usual stuff people my age were listening to in the late '60s. I put a few Françoise Hardy 45s in my suitcase, too, to play for my new friends. I had a Joan Baez album, I remember. I loved her. I mostly longed for my one Dylan album, *'Blonde on Blonde'*. I had seen him when he played at L'Olympia a couple years before when so many people said he was terrible, but I think he was just tired after the long Europe tour. One afternoon I was in my dorm room listening to Simon and Garfunkel sing *'Homeward Bound'*, in a swoon of nostalgia and longing for France, for my family, my father especially. And lost in the music, singing along with the refrain, I sensed a presence and thought it was my roommate coming in. When the song ended and I opened my eyes, Don was sitting at my desk lighting a cigarette. "I don't have this album," he said, picking up the jacket and perusing the song titles. "Can I borrow it?"

He presumably still has it, along with the other nine, since I had to leave them behind when I left. They were not in my room when I returned from the funeral, and I could not find Don during the brief time I spent there before leaving for the train station and Cape Cod.

Now that I think of it, the same song led me to another encounter, but one which turned out much differently. On that afternoon, only a few weeks after I'd arrived, I was out in the skiff at low tide. I wasn't far from the house, just drifting around with my chin resting on the gunwale, watching horseshoe crabs scuttle through undulating eelgrass. It was mating season, and the bottom teemed with their brown trilobite shells, a throng of clown shoes pairing up and heading for shore. I was lounging there thinking about nothing when I heard the song. It drifted in and out of earshot, almost in time with the gentle lapping of wavelets on the side of the boat. I sat up, looked around. The tender voice of Paul Simon singing about his daily ennui came from way over in the marsh off Pochet Island. There I spotted a figure standing in the knee-deep water, raking for clams with a long pole. Another person sat in a small boat nearby. The water sparkled behind the figure in the boat as the song continued, the words of longing homesickness rushing tears to my eyes. I heard both people sing the comforting refrain until the breeze took the rest of the song and with it the singers' voices. I picked up the oars and rowed closer, snatches of music reaching me as I pulled. The music ended and a loud, fast-talking man excitedly announced, *"Preventable relief of pimple agony!"* I heard more snatches of his pitch, then another song began, something attached to a long electric guitar riff; a hash of male harmonizing.

"Hi," a woman sitting in the boat called out as she raised her hand and smiled. She was about the same age as I, long brown hair tied back with an orange rubber band. She was busy pulling the tab off a can of beer, which spurted into her lap. "Dammit!" she muttered, brushing off her knees. On the seat next to her was a tiny transistor radio, treble blaring. She grabbed it and thumbed the volume dial.

"Hello," I said, pulling in the oars. "I like that song. I heard it all the way over there." I pointed.

"Yeah, it's a good one. Want a beer?" She held one up and I shrugged. "Sure, yes." I paddled the boat closer with my hands. She opened another can and passed it over.

"So, you're living up there," she said, pointing her chin at the bluff and our cottage. "Nice to see some signs of life at that place. You must have a great view." I nodded. "Are you renting it?"

"No, it's my parents'." My mother's, I corrected myself.

"Lucky you," she smiled, sipping. "I'm Sylvie. That's Ray clamming over there."

Ray had his bare back to us, intent on tugging the rake through the mud. His shoulders moved with a rhythmic jerking, what almost looked like a dance if he hadn't been holding the tool. The sleeves of his shirt were tied around his head, the rest hung down like an Arabic scarf over his long dark hair. A child's plastic life preserver floated next to him, tethered to his belt. Every so often he would lift up the rake head, pull out a clam and toss it into its center.

"I'm Elli. How did you know I live up there?" I said. Sylvie picked up a length of rope and looped it around the oarlock on my boat, tying us together.

"Because I've seen you. I see you fishing, and I see your boat tied up to your dock when you're not."

"Oh, right." I felt embarrassed for asking a stupid question. Eventually I got used to her direct, slightly patronizing manner of conversing, but that first time was a little disconcerting. Ray waded over, dragging the life preserver. He was a handsome man, tanned and flush with health, unhurried in his actions. He smiled at me, white teeth nestled into a black beard.

"I think I have enough," he said. He laid the long rake across the seats, then lifted a mesh bag from inside the ring where it had been suspended. It bulged with fat, thick-shelled clams which clacked softly together when he dropped them into the boat.

"I'm making chowder," said Sylvie. She glanced at Ray. "For supper. Want to come?"

I was dying for company so I accepted heartily. She told me they lived on Sipson's Island. I knew it from the map. It was about a mile and a half south of Barley Neck. I wasn't sure I could row that far, and said so.

"So let's drop off your boat and you can come with us now," said Sylvie. "Someone will bring you back later."

Their boat had a rusty oil stained engine clamped to the stern which Ray readied while I slid my oars under the seat and Sylvie tightened the rope between us. The engine started with a roar and with a noxious puff of black smoke we were off. It was a short ride, and as we neared the little dock, Sylvie untied us and gave my boat a shove which settled it gently against the gray boards.

"I'll be right back." I tied the boat, then ran up to the house on steps dug zig-zag into the hill, and grabbed the pan of cornbread I'd baked that morning. I turned on the porch light for my return, and left. When I got back down to the water Sylvie and Ray were smoking a joint. Ray offered it to me, but I shook my head. I wanted to be level headed. Normally I would have been happy to be stoned, but living by my wits in this foreign place had made me newly prudent. I needed to be as clear as possible, at least until I settled in.

Sylvie shrugged. "Is that cornbread you have there?" I nodded. She turned to Ray and they laughed.

"Ha! Cornbread is the perfect thing to have with chowder!" said Ray.

"It's a classic!" Sylvie added.

"A tradition," said Ray, solemnly. He and Sylvie giggled about it while I sat there with the pan on my lap, grinning stupidly, wondering what the hell I'd gotten myself into. I took a deep breath and turned my face into the wind as Ray swung the boat around and sped up. The bow lifted out of the water then settled as the vessel planed, leaving a graceful, sunset-tinted wake as we headed south.

But it turns out they were right, cornbread really is perfect with chowder.

Chapter Three

Sipson's Island is shaped like a long triangle, a 25-acre wedge of land that lies with its blunt end facing the mainland and its tip pointing the way out to sea. The island's western flank is one side of a passageway through which much of Pleasant Bay's traffic must travel to get to open water. "The narrows," as it is called, is just wide enough for two boats to pass at high tide. From that shore the island's sandy cliff rises to twenty feet before tapering downhill to its eastern facing stretch of stunning, white sand beach. Between that and the barrier beach is marshy, shallow water only passable at high tide. On the mainland side of the narrows is a small landing with a dock, a couple of parking spaces and a dirt road that winds through the woods to town. The island's name comes from the brothers Sipson, the last members of the native Nauset tribe who lived, fished and hunted on the shores of Pleasant Bay and were eventually all but eliminated as English settlers took over the land.

We pulled up to a rickety pier near the beach. Sylvie tied the boat, then jumped into the shallow water. Ray cut the engine and the sound of barking dogs took over, coming closer as we waded to shore.

"Hey guys," said Ray. Two black mongrels came flying out of the bushes, wagging tails and barking delightedly. One of them came over to me and jumped up to investigate the pan of corn bread, but stopped immediately at a snap from Sylvie's fingers. I patted its head.

"That's Rollo and the other one's Roxie," she said. "Mother and son. Very friendly, don't worry."

They scrambled through an opening in the vegetation, and we followed. The land was densely covered with rugged, waist high brush that supported a froth of exuberant brambles with fat lethal looking thorns. Here and there were the same trees as those surrounding my mother's studio, which I later learned were cedar. As we walked up a slight incline, the underbrush petered out, replaced by sparse grasses under oak and elm trees. We arrived at a clearing where a small wooden house sat in the sun. It had a little veranda made of roughly squared-off logs. Ray set the bag of clams on the deck and walked off down the path. "I'll get some stuff from the garden," he said over his shoulder.

"And start the generator!" Sylvie called after him, then disappeared inside.

I stayed on the veranda looking around and wondering what a generator was when Sylvie came to the door and pulled on my sleeve. "Come in, have another beer while I open these quahogs." She handed me an open can and grabbed the bag of clams. I followed her inside and looked around while she dumped them in the sink and turned on the little transistor radio again. A emphatic voice urged us to go out and buy a tube of Tan-Ya for the beach, then the noise morphed into a song.

"Baby don't go-o-o-o, baby, baby please don't go-o-o . . ."

I stood in a large open, well lived-in room, with an emphasis on seating. They must have lots of company, I thought, counting chairs. The house was split in two. The half I was standing in was double height and open to the roof. A jungle of plants hung from the rafters around a complicated mobile made from feathers, driftwood, starfish and other beach finds. From high windows light filtered down through the plants onto a large, oval table. This central piece of furniture was surrounded by a dozen chairs of all shapes and sizes. Some were painted brightly or had a colorful cushion pressed into the seat. Everywhere I looked were more plants; they sat on windowsills, crowded the center of the table or were arranged on stands in corners. Some were flowering, others pushed meandering tendrils into space, or dangled frondescence from above. They gave the house a cool, fragrant atmosphere. I decided on the spot that I needed some for my place.

A wood stove sat opposite the door on a brick hearth. Chips of brick and small stones were pressed in swirly patterns into the plaster wall behind. The stove was a big, home-welded thing made from an oil barrel. Thick green glass was set into its loading door in a diamond pattern. A fat stovepipe emerged from the top, made a horizontal turn, angled up, ducked under a rafter, and disappeared through the wall. Smooth chunks of driftwood were heaped up around its base. A pile of newspaper listed against the wall behind.

The other half of the house was a galley style kitchen with stairs leading up to the bedroom which overlooked the hanging mobile and plants. The bathroom was beyond the kitchen. Mounted on the wall behind the table was a long, sagging shelf full of record albums, their spines furry from being flipped through. Under the shelf sat an impressive, high-end stereo system, one of those Do Not Touch turntables with the smoked plastic covers. The stylus was slim and tapered, not like the clunky child's toy my roommate at Bard had, or the one on the booming console my mother used in her studio at home.

"Go ahead. Pick something out. I think Ray's got the generator going by now." Sylvie clicked off the radio and turned back to the business of shucking clams. The thick shells clanked into the sink with machine-like regularity as she filled a bowl with their sloppy innards. I raised the turntable cover and saw that the last record played had been The Band's *Music From Big Pink*. I didn't know it, but I lifted the stylus and settled it onto the black vinyl edge as the record began to spin. The voice of Richard Manuel made Sylvie smile. She gestured for me to turn up the volume. I sat on the chair nearest the kitchen while she sang along with his plaintive, horn-backed lament. I tried not to stare, drinking in their harmony. "What can I do to help?" I said when the song ended. She pointed to a bag of potatoes on the draining board and held up a big knife. "Want to chop them up for the chowder?" She laid a cutting board on the table and I started slicing. I didn't know about chowder, so I made fat discs. I thought they looked right for any number of French dishes, but Sylvie took the knife from me and swiftly cubed a potato. "Chunks," she said,

35

and smiled broadly at me. "OK?" I'd been remembering a meal our cook used to make, with thin potato slices, onions, bacon and Reblochon cheese. She put potato slices into a pan in a continuous spiral, the other stuff between the layers, then baked it. When it was done she would invert the whole thing onto a plate. I loved slicing into the crusty, fragrant brown flower. I swept aside a moment of homesickness and got down to business.

"There were still a few peas left to pick, maybe just enough to throw into a salad," said Ray, coming in through the screen door. He had a mass of greenery folded into his t-shirt which he let spill onto the table. Two other people entered with him. "This is my brother, Sal," said Ray, putting his hand on the shoulder of a man who looked a lot like him. "And that's Sandy," he added, nodding to a woman who lingered near the door, undoing a pair of elaborately buckled sandals. She had a sheaf of reddish-blond hair fastened on top of her head with a rubber band, and stringy bangs which she shoved aside. Her mouth widened into a huge, white-toothed grin. Could a normal human really have that many teeth? Ray pointed to me. "That's Elli. She lives in the empty cottage on Barley Neck."

"Far out!" Sal exclaimed, bouncing on his heels. "That's cool, man. I've wondered about that place for a long time. I really like that house. I made up all kinds of stories about why no one lives there. To tell the truth I was about to go snooping around some evening, look in the windows, check it out. Is it yours? If it is, you're lucky."

I was at a loss for words, Sal was such a flurry of enthusiasm. He was nearly the twin of Ray, the same handsome face framed by long, almost-black hair, but where Sal was burly Ray was slim and athletic. They both had inquisitive, smiling eyes and scruffy beards, cutoff jeans and bare feet. I opened my mouth to answer Sal but he turned to Sylvie and said, "The daisies have bloomed! You have to go and see them tomorrow."

To me he said, "There is a huge field of daisies out there sloping all the way to the bay. It's where the geese like to hang out, so it's always fertilized." His eyebrows jigged as he nodded enthusiastically.

"Let's go at sunrise," said Sandy, coming in and sitting down. "That would be groovy!" Taking off her sandals had reduced Sandy's entire ensemble by about half. She had on the tiniest bikini I'd ever seen, and the cloth did not quite contain her magnificent breasts. They smashed into each other in the middle of her chest, fighting for position every time she moved. A tiny silver fairy on a chain dipped in and out of her cleavage like a coy actor dancing on and off the stage. I found it hard to look away. I chopped more potatoes. Sal rattled around in a cupboard under the countertop and came up with a huge colander. He scooped up the greens from the table and dumped them in. While they rifled through the colander rinsing and discarding, he and Sylvie began a long discussion of how the endive was a little brown at the top and what it meant. Sal had found some wild asparagus and Sylvie cooed over it. The dogs came in and stretched out under the table. One of them licked my ankle.

Ray, who had gone upstairs, leaned over the railing and said, "So, Ellie, where did you come from?"

I looked up, briefly flustered. "Uh, Bard. Bard College. In New York."

"Oh, wow." said Ray. "That's a good school."

"Yes, but I was expelled."

37

"OK, we won't ask," said Sal, laughing. They all chuckled along with him, waiting for my explanation.

"And before that, I came from France."

Sandy perked up, thrusting her chest at me. The silver fairy burst forth from her cleavage and flopped to one side. "France!" She said it in a long, drawn-out sigh. "What were you doing there?"

"It's where I grew up. In Paris. But I'm American." I had explained my story many times at Bard, so I had it down. I told them about my parents, my mother the painter, my father the antiquities dealer and Bard alumnus.

"So, how does the house on Barley Neck figure in all this?" said Sylvie. I told them what I knew about my parents' life before we left the country, but as I recited the few facts I became aware of how little I actually knew. "My father used to drive to Provincetown from New York," I said. But what I was thinking was that he never mentioned Barley Neck. "My mother has a painting studio in the woods next to the house." And she used to go fishing in Pleasant Bay, I thought, though I didn't say it, because I wouldn't have been able to elaborate. "And there are little beds in the house where my sister and I used to sleep. Very cute."

No one said much, or asked me any further questions. I suppose it did sound a little vague, so I added, "All I really knew when I came here was that we have a cottage in Orleans, on Pleasant Bay. I found it, and now I live there."

Right then the record came to an end, and Ray came thundering down the stairs to turn it over. Before he did he looked at me and smiled. "Cool," was all he said.

Sylvie got the chowder simmering and we were setting the table with an assortment of bowls and spoons when we heard a car honking a little staccato pattern. Sal lept up and ran out. "More guests," said Sylvie. We rearranged the table and three more people arrived, having driven to the opposite shore and signaled. Sal rowed over to get them. This was a routine they were obviously used to, and accepting of. I remember thinking it would have driven me crazy.

We sat around the table laughing and talking, eating the marvelous chowder. I was happy to see my cornbread wolfed down by a grateful crowd. Based on a little note scribbled by my mother in the margin of the cookbook, I had learned to add a can of whole corn kernels, which makes it much better. There seemed to be an unending source of beer somewhere and a perpetually full can in front of me. I had let go of wanting to be straight and had toked on every joint that came my way, so after an hour or two I felt the strain of the past weeks slowly dissolve, the miserable feeling of dread that had been hanging around was suddenly gone. I felt bright, dynamic, in control. Beer and grass will have that effect on anyone, I suppose, but this seemed different. It felt as if I had finally entered fully into the new life I had begun. I was there. Where that was, I wasn't sure, but it didn't matter.

Sylvie was in fine form that evening, too. She kept jumping up to play us another song, and another one still, pulling records from the shelf and flinging them onto the turntable with comic enthusiasm. She danced around the table, pulling each of us from our chairs to frug wildly with her until the song reminded her of the next she wanted to hear, and she'd leave her partner to flap through the shelf again. Sandy undulated to her own rhythms over in one corner, watched openly by Sal and furtively by the rest of us.

Eventually the generator ran out of gas and the turntable slowed, distorting the music until it growled to a stop along with all conversation. Ray got up to fiddle with a backup music system -an eight-track tape player hooked up to a 12 volt car battery. The thing could go for nearly a month before it needed to be charged. They had played the stereo in my honor that night, using up the last of the gasoline.

It was the first of several memorable dinners I would enjoy at their house. I came to understand that Ray, Sylvie, Sal and their friends had much more in common than simply age or nationality or hitchhiking distance from Boston. They were part of a much broader fraternity, the population of young people who had stopped conforming to the rules, who had turned their backs on the world in which they'd been raised. They didn't care anymore about their parents' opinions or standards. Their desire was to band together in unspoken agreement to enjoy and test the boundaries of life, to reject war and violence, to use their freedom to invent a self. Long hair, bare feet, love of music and marijuana were all signs that a person had an understanding, and belonged. They were part of your tribe. Birth control made free love possible, psychedelic drugs opened the doors of perception. It was the sixties, 1968 in particular, perhaps the most momentous year in that world-altering decade, but of course no one knew it at the time. The spectre of the Vietnam War hung over us all, as did the dream-snuffing murders of Martin Luther King and Bobby Kennedy, and although the people living on the island were politically informed to a certain degree, no one talked about it much. After all, on Sipson's Island one lived at such a distance, jutting into the Atlantic with the rest of America

40

fanned out behind. Like a bride towing a heavy veil, the impulse was to cut free, and mentally that's what they did.

    I got a ride home in the early morning hours with the other three guests. Sal rowed us across the narrows to the little landing and we piled into the car, then trundled in silence along the dirt road through the woods, spring green underbrush tipped orange here and there by first light. When they dropped me at home I didn't immediately go to bed but instead stood on the edge of the bluff, watching little ripples picked out by the sun to reflect its sparkle. Way in the distance, I found the band of green that is Sipson's Island. I was still stoned and a little drunk as I stood there swaying pleasantly, reviewing the evening and watching the bay come to life. As the sun lifted above the barrier beach I watched the line of morning light travel across the tree tops of the nearest islands and jump down to warm the sand along their shores. A heron, concentrating on fishing, long legs stepping gingerly through the marsh grass, made me hold my breath in suspense. A trio of bats swirled and looped past, disappearing into the trees to sleep. I watched as the sun's rays reached the sand at the bottom of the hill where I stood, picking out a trail of footprints which skirted the tideline and disappeared around the corner. The footprints looked fresh. Puzzled, I stumbled down the zigzag path to get a closer look but overbalanced near the bottom and rolled onto the sand beside the dock. I heard someone chuckle softly, or so I thought. The incoming tide oozed into the footprints as I lay there, slowly filling the hollows of toe and heel before erasing them. Maybe the sound I heard was the gurgle and bubble of water moving over mud. But as the sky lightened

I saw a man about 30 feet away, lying on his side, back to me, talking softly to someone. It was Moony, explaining and drawing in the sand with a stick, the way he'd shown me the outline of a flounder. But there was no one else there, he was completely alone. I crouched low and watched. Moony spent long minutes lying still as though listening to someone, nodding and gesturing, then talking again in low, thoughtful tones. I couldn't make out a single word. I stayed still until I felt the tide creeping in between my toes, covering them. Moony felt it too, and folded his legs away from the water, then sat up. I ducked. When I looked again he was making some kind of signal, holding up both his hands, palms facing the water, as he looked out across the bay. Then he put his hands on the sand to push himself up. That's when I crawled quickly to the path and scrambled up the hill, trying not to fall. At the top I ran for the porch door and stood inside watching, but Moony didn't come up. He must have walked along the shore to the road, and gone home. I knew he lived somewhere on Barley Neck Road, toward town.

I got into bed and lay there trying to understand what I'd just seen. I knew I hadn't smoked or drunk enough to be anywhere near hallucinating, but I couldn't think of any other explanation. The sight of Moony lying there on the pebbly shore at daybreak, relaxing and shooting the breeze with an invisible friend while the tide rose around them, was baffling enough to keep me from falling asleep. Suddenly I remembered the drawing Moony had made in the sand, jumped out of bed and ran back down the path to the shore. If it was there, then I had not been dreaming, or seeing things. I got to the spot at the moment the water was about to cover the last of it, three lines meeting at a point, like a drawing of the tip of a pyramid. I studied the drawing for a few seconds, then the lines filled with water, and it was gone.

By the time I got out of bed that afternoon, I had almost convinced myself that the whole thing had been a dream I'd had while lying passed out on the bluff. But there was the puzzling fact of the dream's unusual continuity, which nagged me. Also, I walked down to the dock again and found my espadrilles some way from the path as though they'd been flung off. I had no reason to get in touch with Moony, but I spent some time trying to concoct a need for him to come over to fix something, thinking up a question I might have about fishing or home maintenance that would make a trip to his house necessary. I really wanted to see him, to find out if he'd seen me, to at least detect something in his manner that would confirm that my dream was real. But the hours passed, and eventually I gave up trying to figure it out. And anyway I was tired, and needed some sleep. I planned to go into town the next day to see if I could find a job.

Chapter Four

It was the third of June, a Monday. I figured if I made myself look clean and college student-like I could ride my bike into town and check the store windows for Help Wanted notices, or ask at the market if they needed anyone. I had seen a newspaper for sale called The Cape Codder, and I wanted to buy a copy to check the classified ads. Sandy told me she worked as a waitress at the The Foc'sle, the place where Ed had stopped to get directions to the cottage when we drove here from New Bedford. I planned to go there as well, to see Sandy and ask if they needed any additional staff.

Luckily I wasn't particular about what I did for work, I only wanted to earn a little money to pay for some food, some clothes, and a radio. The dinner party made me want to be part of human life again after being on my own for so long. I was proud of myself for overcoming my initial fear of living alone in such a quiet, deserted place, and as I rode into town I felt I could now do anything and was eager to get on with it. It was more than that, though. I knew without a doubt that something life changing was going to happen that day, that I was already on the way to it, as if I'd stepped onto a train with only one destination. I can't explain how, but I was so sure I'd be set up with a well-paid gig by the end of the day that I splurged on a huge breakfast of eggs and sausage at a place called The Homeport, another restaurant with a whaling-themed interior. I left the waitress a nice tip, got back on the bike and rode across town to the supermarket. Inside, I scanned the notice board but no one was advertising jobs, not there or anywhere else it seemed, except for a scrawled-on business card from Teddy's Garage looking for a capable mechanic. A huge black thumbprint all but obliterated Teddy's phone number. There were several flyers for cottage rentals and a few handwritten notes looking for roommates, but it seemed the mental image I'd formed of myself behind the counter of a bustling *charcuterie* would not be realized. The market didn't even have a meat counter, only some sliced bologna and salami in plastic packages. I bought a copy of The Cape Codder and left, walking my bike along Main Street. Within half an hour I'd looked at every shop window in town, and none yielded any of the hand lettered "Inquire Within" signs I'd imagined. Slightly dejected but still confident, I sat on a bench in the town's center, leafing past the small town news items in the paper, looking for the classifieds and fanning myself now and then with the corner of a page. Behind the bench was a small cemetery, the lichen-coated stones fallen flat or leaning into each other, a drunken gathering of the town's departed citizens. I watched as cars slowed for the stoplight, cigarette smoke drifting from open windows, radios blaring half-minute excerpts from top ten songs. I heard again the high-energy disc jockey rattling off a phone number. *"This could be the very chance you've been waiting for!"* segued into a song about a kookie, snoopy, spooky girl, something like that. I couldn't make it out.

I had just found the Want Ads when I heard my name called across the rumble of downshifting, engine revving and radio noise.

"Hey! Elli! Over here!"

Diagonally across the intersection, in the doorway of the The Foc'sle, was Sandy in a black miniskirt and apron, jumping up and down and waving at me. I put my hand up and she beckoned, then disappeared inside. As I crossed the road I thought about the day I arrived on Cape Cod, when Ed left me in the car to go and ask about the location of my parents' cottage. How could I have been so naive and yet so bold? I stood outside the bar, mulling over whether it was brave or stupid, and remembered the glob of gum I'd spotted while I sat waiting in Ed's car. Back then the gum had somehow struck me as a token of my freedom, and suddenly it seemed imperative that I find it again, to confirm that it had happened at all, and that I had indeed found freedom, and that I was both bold and brave. So I dawdled in the parking area for half a minute, scanning the pavement. The only reason I'm admitting this peculiar little detail of my inner life is that while I was standing there searching among the flattened blobs, a little block of folded pink paper, almost exactly the size and shape of a fresh piece of Bazooka, landed at my feet.

"Excuse me dear, I just need to . . ." A tall white-haired man bent to pick it up. He had a bundle of mail under his arm which began to slide as he leaned down, magazines and envelopes spilling toward the pavement. I caught some of it as he straightened, and grappling for the rest, he thanked me.

"I don't even want any of this junk," he sighed. He wore a beautifully tailored jacket over a white linen shirt. I knew good quality menswear when I saw it, having grown up with my father, who wore nothing but, ever. "And I especially don't want this." He held up the folded pink paper before stuffing it into an inner pocket, then winked at me and walked into the The Foc'sle. I forgot about the gum and followed. As soon as I stepped through the door Sandy spotted me. She rushed over and threw her arms around my neck, enveloping me in her patchouli-scented aura. "Sit at the bar," she said, leading me over to a stool. "I'll be right back." I ordered a Coca-Cola, another previously forbidden American treat, and opened The Cape Codder again. The jukebox boomed out Stevie Wonder singing *"Shoo-Be-Doo-Be-Doo-Da-Day,"* as I ran my finger down the Help Wanted column, which contained four inches of motels looking for chambermaids for July and August. The pay was $1.35 an hour. Not too bad, I thought. But what would I do after August? I watched Sandy in her miniskirt winding briskly through the tables, picking up empty glasses and dirty dishes, nodding as someone held up a beer mug for a refill. The bar was not large, only a dozen tables and the long bar where I sat. Big multi-paned windows faced the crossroads at the town's center, their lower half covered by a thick green curtain. It was comfortably dark inside, and smelled of freshly grilled steak. In my teenage years I spent a lot of time with my friends after school,

47

sitting in cafes and drinking *panaché,* a summer drink of half beer, half lemonade, and now I badly wanted one, but I was too shy to ask. Sandy stopped at a table to take an order from two men sitting with their backs to the wall. One of them was the man I'd encountered outside. Even though he was white-haired and clearly old, his eyes were merry with curiosity about his surroundings, which, as he looked around, made him look like a boy of fifteen. His companion, a man of roughly the same age, wore grease-covered jeans, a grimy white t-shirt and black rubber boots. He sat with his legs elegantly crossed balancing a spiral-bound notepad on one knee, which he flipped through mechanically. They made a curious couple. They hardly spoke to each other until Sandy brought their drinks, then they put their heads together and began to discuss something with great enthusiasm, ignoring everyone else.

Sandy came over to the bar and heaved herself onto the stool beside me. A black bib-front apron over a tiny white blouse restrained her splendid bust, yet she looked as good in clothes as she had in her bikini. "So," she said, taking a sip of my drink, "Did you have any luck?"

"Not unless I want to clean motel rooms." I slid the Want Ad section over to her. She glanced at it and nodded. "I did it every summer when I was in high school. Gets old fast."

"It's only two months," I said, still banking on the confident feeling I had on the way to town. If a job changing sheets at a local motel would turn out to be life changing, I was game. I looked at the list of ads. "Which place should I pick?" I asked.

Sandy didn't hear me. She was listening intently to a man sitting on her other side who spoke to her in a low, confidential tone. He had stringy, dirty blond hair and a thick brown mustache. He was also missing an eye, the one on my side, which left him with an empty, squeezed shut socket. I stole a few looks while he talked. The eye hole opened a little on certain emphatic words, and I caught peeks of its shadow-pink interior.

"Has he said anything to you?" he murmured to Sandy. I saw her look over at the pair she had just served, the white haired man and his notepad companion. "No," she whispered back, "and don't get me involved, okay? It's your problem, and you really ought to tell him the truth."

"I know," said the man. "I can't."

"He looks at me with his friendly eyes and asks if you've mentioned the skull. He does it nearly every time I see him. It's breaking my heart," Sandy hissed.

"Oh, Christ. All right. But not this minute. I'd better get out of here before he comes over." The man jumped off the stool, pecked Sandy on the cheek, and left.

Sandy got down also. "Right back," she said, and darted across the room to tend a table. I sat for a moment, rummaging in my purse for a dime while I finished my Coke. I figured I might as well phone a place called The Governor Hancock Inn. It sounded a little upscale. The woman who answered at the motel told me I could come by immediately, if I wanted. When I got off the phone I waited for Sandy so I could say goodbye.

"What was that about?" I asked Sandy when she stopped beside me.

"Sticky situation," she said, looking over her shoulder at the two men. "See that white haired guy over there? That's Martin. Martin Meyer. He's this classy dude who lives out on Sipson's. That's where . . ." She swatted her forehead. "Oh, right, you've been out there. So he, like, owns the place. The island, I mean. I've seen him at Ray

49

and Sylvie's place a few times. He's pretty laid-back about everything. And he's funny, too. Sylvie says he's got a big collection of far-out stuff at his place. Weirdo antiques and oil paintings, I think. Sometimes she cleans his house or cooks dinner for him when his housekeeper is off."

While she talked I kept an eye on Mr Meyer. He took the wad of pink paper from his jacket pocket and began to separate it into pieces. I could see they were those While You Were Out slips for when someone takes a phone message. He rolled his eyes as he read each one aloud. Then he fanned them out, plucked two from the array, and crumpled the rest. When he finished he looked up, right at me, as though he knew what Sandy was telling me. He did indeed have kind eyes. They were dark brown, nearly black, but they each held a speck of light, two shimmering, animated points which skittered around, glancing off me on my barstool, before settling back onto the pink paper.

"Anyway, one day he lent Bill, that's my friend, this skull. A human skull. I think he dug it up out there on the island. Bill's an artist, and he wanted to paint it, so Martin let him borrow it. But that was over a year ago, and now Martin's wondering where it is."

Meyer lifted his glass then, and I nudged Sandy. "He wants another cocktail," I said. Sandy grabbed my arm to pull me along. "Come and meet them. You guys all live out there, so you should know each other."

"Not right now," I said, backing away. I didn't want to stay there any longer. I wanted to nail down a job and get on with things. I was feeling sweaty and slightly hungover and a bar was not where I'd hoped to end up that day. "I'm going over to the Governor Hancock. I'll see you later."

"OK." Sandy turned to go.

"Wait," I said. "What happened to the skull?"

"Oh yeah. He backed his car over it by mistake in his driveway. Don't ask me how that happened." She walked away, chuckling.

Two hours later I was riding my bicycle down the road to the house, a rayon uniform strapped to the baggage carrier. It was a rather ugly thing, custard yellow with little brown dots. A white rayon apron added to the misery, but it meant I would not have to come up with any clothes to wear while I made money to buy some. After my interview I rode back to the center of town to look at radios for sale in a place called Western Auto, and with a feat of self discipline, did not spend the $27 it would cost me to get one. I needed food first, then clothes, then music. I lingered in front of the building next door to admire the sign hanging in its window. A fat grinning man wearing a fez lifted a tiny white cup to his lips. Tendrils of steam rose from the cup, spelling out 'Turk's Head' along the top edge, and below the man's ample belly, 'Coffeehouse'. I opened the screen door and stuck my head inside. A scuffed wood floor, a dozen tables with mismatched chairs. Opposite, a small stage covered by an Oriental carpet. A tipped-over stool and an ashtray were the only items up there. The place smelled of cigarettes, coffee, and sandalwood incense. Along one wall three sagging shelves were loaded with coffee mugs: corny joke mugs, holiday mugs, teacups with saucers, thick glass goblets, beer steins, small cups for espresso, handle-less cups for god knows what. The other walls were hung with posters of famous paintings, singers with guitars, one of the Hindu god Ganesh, the Remover of Obstacles. A huge sofa took up a side wall. Through a half-open door I saw a counter piled with dirty dishes. Beyond that was a man sitting in a chair picking out notes on a guitar. A cigarette burned in an ashtray on the floor, the smoke swirling around his feet, the opposite of the Turk on the sign. No one else was there. I made a mental note to return, maybe with someone else.

All in all, the trip was not the vision of golden opportunity I'd had on the way into town that morning, but it was something, and my mother seemed quite pleased about it when I told her, so much so that she offered to send me money for clothes, since I hadn't mentioned the uniform. Moony would get it to me, she said.

I spent the next two days learning the chambermaid job, working the 15-room motel with a girl called Becca. We stripped beds, vacuumed, and trundled stacks of yellow towels to and from the laundry room. I found wiping pubic hairs off the bathtub disgusting but other than that the work was all right and the tips were a bonus I had not counted on. Between tips and what my mother was sending I thought I might go and get the radio after all. It was still early in the season, so the hotel was only a third full. We were usually done by noon. I would ride directly home, take off the stinking uniform and jump into the bay. On the fourth day I arrived at work to find Becca sitting in tears on one of the beds, watching television.

"Isn't it horrid?" She stared at the screen and blew her nose into a wad of toilet paper. Of course I hadn't heard that Robert Kennedy had been shot the night before in a hotel in Los Angeles. He was still alive but undergoing emergency brain surgery. We watched the news coverage for a while. I didn't understand why someone would do it. Another Kennedy! Everything I'd heard about him since I had come to America was that he was busy giving people hope again after the murder of Dr. King and the ongoing mess of war in Vietnam, not to mention his own family's struggle. Who could object to hope? I felt dizzy, and suddenly afraid.

The couple whose room it was came in wearing bathing suits. Becca and I leaped up from the bed and we all stood there not saying a word until the woman went and flung open the closet doors, pulling things off hangers and tossing them onto the bed. "Swimming in a pool," she muttered. "I can't do it. Just take me home. I do not want lobster or sunshine or drinks overlooking the bay. I want . . ."

"Thank you, maybe just leave, all right?" said the man to us, and we did. As we walked along the row of rooms pushing our supply cart we could see through open doors people sitting on beds watching as Walter Cronkite talked the country through yet another catastrophe, delivering the facts with solemnity, though everyone could tell, as with most loving fathers, that he himself could not entirely maintain an objective demeanor. We all saw the pain on his face.

The owner met us and suggested we go home. He asked us to phone him later, he'd let us know when to come back. Becca took off, and I got on my bike and rode to town. The crossroads were deserted. I rode down to the harbor and hung around for an hour or so watching tourist kids feed doughnuts to the gulls, but I felt foolish in my uniform and decided to just go home. I could phone from down the road later on. I was nearly there when a car slowed as it passed and Sylvie leaned out the window.

"Hey," she said, crunching the gearshift into neutral.

"How are you?" I could tell she'd been crying.

"Shitty. I was looking for you. Come to town with me, OK?"

53

"I need to change first."

She glanced at my uniform. "Yes you do."

When we got to town she parked in front of the Turk's Head and we went inside. She threw herself onto the far end of the sofa and tucked her feet up. The place was empty but I could hear noise from the kitchen and smell coffee brewing. A minute later a woman carrying a small tray emerged. She wore a pair of wide legged linen trousers and an embroidered blouse tucked into a macramé belt. Her long dark hair was streaked with gray and had tangled itself into a complicated silver necklace which lay heavily across her chest. Bells dangled from every part of the piece, tinkling each time she moved. She went over to the shelf and plucked two mugs from the array, then brought them over and set them on a little table in front of us.

"Hi honey," she said to Sylvie. "I thought you might come in today." As she poured coffee from a glass pot she turned to me and smiled. Her brown eyes were heavily lined in black. She had on red lipstick and giant hoop earrings. "Who's this?"

"New friend from out on the bay. Elli, this is Joyce."

Joyce extended her hand. Her wrist was encrusted with silver bangles. Every finger displayed a ring with a jewel. "Pleased to meet you on this awful day," she said as I took her hand.

"What's the latest?" asked Sylvie.

"I don't know. I can't listen to it any longer. It's too depressing." Joyce got up, crossed the room and fiddled with some stereo equipment near the stage. Spanish guitar music floated over to us as I sipped my coffee. It was delicious, rich with a chocolate bitterness I could never seem to achieve at home. Joyce picked up a single maraca from the stage and tapped it against her thigh in time to the music. With the other hand deep in a pocket she swayed there in place, eyes closed.

"I knew I'd find some peace here." Sylvie sighed, a guttural moan. "Lots of yelling back home. Sal took off in the boat because Ray's mad at him. Slugs ate most of the broccoli plants. Why that's Sal's fault, I'm not sure. Ray has been glued to the radio since early this morning. He even yelled at Martin when he knocked, and that's not cool. I went to Martin's place to apologize, but he wasn't there. His car's gone, so he's somewhere in town. I really need to find him. You haven't seen him, have you?" She paused, bit off a sliver of thumbnail. I heard it snap. "Oh, right. You don't know him yet. I forgot. He's probably at the Foc'sle. I'll check in a while."

I didn't mention having seen him a few days before. It seemed irrelevant in the face of nation wide grief. Robert Kennedy had only entered my sphere of knowledge a few months before, and to tell the truth I had not paid him much attention other than noticing he was pretty cute for a politician, and the brother of JFK. Now I wanted to understand more. I wanted to sit and watch Walter Cronkite. But Sylvie seemed to need me, so I settled in.

"This is a nice place," I said, looking around. I noticed the Ganesh poster had some gold highlights which glimmered in the light from the windows. It made me think of a client of my father's, another Sirhan like Kennedy's killer, but this one an old man who collected illuminated manuscripts. He would buy only those with the most gold leaf, and paid a lot for them. Once, after Sirhan left our apartment with one my father said, "When I was a boy, I used to watch my father make fake ones at the kitchen table. Adding the gold takes a certain skill that not too many people have. Sometimes I'm tempted to try it." He chuckled, then added, "But that one was real." He told me that some of my grandfather's forgeries are displayed in museums now, unbeknownst to the curators.

Sylvie swigged the last of her coffee. "It's a great place. It's where I come when I want to get away from men." Joyce heard it, turned to us and winked, then went back to her Spanish reverie. "But it's also a great place to hear some live music. Joyce knows every folkie in the business, and she talks some of them into driving to the Cape to play. I saw Tom Rush here last summer."

I did not know who that was so I nodded, but shrugged involuntarily. Sylvie stood up. "I'm going across the street to check if Martin is there." She waved her hand in the direction of the The Foc'sle "He loves Warhol, so he was already freaked out, and now this."

"OK." I hoped the look on my face expressed empathy but in truth I didn't know what she was talking about. I knew who Warhol was, but what did he have to do with it? Sylvie turned in the doorway and said, "Joyce, put on some Tom Rush, will you? Elli wants to hear. I'll be right back."

The guitar music had wound down, anyway. Joyce deftly switched albums, and a folksinger started. Slow plucking of guitar strings, then a somber man began singing about love's memories. Joyce sat down and hummed along.

"What happened to Andy Warhol?" I said.

She shook her head. "Another lunatic with a gun. A few days ago."

"Is he . . .?"

"No. He's in the hospital, too."

An image appeared in my mind, a symmetrical *tableau vivant* of Bobby Kennedy and Andy Warhol in side by side hospital beds hooked up to fluids, hair parted in mirror image, one white, one dark, with twin doctors bending over them and nurses standing in formation on either side. I shook my head to delete it.

"Why?"

"That, honey, is the question of the hour, isn't it?" She got up, went into the kitchen and returned with the coffee pot. She poured us another cup, and simply by making small talk she quickly got out of me not only my address but my parents' whereabouts and the circumstances of my living in Orleans. Warm but not overly familiar, she had the rare quality of being a good listener, and gave her full attention to every word I said. She was also close to my mother's age, and as we talked I felt myself mentally curling up in her lap, momentarily letting go the willpower it took to cope alone in my new world. She had lived in Paris fifteen years before and wanted to know about the riots, but I had nothing to offer. During our phone conversations my mother barely mentioned anything happening outside our apartment, so I didn't know. Joyce told me that she had come to Orleans on a whim, with Sylvie, while they were working together. She didn't say what kind of work and I was about to ask when a trio of customers came in and she got up, saying, "If you ever get lonely out there, you know where to come, right?" I nodded. The Tom Rush ended and she floated across the room to turn it over.

Sylvie came back half an hour later, followed by the white-haired man I knew to be Martin. Joyce, en route to a table with a plate of sliced cake, touched his shoulder and gave him a little cheek kiss. Martin sat down with Sylvie and me and introduced himself. "I think we've already met," he said. "You rescued my silly magazines, remember? But I didn't get your name."

"It's Elli," said Sylvie. "She's a friend of ours. Lives out on Barley Neck in that empty cottage."

"Lovely. Good to meet you, Elli. I'm Martin."

"She comes from Paris," Sylvie added.

"Oh yes?" He looked me over. I gave my usual account while he nodded along. When I finished he said, "It's a painful day for the planet. I sure wish I were in Paris right now." He paused, looked at the door to the kitchen. "Though I don't know if that would be any better, come to think of it." He seemed to be talking to himself, but he asked Sylvie, "Is Joyce bringing us something?" He looked longingly at the kitchen door, then continued, "I wish I could get away, away from men in love with money and politicians who care only about manipulating the world to get them more of it."

"What's that got to do with Bobby Kennedy being shot?" Sylvie said.

"I don't know exactly, but I suspect everything."

Joyce emerged from the kitchen with a pot of coffee. She selected a cup from the shelf and put it down in front of Martin, then poured. The cup had a picture of Robin Hood taking aim with his bow and arrow. I watched Martin put cream and sugar in his cup and stir. His long fingers held the little spoon with grace. Each bend of knuckle was a precise procedure. It reminded me of a heron stepping gingerly through the marsh, hunting. He was dressed in another linen shirt, this one royal blue, with mother-of-pearl buttons cut in the shape of little white birds. When he reached for the cream I glimpsed a small tattoo on the inside of his wrist. It was an Ouroboros, a snake eating its own tail. There was a book in our Paris apartment, something in Greek, with a similar image embossed on its cover. When I was little I used to run my fingers over it, around and around. Martin was talking to Joyce and Sylvie, reassuring them that he was fine, that Ray's outburst had been understandable, given the circumstances. Meanwhile the phone in the kitchen rang five or six times, then stopped, then started up again. Finally with a *tsk* of annoyance Joyce left us to answer it, but was soon back.

"He's dead," she said. It was just a whisper.

Sylvie dropped her head into her hands and let out a muffled sob. Joyce started to cross the room to inform the other customers, but Martin grabbed her arm. "Let them finish. They'll know soon enough." She nodded and sat down, laying her arm across Sylvie's shoulders. I felt out of place, as though I were witnessing a private grief shared by family members. I felt stupid having wasted the months at Bard smoking pot and listening to music when I should have been learning the fundamentals of my heritage. I did not understand the impact of this event. I felt I ought to leave them to it, and got up.

"I need to go and check at work," I said, which was sort of true.

"Wait. Don't go," said Sylvie. "We need to be together today. All of us. Don't you think, Martin?"

"Yes, you're right, we do. Let's go back to the island. Come and have supper with me."

And so I was pulled along. We stopped off at The Governor Hancock first, where I found no sign of life. I left a note to say I'd been there, then Sylvie and I drove toward the bay. Martin drove his own car, and would wait at the landing to ferry us across.

When we got to the island Martin told us he'd need an hour or so to sit, but then we should all come. "Bring whatever food you want," he said. "Min has made a pot of chicken stew." Min was the housekeeper, Sylvie explained after he'd left us on the path, and Martin needing to "sit" meant he wanted to meditate, another thing I had no idea about, except that I knew the Beatles did it with some Maharishi in India.

The evening didn't quite turn out as planned. Sylvie and I went directly to the vegetable garden which was located in the center of the island. The natural concavity of the landscape had been further hacked out of the underbrush, and Ray and Sal rowed boatloads of horse manure from a neighbor's corral across the narrows to improve the sandy, acid soil. They were always having to lop off encroaching vines, pull up milkweed and uncurl briars from the rows of vegetables, but overall the thing was quite lush and healthy. We picked a large bundle of salad greens, fat pea pods, asparagus and a dozen spring onions. Walking along the path to the house to put together a salad, we heard Jimi Hendrix's guitar screaming through the trees, making the birds flap around looking for a place to settle. We found Ray sitting at the table, staring at his hands. Sylvie dumped the vegetables in the sink and went over to him, put her arms around him and kissed his neck. While they murmured to each other I began to wash the greens and toss them onto a dishtowel. Sylvie turned the music down after a few minutes and I could hear what they were saying which made me uncomfortable enough that I went outside to wait on the porch. Somehow she and Ray had turned the misery of Bobby Kennedy's shooting into a discussion about some problem in their sex life. I sat outside the door for a long time watching the water glinting through the trees, then wandered down to the garden again and for lack of anything better to do, began pulling weeds. I had never pulled a weed in my life, but I could certainly tell the difference between lettuce and grass, so I killed some time doing that while I waited. The dirt was warm and fragrant and the grass came out with a satisfying muffled rip. I spent an hour happily employed before anyone came, and when I turned at the sound of footsteps, there stood Martin holding a wooden salad bowl and beckoning me with his chin.

"C'mon," he said. "Those two are still talking. I don't know when it'll end. Let's go up to my place. I'll give you a glass of wine while we wait."

I followed him up a small incline through more of the endless brambles until we came to a clearing. Patchy, dried out lawn surrounded a two story structure that looked like one of the old barns I'd seen in the Hudson Valley around Bard. Its clapboards had been painted white at one time, but had been left to weather to a diaphanous gray. Each clapboard had a groove cut into the lower edge which made an allover pattern of thin, dark wood stripes. On the second story an immense x-braced panel was rolled to one side. In the space were a pair of glass doors. Under them, a thin metal staircase spiraled up to a tiny balcony. We followed a shell path around the house, ducked under the fronds of a willow tree, then stepped onto a tidy skirt of lawn with panoramic views of the water. The barrier beach looked insubstantial, just a stripe of white holding back the mighty Atlantic. I wondered what it was like to see it in winter with the north wind pushing huge waves onto it. How did mere sand withstand ocean storms? I turned to ask Martin, and gasped at what I saw. He was opening a screen door in a wall of glass. The house's entire east-facing facade was made up of different sized, pieced-together windows. Most of the upper ones had screens, but the hundreds of mullions in those below made a patchwork of reflected light and color. Mirrored, the barrier beach stretched a wobbly white line across the panes, the marsh glowed brilliant green, the sky was a mosaic of blues. There I stood as well, fragmented like a cubist painting. I started to fool with it, shifting my head to split it in two, shooting a hip into the next frame, extending my arms to look like disconnected puzzle pieces.

"Ahm-m." Martin, framed in the middle of it all, held the door for me, smiling at my antics. I stepped inside, then stood there for another stunned minute taking in the room as he inched around me into the kitchen area, put down the bowl and picked up a bottle of red wine. "This stuff is good," he said, waving it at me.

"Great, thanks," I murmured, completely distracted by the dazzle and sumptuousness of the space. Sixty feet long and half as wide, the entire downstairs was one big room. At one end a kind of office was set up, with a big desk against the wall, bookshelves surrounding it. The center area was taken up by an enormous coffee table made of lustrous black wood inlaid with a pattern of twigs. Surrounding the table were five oversized white-upholstered chairs. On one end of the table, splayed across its width, lay a carved wooden horse, eyes closed, its front legs crossed in sleep. A glossy black burl made up the horse's rump. I wanted to rest my hand on it, to feel the smooth, cool surface. The rest of the table was strewn with books, piles of magazines, a giant silver candelabra, a bowl of oranges, a grouping of phallic cacti shooting up from a shallow pot. I reached out to touch one just as Martin put a glass of wine on the table in front of me.

"I wouldn't, if I were you," he said. "I don't know where we keep the tweezers, and Min has gone home." It made me feel like a child and I felt myself blush as I sunk into one of the chairs. I was a little uneasy anyway, being there with this man I did not know. Even though he was old, he gave off a kind of vibrancy, a person excited by life, and in control of that emotion. He would laugh if he could read that now, but it's what I thought, and in a way I wasn't wrong. The room itself confirmed it. Martin had power, even though it was the last thing he wanted, or wanted anyone to think. He shucked off his sandals and put his feet on the table, sipped his wine while I looked around. I didn't know what to say, so I said nothing. The place was uncluttered, but not spare. It had clearly been arranged for presentation rather than for pure comfort, and it was full of beautiful things –not exactly the type of *objets* I grew up with, but I recognized the habitat of a collector. Then I saw something across the room which was surprising to me, a thing out of place yet so familiar. It was a painting I knew by Robert Motherwell, two huge black monoliths hovering in a field of yellow ochre, holding a triangle of white between them. We had a framed print of it in the apartment back home, but could this possibly be the original? It was nearly six feet across. I took a sip of wine while I stared, worrying idly about spilling on the creamy upholstery. As a kid I used to gaze at the image, wondering why I loved it so. It was a grouping of blobs, of smudges, but somehow it affected me.

I pointed to the painting. "We have a copy of that in our apartment. It's in the bathroom, over the tub. It's part of the fun of taking a bath." I stood back, studied the picture. "Ours has a darker brown area on the lower right. I always thought was paint, but now I see it must be a water stain." I glanced at Martin. I was saying something stupid, clearly, because he was staring at me, the corners of his mouth fighting a smile. I took another sip of wine, put the glass hurriedly back on the table. "Is it the same one?" I asked. I couldn't see a signature.

He raised his eyebrows. "Well, I haven't seen yours, but that's a Motherwell. Excuse me, but I'm smiling because I have never met anyone of your age who knows of his existence, not to mention takes a bath under *Afternoon in Barcelona*. He laughed. "Show me where the water stain is on your copy, will you?"

I thought he might be making fun of me, but I got up anyway, went over to the canvas and waved my arm in an arc across the general area. "It's sort of orange-brown," I added.

"Wonderful!" he exclaimed. "Does it improve it? Now that you see the original?"

I looked at the painting. "Actually, no," I said. "This is much better." Of course it was. The black was lustrous, almost throbbing. It was a great comfort, seeing it there. I felt it connected me to this new place, and to Martin, in a way. I felt my bathtub contemplations confirmed, and I relaxed.

"Your house is very interesting," I said. A more articulate word existed for what it was, I was sure, but I couldn't come up with it at that moment. Many other paintings and photographs hung on the walls or leaned against them. Wood and stone carvings, pottery and glass sculptures stood on the floor or on tables and stands throughout the room, even on the kitchen counter, where, poised over a shallow marble bowl half full of garlic cloves, Martin had placed a bronze statuette of a man with a sack slung over his shoulder broadcasting seeds, sowing the wide bowl with garlic. His things were not arranged immaculately as if on display; the place looked more like the personal lair of someone who has a good time with his

64

stuff. As on the outside, the walls had been left alone, boards painted with thinned white paint, letting the wood's grain show through. The floors were plain as well, simple pine boards except for under the coffee table. There Martin had a woven carpet. Not a kilim, which I knew so well from my father's world, but something similar I could not identify. Orange background with a white and black diamond pattern. It had been stitched to something thicker to make it more plush. The light fixtures were handmade paper, the furniture was birch or something. Light, not heavy and dense. Modern.

Martin glanced around the room, said "Yes, I like it here, thanks." He went over to the kitchen and lit the stove under a big blue pot, then began to pull plates and bowls from the cupboards. "You can put these on the coffee table, OK?" He held them out to me and I distributed them, then went back to the kitchen for cutlery. On the way past the fridge I noticed a picture of Einstein taped to the side. He had a goofy look for the camera, and held up a forefinger. In red letters across the bottom it read, *"Energy cannot be created or destroyed, it can only be changed from one form to another."* Someone had written the word MATTER across his mustache in red crayon, and colored his lower lip as well. I stood there trying to work it out. I noticed Martin eyeing me as he lowered the flame under the pot. I read the quote twice, hoping I understood it. The graffiti part was a mystery. I supposed it had something to do with the look on Einstein's face.

I tilted my head at the picture, about to ask about it, when Martin spoke.

"Know what this is?" He held out a wishbone, cutting off my question.

"Yes."

"All right, then help me for a moment." He placed the bone in the traditional position, curled into a pinkie. I took the other side in mine. "I need to make a decision," he said. "Ready?"

We pulled, he perhaps with a little more gusto than I, and so I came away with the stem. "You got your wish," he said, turning back to the blue pot on the stove. "What was it, if I may ask?"

I hadn't made one, so I said, "I want to know about this Einstein thing on the fridge."

"Ha!" The sudden guffaw crumbled to an affable chuckle. "Oh god! It's kind of a joke, but sure!" He draped an arm over my shoulder. "Let's see, ah, where do I begin?" He gave me a gentle shove toward the coffee table. "Let's go and sit. I need more wine for this." He opened the fridge. "Want some cheese?"

"Sure." I sat down and picked up my glass while he rooted around, tossing things onto the counter. "You don't really have to explain," I added.

"No, no, I want to. Everyone needs to know this stuff. And it pertains to my decision, so. Hold on." He unwrapped a wedge of cheese and laid it on a plate, added a knife and half a baguette –a baguette!– and brought it over. "The thing is, it's not too difficult to grab onto the basic idea, you likely even learned it in school. We've all heard of the equation e=mc2, right?" He drew it in the air.

"Yes, but I never really understood it."

"Okay. Everything is made of energy. Vibrating energy. I mean everything –this table, this cheese, the house, the island, the water, you and me. Sound is a vibration. So are thoughts. That's the 'e'."

"Uh-huh."

Now, you can look at energy as matter in a chaotic state, but actually, matter is just extremely structured energy."

"Okay." I was already lost.

"No, that wasn't clear enough. Try this: Everything is energy vibrating. The rate at which it vibrates makes a wave, a pattern. If there is some other energy vibrating at exactly the same frequency, the two will naturally attract." He shook his head. "No, that's putting it too simply. Too simply."

He sat staring at the table for several moments, until I murmured, "I see. . ." But I was thinking, So if there is a cheese somewhere else vibrating with the same frequency as the one on the table, would it show up here? Or why doesn't our cheese fly off back to the Netherlands, to the hunk it was sliced from? It was ridiculous.

"Okay. Back to e=mc2."

"Uh-huh," I said.

"Right. Now, matter cannot be obliterated . . . "

There was a knock at the door then, and Sylvie strode swiftly in, followed by Ray. She set a bottle of Chianti on the kitchen counter, then slid it on its straw base, idly knocking it from hand to hand.

"He's not already talking about kooky quantum theory, is he?" She tilted her head, looking at Martin with one eyebrow raised. "Elli, don't pay attention. He used to be a respectable chemist until he discovered beat poetry and peyote buttons."

I didn't know what to say. I was trying to un-visualize the flying vibrating cheese and remember the exact wording of Einstein's quote.

"Aw c'mon, Sylvie. It's neither kooky nor theory. It's only a kind of science you refuse to understand." Martin patted the chair next to his. "Come, sit. Let's eat. The soup's getting cold waiting for you two."

Ray had already slid into the chair beside me and lifted the lid on the chicken stew. He picked up the ladle and put out his hand for my bowl. While Sylvie and Martin playfully elbowed each other and poured wine, Ray dished out the meal and we got on with eating the stew, savoring each peppery, aromatic stage of flavor. Ray let out a long groan of pleasure that devolved into a slurred diatribe about Kennedy and the pigs in Washington. The three of them had a long discussion about whether the murder spelled the end of any promise at all for this country and Ray thought it did and cried silently, tears leaking down into his beard. Then suddenly he got angry and stomped off out the door. Martin rushed after him.

"Sorry," said Sylvie.

"It's okay, I get it." I slid an asparagus tip between my lips and crushed it. "I mean, I don't have the same history as you, but I am beginning to see that this is a disaster."

"Yeah, I guess that's what you'd call it," Sylvie picked at her salad, too. "For you and me it won't make that much difference. But if you were a black teenager in rural Alabama, you had hope. For something to change, you know? Now?" She made a little puff sound with her lips. "It's like they picked them off, one by one."

She got up and stood at the glass wall to look for Ray and Martin. When she didn't find them she turned and went over to the stereo by Martin's desk.

"There's something I haven't told you," she said, clicking on the radio. A piece of classical music filled the room, a dramatic cello-sawing which she zipped past immediately, passed over a few jabbering advertisements until she settled on young men harmonizing a sweet, poetic song. "The fucking Vietnam war. It must have occurred to you that Ray and Sal are draftable material, right?"

It hadn't. I wasn't clear about the system which obliged young men to fight, and though I was aware of the war because certainly it was discussed at Bard, for some reason I had left the subject behind along with my books and records. I had a vague idea that people volunteered to be in the military, and not much more. "No, actually," I said. "I don't know how the draft works over here."

"They should both be there. But they refuse to go, and neither of them wants to move to Canada. They have a mother in Boston, for God's sake, and they already lost one brother to that senseless bloodbath."

I was stunned. "I'm so sorry," mumbled.

"Yeah. Everyone is. See, their father fought in the second world war. He was a hero, and those boys grew up playing war and taking to heart Kennedy's 'Ask not what your country can do for you,' speech. They were more than ready to do for their country when the time came. Especially Marco. He was the oldest, and he went over there, gung-ho and ready to come home and be respected for his patriotic exploits. But he was blown up in an underground tunnel because he tripped over a root and triggered a bomb. That's what they think, anyway."

"Jesus. I'm sorry," I repeated.

"So Ray and Sal disappeared. There was no way they were going after that. Ray had been here once for a summer weekend and camped out on this island, not realizing it was privately owned or had a house on the other end. When he and Sal ran, they came here. Just by chance it was the year after Martin's wife died, and he was by himself, suffering and lonely. He asked them to stay and even encouraged them to build the house we live in. They take care of the place when he's not around, and in return he keeps their secret and has protected them all this time, and so far it's worked."

"That sounds impossible. How could . . ."

"It's because no one in town dares to challenge Martin. Or maybe they don't know, it's hard to say. Of course nobody thought the war would still be going on as long as this, but here we are."

"So, Ray and Sal can't leave?"

"That's right. Not until the war ends."

I couldn't quite grasp the actuality of what Sylvie had just explained. I stood there with my mouth hanging open while I tried to work out the details of how they managed.

"I won't say anything, of course."

"Of course. Or we will kill you." She sang along with the radio for a while about seasons and the turning of the planet, a playful smile on her face, then stopped abruptly and said, "Just kidding. C'mon, Elli. We know you're one of us, but seriously. You cannot say anything. To anyone. Got it?"

I nodded, but didn't know how to move past it. I looked around Martin's house with renewed interest. Knowing that he had helped Ray and Sal in those circumstances made him seem even more impressive, and tragic.

"So. What do you think of Martin's art collection?" Sylvie asked, to change the subject.

I pointed to the Motherwell and told her about the one-fifth size we had hanging over the tub at home.

"Want to see another?" She got up and beckoned for me to follow her. We took the staircase by the kitchen to the bedroom. A large room under the eaves extended to the little balcony I'd noticed on the way over. Unpainted rafters separated swags of white fabric which billowed slightly in

70

the breeze from the open doors, giving the room a tent-like atmosphere. I felt shy and intrusive looking at Martin's bed, another expanse of white broken by a fuzzy black mohair blanket folded back on one side, as though he'd just gotten up from a nap. Another large kilim-type rug lay on the floor next to it, with a pair of red *babouche* slippers lined up on the border of its zigzag design. The late sun sent orange light in through the balcony doors, making another pattern across the floor. The room felt cozy in spite of the sparse decor, and there was a scent around the bed, a whiff of sandalwood and cigarettes, like in the Turk's Head.

"Check it out." Sylvie stood at the foot of the bed, aiming her thumb over her shoulder at the wall behind her, where a little canvas hung at bed level, a long rectangle of fat black splotches bumping into each other in places. "I want to understand it, and I'm working on it," she murmured, her eyes scanning back and forth across the canvas, "but it's like you have to remember being little again, with your crayons, you know?"

I nodded, still engrossed in looking around the room. I stepped closer to study the painting. I noticed that the edges of black were painted very carefully, not slopped on in a quick gesture, as my mother seemed to do. The white was very white in places, slightly beige in others. It gave the black shapes such stature, pushed them forward to quiver off each other with quiet intensity. Of course I didn't have those words back then. It's only now on reflection that I can come up with a proper description. Back then I said, "Yeah. But still, you want to keep looking. I guess that's all there is."

"I forgot – your mother is a famous painter, right?"

"Yes. But don't ask me to explain her art, either."

"I wonder if Martin knows her stuff. We'll have to ask. He knows everyone –I mean in that world. In this one he just tries to get away from people."

I laughed. "He seems pretty friendly to me."

Sylvie sank down on the rug and leaned against the bed, stretching out her legs. "He's had a weird life. He inherited all this money." She spread her hands to include the house, the whole island. "His father invented a drug, basically a syrup to make unhappy women controllable. That's where it came from."

I sat on the floor across from her in the criss-cross pattern of sunset light. It glowed orange on my knees. "I guess it was a big success," I said, looking around.

"Yeah. Huge. But he grew up a pretty unhappy kid. Lonely. His mother had him and then spent years suffering, being depressed. She drank a lot of booze. He told me once she said to him: 'I barely survived your birth. You got your spoink all over me once.'"

"Spoink?"

"Yeah, you know, doo-doo."

"*Merde.*"

"She said it was the last time she changed his diapers. She had the maid do it. I guess that was normal for rich people. She told him that's why she never had any more kids. It was too disgusting."

"That's horrible."

"Yeah. She drank all day in secret. His father was a chemist, and he tried all kinds of drugs on her to get her to cheer up. Finally he invented Nervilex, which worked, mainly because it was loaded with lithium salts and opium, and in combination with the booze, she got happier, just when Martin went off to college."

"Nervilex. That's what made him rich?"

"Yup. His parents died when he was in his 30s. By then he was living out on the west coast with his own family. Get this: his father died in the back of a car. He was being driven home one night, through a section of Brooklyn where they were working on the road. The driver hit a can, a big container of gas. It landed on the hood of the car and bounced through the windshield, right into Martin's father's head."

It sounded complicated. I was trying to picture the can and its trajectory when she added, "His mother died almost exactly a year later, falling down drunk in the garage. She hit her head on a can of gas. Freaky, right?"

"Very strange."

"Martin is a chemist, too. Or was, I should say. He went into the family business because his father told him he lacked the social skills for anything else. So he spent his twenties sitting on a stool in a pharmaceutical lab, dribbling concoctions together, hoping for another product that worked so he could get rich and move away."

Sylvie crossed her arms behind her head and looked up at the ceiling. "He told me he used to stay up all night listening to jazz. He loved Artie Shaw. Opera too. He met a man at a record store, some beatnik poet. He was Martin's only friend back then. They'd get drunk together and play records, read poems out loud to each other. He's the one who introduced Martin to abstract art. They used to go to galleries around the city, and his friend would always talk about how they should go to Provincetown. He said that's where he'd get famous, and where they could make it as actors, and he would be able to hang around with artists, reading his poetry in the sun. Martin really liked the idea and tried to figure out how to get away from his father so they could go. But then one night his friend got drunk and tried to talk Martin into stealing some laudanum from the lab. That's like heroin. He wanted them to get high together. Martin wouldn't do it but the guy kept asking, then begging. Within a couple of months Martin stopped seeing him. The friend would come around and bang on his door, yelling. Fortunately right around then he was asked to hand deliver some formula to Berkeley Lab in California, and he decided not to come back."

"So, how old was he then?" I was confused about the time frame. I knew nothing of the infamous West Coast except what I'd heard my Bard friends discussing, but that was Jimi Hendrix and love-ins, not poetry, Artie Shaw and laudanum.

"It's easy with him. He was born in 1900. So, whatever year it is, he's that old."

"Sixty-eight. Hm."

"Seems much younger, doesn't he."

"Uh-huh." I would have said fifty.

A door slammed, and footsteps crossed the floor below. Martin called out, "Sylvie?"

"Coming." She leapt up and grabbed my hand, pulling me along. Martin was in the kitchen driving a corkscrew into another bottle of wine as Ray sat bent over, cradling something in his lap.

"Look at what he found." Martin tipped his head toward Ray, who opened his hands and held up a ball of quivering yellow fluff for our inspection.

"What is it?" Sylvie said, stepping closer.

"A gosling. Canada goose." Ray held it up to his face and peered at it. "It was just sitting in the sand. No other geese in sight."

"We left it alone for a while to see if it would be rescued, but it followed us," said Martin. He brought the wine bottle to the table and sat. I knelt next to Ray's knees and touched the down on its tiny head.

"We walked around the whole island. Nothing." Ray looked at Sylvie for approval, but she frowned and said, "Well there isn't much daylight left. What are you going to do with it?"

"I don't know."

"I suppose if you put it back it would die," Sylvie stood, hands on hips, contemplating the situation. "What do they eat?"

"No idea." said Ray. The gosling waddled off his hand and fell into his lap, pushed its beak into the fuzz on its chest, and closed its tiny black eyes.

"I guess you'd better find out," said Martin. Ray smiled at him, his own red rimmed eyes closing like the little bird's. It was the beginning of a friendship. That goose lived on the island all summer. Ray named it Bobby, though we never found out if it was a male or female. Bobby was a much better watchdog than either Rollo or Roxie, and could be quite intimidating if anyone except Ray got too close.

Ray's head began to nod, and he joined the little gosling in a doze. Sylvie turned from him and whispered to Martin, "I showed Elli the other Motherwell painting."

"Oh, yes?" Martin turned his excited eyes my way. "What do you think?"

"It's okay." In truth those black throbbing blobs had thrilled me, but I found I could not separate them in my mind from Martin's white-covered bed with the black blanket so clearly folded back from his post-meditating body. It was too intimate a scene for me to dwell on, and besides, after three glasses of wine I was too foggy to offer any naive opinions of modern art.

"There should be a window there instead." I said, then immediately regretted it, because it's not at all what I thought, but I did not want to talk about his bedroom or anything in it.

"Maybe you're right," said Martin. He looked at me and smiled indulgently, as if I had expressed his own doubt about the decor.

"Elli's mother is a painter," said Sylvie.

"Oh?" Again, Martin aimed his nearly-black eyes at me.

I nodded. "She's pretty well known in Paris, I guess. I don't know about anywhere else."

"What's her name? Maybe I've heard of her." Martin took a sip of wine and glanced at Sylvie, who had gotten up and was busy clearing the supper dishes. When I told Martin my mother's name delight lit up his face.

"Of course I know her work. I have some photos around here somewhere. I'll show you." He went over to his desk, opened a filing drawer and began flipping through folders. "Have a look," he said, settling on the arm of my chair and handing me a packet. He looked over my shoulder as I laid them out on the table. There were four color Polaroids of large framed paintings. It looked like they'd been taken in a gallery. I recognized two of them from photos pinned up in our apartment. I think they were things done years ago, and likely had been sold. I said so to Martin.

"These others I've never seen. But that's not unusual. My mother has piles of them in her studio. She's been painting since before I was born."

"I've been an admirer of her work for a long time." Martin moved back to his own chair, and Sylvie came and sat again, too. She picked up the photos, looked through

76

them and selected one. "Nice," she said, tossing it back on the table.

"Her old studio is in the woods next to the house," I said to Martin.

"Really?" He leaned forward excitedly. "You don't suppose I could come over and look at it, do you?"

"Sure. It's empty, but you're welcome to come and see."

We made a date for two days later, in the afternoon after I was done at the motel. Martin said he would come in his motorboat. Sylvie announced that it was time for her to go, and said she'd drive me around to my house, or I could stay with them for the night.

"If it's not too much trouble, I think I'd like to go back home," I said. "I have to go to work in the morning."

"No trouble at all," she said, but in the end it was Ray who rowed us over to the other side of the narrows and drove the winding roads which skirted the various inlets and estuaries of Pleasant Bay and out onto Barley Neck, a distance of only a mile or so by water, but a five mile trip on land. The little gosling huddled in his crotch for the entire time while we sat in silence.

When we pulled into the driveway I thanked him and he apologized for his earlier behavior. "I can't understand how we're supposed to proceed from here," he said, scanning my face as if the answer was to me an obvious course of action. His eyes skittered back and forth across mine, perhaps waiting for a gem of old-world wisdom, even though he was older and more experienced in the basics of getting through life. I thought of the idyllic hour I'd spent in his garden, pulling weeds. It had been one of the most peaceful and satisfying I'd ever lived. The pain of my father's death, the worry over my immediate future, the shame of dropping out of college all vanished from my thoughts where they had been a constant chorus for the last month. Instead I'd thought of nothing at all, and I was happy.

"Your garden is a good place to be." It just came out of my mouth, sounding banal. But Ray nodded thoughtfully, and smiled. His white teeth glowed in the dark of the car as I grasped the door handle.

"Oh wow. You're so right," he said. "So right."

"Thanks for the ride." I closed the door softly so as not to wake Bobby. When I got inside I picked up a little blue and white glass blob from the shelf, one of my father's collection, a protection against the evil eye. He always kept one in his pants pocket. I climbed into bed with it in my fist and drifted off to sleep.

Chapter Five

Martin didn't come to my house as planned. Instead I came home from work to find a note from Sylvie wedged into the porch door:

"Martin had to leave for a few days. Problems at his place in New York. He asked me to let you know he's sorry he can't make it over to see the studio, but wants to when he gets back. C'mon over and hang out with us po' folks whenever. Just yell if you come by bike and I'll row across."

She signed off with a peace sign dotting the 'i' in her name.

That was fine with me. I had been feeling a little sidetracked from my solo habits after the events of the past week, and wanted to get back to fishing and cornbread, memorizing the map and other novel pastimes of my new life which kept me feeling in control, like spending time with my father. I had developed an evening routine of sitting on the front lawn in one of the wicker chairs wearing a suit of his that I found in the back of the closet. The suit was so old it looked like something from a gangster movie. Its original white linen had yellowed and was so flimsy from being chewed by bugs that I could have torn the pants off at the knees as easily as a piece from a roll of paper towel. I smoked a few cigarettes, trying to summon him through the taste of tobacco. I even wore his old gray felt hat which was much too hot, but smelled faintly of the hair oil he used. I sat there with my eyes closed, imagining not only myself and my sister as kids crawling around on the lawn, but my mother back in the house, maybe chopping up onions for supper, or coming up behind me carrying two glasses of red wine. It was a bit of a mental strain being my father twenty years ago, and filling in the details I no doubt got many things wrong but somehow it made me feel good. I'm sure I looked ridiculous with his pants rolled up and the jacket sleeves turned back a few times. Nevertheless, sitting in the chair wearing my father's suit and smoking, pretending to be him looking out over the bay and luxuriating in his good fortune had become my time with him. It took the edge off my longing to have him there, so to speak, and gradually, in the weeks after his death my fantasies became a pretty effective way for me to say goodbye and allow him to be dead.

I was in that state one evening, having a final few puffs before going inside to heat up some food. I'd concocted a dinner by adding fried onions and potatoes to a can of Campbell's mushroom soup, my favorite cheap and versatile ingredient. I made many meals from those quivering blobs of beige sludge. I could add almost any vegetable to it as long as it was fried first in lots of butter. Pour the whole thing over some minute rice and life was perfect. I loved American food products. So easy! My only culinary disappointment, I was shocked to learn, was that it was forbidden for me to buy wine to go with my dinner until I turned 21, nearly a year away.

Normally I would have been alerted to Moony's presence by the sound of his car in the driveway, but this evening he had walked along the shore and come up the path. When his head and shoulders appeared in front of me we both experienced a moment of shock before I leapt up and ran inside, and he retreated backwards to the little dock below. I snatched the hat from my head and yelled out the porch door, "Wait, Moony! Don't leave!" I quickly stripped off the suit, tearing it irreparably in the process, and reappeared on the lawn a few moments later in my shorts and t-shirt. I called down the hill to him. He came, climbing slowly up the carved-out steps, looking embarrassed and holding a paper bag.

"I brought you something." He held out the paper bag. I thanked him silently for not commenting on my previous costume, and took it.

"A friend of mine had it in his garage, just sitting there. Your mother told me you might want one." Inside the bag was a small AM/FM radio, a desk model with green flowers printed on the speaker panel in front. I was overjoyed at the sight of it and kissed Moony on the cheek which made him plow his fingers through his hair a few times. Inside, he dragged the bookshelf away from the wall to expose one of the few outlets in the house.

"You'll need an antenna if you want to use the FM part," he said. I didn't know what FM was or what difference it made, I only knew I would soon have music.

Sure enough, when Moony plugged in the radio a song came bursting forth, its bass line throbbing the speaker flowers into a blur as a trio of horns blasted backup, and Moony and I stood there grinning while *'Poke Salad Annie'* wound down, the DJ yelled, "It's a Solid Gold Weekend!" and launched into another hit. I was overjoyed.

Eventually Ray explained to me about AM versus FM stations, and fixed me up with an antenna which pulled in the brand-new WBCN, a station in Boston which he had only recently discovered. It was one of the first in the country to trailblaze a kind of role for radio in the political and cultural arena of young people as well as to launch the careers of many now famous artists. But in the summer of '68 it played the music I already loved and introduced me to so much more. I learned a lot about American culture and formed my most abiding political opinions that summer, often listening late into the night.

I often met up with Sylvie and Sandy at the Turk's Head after work. The summer was in full swing by then. Main Street had tourists strolling up and down the sidewalk, the benches in front of the cemetery were usually crowded with families. Kids ran around unguarded, vaulting off the headstones into the lush mowed grass. A funk of hot tar and exhaust fumes wafted over them, mixed with a sugar-sick smell from the taffy shop across the street. The Turk's Head was always dark and cool, somehow the cartoon-jumpy center of town atmosphere did not penetrate. The three of us would sit, telling stories and drinking cup after cup of Joyce's excellent coffee. Sylvie worked for an attorney in town whose clients were almost all people with summer houses. They paid the attorney a yearly retainer to do what legal work there was, but since very little came up he mostly acted as a caretaker, hiring carpenters and housepainters and other maintenance people. Sylvie organized most of it while her boss sat in the The Foc'sle reading the paper and drinking scotch. Sylvie had a vast network of friends who would do anything for her at a moment's notice, because she charged the owners an inflated rate and passed it on to them. These seasonal homeowners all used this same lawyer and referred each new arrival to him.

"They sit around sucking down cocktails together and boasting about their bathroom makeover or whatever. The next day I'll get a call from another one wanting theirs done. Keeps us all busy and everyone's happy." She also had a lucrative side income dealing pot from the office, which her boss knew nothing about. Sometimes Sylvie would phone Sandy at the The Foc'sle and get her to keep her boss there for another drink so she could conduct a late day transaction. Sandy would get her reward in the form of a constant supply, and she was almost always high. Even when not, Sandy was one of those naturally buoyant people who seem to gambol through life oblivious to sorrow or struggle. I studied her, trying to deduce her formula for happiness, but of course I didn't get anywhere. I've learned we each have to concoct our own.

Joyce often sat with us when business was slow, or she would turn up the volume on the record player and huddle with Sylvie at another table for a private conference. Sylvie was usually in tears during one of these talks, and didn't share any of it with us after. I assumed it had to do with Ray and didn't ask. Her friendship with Joyce went back several years to when Sylvie was in college and Joyce ran a little gypsy-type scam selling magazine subscriptions. She'd recruited a small band of college dropouts who would drive around with her to various New England

83

campuses. There they would mingle with the students, telling some sob story to get them to buy the subscriptions from which Joyce and her crew would get a kickback. Sylvie quit school to join them. I don't know exactly how the scheme worked, but apparently it was quite a good income for a while, until Joyce got in trouble and the whole thing fell apart. Sylvie said she was getting to old to mix with the students anyway. I learned that Joyce was the daughter of a multimillionaire who had secured a patent for a certain process in the refining of gasoline from oil. She grew up in a ritzy Boston suburb and attended Smith College, but had been disowned by her family because of her involvement with a man whose cousin was Malcolm X. "I think she made a deal with her father," Sylvie speculated. "He'd take care of her if she left Boston. I guess Cape Cod is far enough and white enough." Joyce was also linked to Martin. She had known him through friends in the folk music scene around Harvard Square, where he had spent time before coming to the Cape.

"He belonged to some weird church there for a few years," Sylvie told us one day when we were on that oft-discussed subject. Martin had been gone for about three weeks at that point "They ate very specific foods and practiced some combination of Chinese medicine and physics. Like Karate I guess."

"Not exactly," Joyce interjected on her way past with a tray. "They were practicing Tai Chi. It's a way to move energy around. Chi is the energy. It travels along certain pathways in your body."

I remembered the conversation Martin and I started to have about vibrating energy. The wedge of cheese reappeared in my mind and I looked around the room, squinting at the chairs and tables, trying to visualize them as buzzing clusters of atoms. I studied the inside of my forearm, dumbfounded by the idea that even more could be going on in there. I made a mental note to ask Martin to finish telling me about the Einstein clipping stuck to his fridge. All I recalled was the idea that things were attracted to each other based on a harmonious pattern of vibration. And that he had included our thoughts in his list of things doing it.

"Thought is energy," I heard myself say. It just came out of my mouth.

"Oh, man, are you on the same trip as Martin?" Sandy leaned closer and studied my eyes. "Freaky," she added, sliding her arm along the back of my chair and nodding eagerly across at Sylvie.

"She's right. He talked to me a lot about that stuff, and I sort of get it." Sylvie took a gulp of coffee, her eyes growing darker with concentration. "I try to imagine a sort of vast, endless zone, like space. But it's a continuously vibrating mass of pure energy, like atoms or particles or whatever, floating around all disorganized. Until some of them attract each other because their pattern matches and they become something: matter. Which is everything." She shrugged dismissively. "I don't know. I'm not sure I believe that we all conjure up our own realities from our thought vibes drawing a bunch of atoms like a magnet."

"Besides, we're all seeing the same things." Sandy looked around the room and then from me to Sylvie for confirmation. "Right?"

"It's confusing, but if you think of your thoughts as energy, and energy is what makes up atoms, and atoms are what make up things, like this chair, or you, Sandy, then thoughts are part of that vibrating mass, too. And so thoughts can hook up with other matching energy in that field of possibility. At least that's what I'm told." Sylvie shrugged. "I've never seen any proof."

"Oh wow," Sandy said. "That's intense. Too heavy for me." She got up and headed for the bathroom.

"I wouldn't mind attracting something with my thoughts," I said, imagining a bag of new summer clothes. The check from my mother had arrived, but it was taking an awfully long time to clear. My summer outfits were decidedly odd. For lack of anything else I now wore my mother's shorts and blouses in public, not only while I was out fishing. I had bought myself a bathing suit and some underwear with my earnings, and cut off a pair of dungarees for shorts. Sylvie and Sandy gave me a few things but I was a Parisian woman, certainly not used to parading around in public in my mother's 20 year old cast-offs. On the other hand I harbored a secret delight in the fact that nobody seemed to care. Sandy pointed out that my handful of 1940-era linen blouses with their corny designs were beautifully made. "You look bitchin'," she said.

Sandy left shortly after, and we returned briefly to the topic of energy, atoms and matter, but only in a superficial way, mostly because Sylvie had already exhausted her sketchy knowledge of it which was culled from much further-ranging sessions listening to Martin talk about it, which he tended to do frequently in those days. She told me he made a few trips to Boston to the library at MIT to peruse what material he could find, and spent long hours scribbling away at his desk, or meditating, doing what he called "thought experiments," trying to conjure something by concentration. Although I hadn't heard him use the term, I now understand that he was using elements of quantum mechanics, specifically about entangled particles, to validate his hypotheses about time travel, which no physicist, even an amateur one, would ever admit to doing.

All this was before his return from Brooklyn Heights in New York, where he still owned a substantial mansion inherited from his parents. He spent the winter months there, and in another house somewhere in California off the coastal highway. He had spent decades collecting works of art and had turned these houses into private museums with full-time staff who took charge when he was on Sipson's. Now and then he would lend a painting to the Metropolitan art museum or meet with the curator of a specific traveling exhibition, and would oversee the details of contracts and transportation, spending time among a vast network of creators and collectors in the world of contemporary art.

As soon as Martin appeared on the island again he sent Ray over to my place with a note apologizing for delaying his visit to my mother's studio and asking if he might see it at my "earliest convenience." I asked Ray to tell him to stop by the following afternoon if he wanted, or any afternoon after four, which would give me time to strip off my uniform and have a swim to wash off the smell of the ammonia-laden cleaning products we used at the motel.

He showed up the next afternoon with a bouquet of white iris, a favorite of mine. He looked almost as pale as the flowers, as if he'd been kept in a box since I'd last seen him. He wore a loose black Moroccan shirt and white linen trousers which he had bunched to his knees for the the boat ride over. They slid down as he picked his way across the parched grass to the porch where I sat drying my hair with an old towel.

"Hello my dear," he said as I scrambled to fix myself.

"Oh, hi, come in." I held the screen door for him as he stepped gingerly inside, proffering the iris. He made a little bow at my delighted thanks and followed me into the house. I left him admiring the fireplace while I went into the kitchen for a vase. I spied on him from around the corner as he lifted one item after another from the bookshelf, examined it, and put it back. When he saw one of my mother's little paintings he rushed over. It was a blurry red and pink swirl with a dark blue slash along the bottom. He put his face about three inches away and stared into its center.

"Yup, that's hers," I said, placing the vase of iris on the coffee table. They instantly transformed the somewhat shabby cottage into a chic summerhouse.

"Very interesting." He scrutinized every bit of the picture, then looked around the room for others. I pointed to one hanging on the wall by the front door and he stepped closer.

"I can say for sure those are very early examples. They were here when I arrived, and no one has lived here for sixteen years." I sounded like a museum tour guide.

His eyes widened. "So, these are from the fifties?"

"Or even before. Let's look at the back. Maybe she wrote the date." I lifted the picture off the wall, blew a puff of dust from the frame, and turned it over. There, in careful script, was her name and below that the year: 1947. Her signature had evolved since then. Now it was indecipherable except for the 'B' in Bang. 1947 was the year of my birth. I made a mental note to ask if she remembered painting it. Maybe she did it while pregnant with me.

"Hm," was all Martin said.

"Would you like a glass of water, or something?" I turned to the kitchen and added, "Have a look at the back

88

of the other one if you like." Martin was taking it down when I returned with two glasses.

"I really like her work," he murmured, hanging the picture back on the wall. "I had quite an experience once, looking at one of her pieces. She's very good."

"Shall we go out to her studio?"

I walked ahead of him on the path through the woods. The briars had grown since I'd last been there and were now intertwined with shiny new leaves of poison ivy. I used a dead branch to push them away as we made our way to the door. Martin looked up at the roofline's dramatic slant, nodded his approval, then entered. As soon as he saw the streaks of paint on the wall he said "Oh! Oh, my. Oh, my my my." Standing directly in front of where a canvas would have been tacked up, he reached out to run his fingers along the paint marks that had been left, up one side and down the other. He touched every one. He spun slowly around, looking at every part of the nearly empty room, then went back to staring at the white part of the wall and nodding again. I began to feel in the way, as though I were witnessing some private, intimate moment. I gestured toward the pair of lounge chairs facing the window and said, "Here, have a seat while I go and make us a cup of coffee, all right?"

"Mm-hmm," he murmured distractedly.

As I walked back to the house I thought surely there must have been some important connection between my mother and Martin that he was not telling me about. He seemed more than merely interested in the scraps of her work I'd shown him. It was almost as if he'd been actively involved with the paintings, not merely a connoisseur studying her early work or cast-off paint strokes. Of course it was entirely possible that they might have known each other. But why had he seemed only casually interested when I told him I was her daughter, or that her house and studio were a mile away across the water? This day his behavior was like that of someone obsessed.

As I poured water into the percolator and added coffee grounds to the basket I tried to talk myself down a bit. This man was a collector, and hugely knowledgeable about his subject. Any well-known painter's studio would be fascinating to someone like that. Perhaps it would even be akin to an anthropologist finding the remains of a local Indian tribe's campsite in the woods. I could only imagine the significance. For me, the stuff was old hat. I'd seen plenty of Ria Bang Overtons.

When the coffee was done I poured it over two tall glasses filled with ice cubes and added a splash of milk. I set them on a tray with a dish of Lorna Doone cookies and brought it out to the studio. I got as far as the doorway, but had to put the tray down on the grass so I could watch the goings-on inside without the noise of tinkling ice cubes breaking into Martin's reverie.

He stood facing the wall where the paintings had been made, only this time he was gesturing as a painter would, holding his left index finger an inch or two off the surface and making slashes and scribbles. He would pause, the finger twitching, then dive at the painting, making curving, slicing and daubing gestures. Then he'd stop, step back and take a drag from an invisible cigarette with the other hand, contemplating what he had just done. I watched for several minutes, engrossed in the theatrics, then picked up the tray and stood on the step. He spun around at the sound of my entrance, and after a few startled seconds of reaction took the tray from me and headed over to the chairs, saying, "Oh, lovely. Just what I have been craving all day." But his voice was shaky, uncertain. The cubes were jangling crazily as he put the tray down. He looked fragile, almost translucent, as if he'd been drained of life-giving fluids. His white hair stood up in places, brushed against the grain from running his fingers through.

"But, uh, please excuse me," he mumbled. With his head down he crossed the room and stood in the doorway. "I have to go," he said over his shoulder, then plunged into the bushes and ran down the path.

"What? Martin, wait!" I started after him, but stopped. Maybe he was just standing in the woods nearby, having a pee. Then I heard the sound of grinding gears as he backed out of the driveway.

I looked at the wall, half expecting there to be a fresh painting, but it was the same white square surrounded by cut-off brushstrokes. A movement in the trees above the skylights made the light change, and I saw several of those brushstrokes glisten as if the paint were wet. I went over to have a closer look and sure enough, many of the marks looked freshly painted. I touched the nearest one, then looked at my finger. On its tip was a bright dab of green.

Chapter Six

It was the middle of the night in Paris by the time I reached my mother, but she was awake, thank god.

"I'll call you back, just hang on a minute while I find my other pack of cigarettes." We had a regular phone date, but this wasn't it, so she knew something was off, and would need to smoke. It took her a while to go through the international operator but after several minutes the phone rang out across the little parking lot, and I grabbed it.

"OK, what's going on? Is there still a problem with the check?" she asked as soon as I answered.

"Still no cash, but it's not that." During my bike ride there I had thought hard about how to describe what had happened in her old studio, but I didn't know where to begin. Out of context, or what passed for it, a daub of wet paint didn't sound like much. "It's hard to say."

"Try." I could hear her lighting up across the Atlantic.

"Don't worry, everything is fine. But I have a question for you."

"Yes?"

"In your studio. You painted something tacked directly to the wall, which left marks. Do you remember?"

"No, not really. It was a long time ago. Why?"

I listened to the sound of Paris traffic in the background while I contemplated my answer. The distinctive two-tone of a French police siren made me suddenly, overwhelmingly homesick. I could picture exactly where my mother was sitting; the embroidered peonies on the sofa cushion she always held in her lap when she talked on the phone, a heavy cut-glass ashtray balanced on its brocade.

What happened in the studio had frightened me. After Martin left I looked around the room for a spray can or other evidence of some substance he might have used to bring the dried paint to life again, or anything at all to explain what I had seen, but there was nothing. I ran out the door; spooky thoughts of sorcery, ghosts and demons nipping at my heels made me run even faster, away, away. I expected Martin to jump out of the bushes at any second. I ran blindly for several minutes before finally coming to a halt in the middle of the quiet country road and forcing myself to go back for the bike. It had taken all my courage to enter the house to fetch my handbag.

I dove into my story, nervous about the long-distance charges. "I met someone who knows your work."

She was used to that. "And . . ?"

"And he owns Sipson's Island."

"Wow. Lucky man. Is he the problem?" I could hear a slight protective aggression in her voice. "Have you been there?"

"Yes. He has the same painting as we do in the bathroom. The Motherwell."

"Nice."

"Except it's the original."

"Holy smoke!" she said again. "Are you kidding?"

"No." I didn't know how to tell her about what happened. To tell the truth just the sound of my mother's voice and accompanying city noise had soothed me somewhat, and now, standing alone in the waning summer light, all I wanted was to get back to Barley Neck where I could lock the door and think. "He asked me to show him your studio, and I did. He seemed to know which painting had been painted on that wall. Is it possible?"

"I don't think so, how could he? I painted so many in that space, when you were still babies."

I described to her the size, the colors of the cut-off brush strokes.

"Oh, Elli! Of course I remember now. That was an important piece, the first thing I did which truly accomplished what I'd been struggling with, to . . . to manifest, I guess. It simply came out of me. We were about to leave the Cape, and I didn't have a stretcher frame so I just taped a canvas to the wall. God, that was a long time ago." I heard her sigh, take a drag of her cigarette, and exhale. "Yes, honey, I remember it well. The painting is called *'A Swim at Pochet'*. I did it so fast that afternoon. Your father was out in the water and I was home with you and I was jealous of his . . . his freedom." She hummed, thinking. "It sold years ago, to some American collector. My first gallery here. It was a breakthrough for me but the painting itself was done during a very painful time in my life."

I recognized the title. It was typed on the border of one of the Polaroids Martin had showed us the evening of Kennedy's death. I remembered that when I saw the word 'Pochet' I had felt a little tingle of pride that I now shared my mother's knowledge of the area's place names.

"What was going on?" I hoped it wasn't regret over having had a baby.

"Oh, nothing. Way in the past, now." She sighed, exhaling smoke. I could picture it perfectly. "Maybe your friend is the one who bought it," she said.

The thought had not occurred to me, but it made perfect sense. It would explain Martin's immediate involvement with the scraps of image left on the wall. Maybe he had spent time with the actual painting, going over my mother's strokes the way some people air-conduct an orchestra playing on the stereo. If so he would be familiar with each and every one of them.

"You still there?" I could hear tiredness in her voice. I'd forgotten the time difference.

"Yes, sorry. I think you may have cleared something up for me." I wasn't sure what, but I wanted to go home and work it out.

"So, you're all right?" I heard the familiar distraction in her voice, and despite the sounds in the background, a small echo of emptiness between those words. It was a question I ought to have been asking her, but hadn't. A pang of guilt zapped through me.

"Yeah, I'm fine. Don't worry. Thanks Mom. Love you." I hung up, got back on my bike and pedaled toward Barley Neck, deep in thought about my mother's 'painful time', but buoyed by a possible explanation for Martin's strange gesticulations. It did nothing for the question of the wet paint, but that answer would come, I felt sure. Martin had done something chemically to bring those scraps of painting back to life, for his own obsessive reasons.

I was halfway home when I remembered the sight of Moony lying on the shore the night I came home from Sylvie and Ray's house, when it seemed like he was talking to an invisible person. I pictured the sketch left behind in the sand before the tide washed over it, three lines converging in a point. I had pushed the whole thing from my thoughts, explaining it away as a dope-generated vision. But now my brain was connecting it to this new, equally inexplicable event. I wondered if Martin and Moony knew each other, if there was some sort of supernatural power lurking among the islands and inlets of Pleasant Bay that they had both tapped into. Yes, I know it sounds ridiculous, but you already know how my imagination can be whipped up even by the sight of a blob of pink gum.

As I rolled along in the twilight figuring how to interpret everything that had happened, stars began to appear, their random flicker mirrored by fireflies idling the dark hollows of overhanging elms. Spring peepers chirped in euphonious rhythm. Everything was in sync, oscillating, vibrating. When I arrived at my door I looked back down the dark driveway, then out across the water. The bats were out, flutter-darting figure eights across the clearing. I realized I was no longer afraid of this quiet, mysterious place, but deeply curious.

A few days later I came home from work to find another note pinned to the screen door:

Party tomorrow nite at Sylvie & Ray's place.
Honk when you need the boat. Come early
and bring cornbread please!
Sandy

The rubber bulb of a bicycle horn was wedged into the door handle. I pulled it out and squeezed. The blare startled a passing gull who veered off track and clipped a locust branch. Laughing, I brought the horn inside and tossed it on the sofa. I still hadn't gone back out to the studio to retrieve the coffee tray or close the door which I know I left hanging open. I pictured chipmunks and mice having long since dragged the Lorna Doones back to their nests, a colony of ants settling in for the crumbs, so I went. When I got out there I looked around to find all exactly as I'd left it, cookies intact, tall glasses of lukewarm coffee. And the paint was dry, thank god. As I closed up I promised myself I would get to the bottom of that little scene. Maybe I'd take a walk up the hill when I got to Sipson's, and ask Martin to show me those Polaroids again. Surely he owed me an explanation, even if it was only the sudden onset of a headache.

In the morning I went to the bank for some cash and found that the check from my mother had at last cleared. I rode directly to Pilgrim Clothing, a place I would ordinarily shun because the store's show window consistently displayed mannequins dressed in good-girl, shin-grazing skirts and the pure white blouses of Catholic private schools, but this day I wanted high quality. I bought a pair of white linen shorts, a pink skirt with a scalloped edge, a lightweight cashmere sweater and a pair of sandals. Down the street at a place called Celestial Body I found a long embroidered tunic with tiny mirrors sewn along the bottom, and a little sky-blue dress which, when scrunched, nearly fit in the palm of my hand. Then I went to the grocery store, bought the ingredients for cornbread and took it all home.

That evening I stood in the yard in my new dress trying to tie a lopsided wicker picnic basket onto the baggage carrier of my bike with a piece of frayed rope. It was all I could find to transport the twenty four squares of cooling cornbread I'd carefully wrapped to take to Sipson's. My hair was still wet from washing it in the kitchen sink. It hung down over my chest, and wayward strands kept getting trapped in the lousy knots I struggled to tighten. I was not looking forward to the long bike ride. I'd considered rowing the mile or so there but the wind had picked up and was blowing from the south, so it would be against me. By the time I was on the road I was in a foul mood. I'd managed to get grease from the bicycle chain on the dress, so I had to go back and spend some more time doing a quick scrub before it set in for life. Then, as I rounded the first curve, a gust of wind whipped sand into my eyes and I glanced off someone's mailbox trying to steer. That was enough. I sat on the grass by the side of the road convincing myself to give up and stay home, go for a swim and gorge on cornbread, when I heard someone say "Evening, miss." The voice seemed to be inside my head, but it was not mine, it was a man's. I opened my tearing eyes a crack and looked around. I was alone.

"Hello?" I said anyway. No answer, only the screwball song of a catbird running through its repertoire of swiped trills and warbles, ending in a crescendo of *idiot, idiot!* I took it as my cue to abort the trip, and turned the bike toward home. As I lifted my leg to get on I saw Sal standing in dapple-shaded vegetation about twenty feet behind the mailbox. Shirtless, he wore a filthy pair of *culotte*, the kind of trousers buttoned just below the knees, like something from the French revolution. I said, "Hey! What are you . . ." But he turned and ran away through the trees, black ponytail flopping. I'd had only a glimpse, but I was pretty sure it was him. My eyes were still watering liberally from the sand though, so things were blurred and I couldn't say for sure.

"Sal? Is that you?" I called again, but he didn't answer. I waited for a minute or so to see if he would appear, then walked the bike back to the house. I had just changed into my bathing suit when I heard the familiar sound of a Volkswagon Bug engine downshifting in the driveway. Sandy tooted twice, then leapt out of the driver's side. She was wearing cutoff shorts and a bikini top, her normal getup.

"Elli? Aren't you coming?" she called to me from the porch. "I was just in town buying some beer and I decided to stop and see if you needed a ride." When she saw me in my suit, carrying a towel, she frowned. "No? Aw, why not?"

"I'll be right there, just give me a sec," I said, turning back to the bedroom to change again.

When we were on the way I described the man I saw in the woods, and said I was sure it had been Sal.

"He's back on the island, as far as I know. Last I saw he was ferrying some people over in Martin's boat. His friend Theo, and Min." Ray was there, too, she added, in case it might have been him I thought I'd seen.

"It was someone else, then," I said. "But it was strange the way he just took off."

"Tourists," said Sandy. "You never know."

We got to the landing and honked for someone to row us across. Over on the island side a dozen people splashed in the water, tossing a frisbee back and forth. On the beach near the dock Ray and Sal were standing waist deep in a large hole. Others brought rocks from farther along the shore and dumped them in. I noticed Bill, Sandy's one eyed friend who had accidentally backed his car over Martin's Indian skull.

"What's going on?" I asked Sandy while we waited.

"They're making a clambake," she said, rubbing her hands together.

I shrugged. "What is it?"

"It'll blow your mind, man!" Sandy did one of her little happy jigs on the landing as she explained, dancing me through the lining of the pit with rocks and the building of a fire on them. "You let it burn down and then, when you've got a good bed of coals, you dump on a layer of rockweed."

"Rockweed?"

"Yeah. It's gotta be that kind. I'll show you why." She waded into the water, reached in and came up with a fist full of seaweed. Yellow-brown and rubbery, its branches were covered in little egg shaped pustules which, she told me, were full of air to keep the plant growing upright in the water.

She poked a fingernail into one. "When the rockweed heats up, these burst open and make steam."

"Oh."

"Which is needed to cook the next layer, lobsters. Far out, right?"

"Excellent."

"Yup. Also clams, mussels, potatoes, and corn on the cob." She flounced in a joyous circle, swirled the seaweed around her head, then tossed it back into the water. "It all goes in, then more rockweed on top, then a big tarp. Indians taught it to settlers."

Trying to picture it, I wondered idly what the natives used for a tarp and was about to ask, but decided it was the kind of picky detail that could ruin a great image.

The rowboat slid toward us, and we climbed aboard with my basket of cornbread and several six-packs of beer. Sandy talked with the woman rowing while I thought about Martin, wondering if I'd see him at the party. By the time we were across, Ray was tossing the last pine branches into the pit. A fire had already begun to burn, sending long streamers of smoke out over the water. More people arrived on the opposite shore, and Sal jumped in one of the boats to fetch them as Sandy and I walked through the brambles to the house. There we found Sylvie and two other women wrapping potatoes in foil and adding them to a large pile of unhusked corn on a tray. On the stereo, a familiar scratchy-throated saxophone snaked a sensual refrain around through the plants and chairs as the women chatted, and I moved closer to the stereo to see what was playing. The painting on the album cover showed a lineup of overlapping geometric shapes in scribbled color on a white background, linked together by thin catwhisker lines. Charles Mingus. I remembered the album cover from my mother's studio.

"Elli, hey. Haven't seen you for a while." Sylvie kissed my cheek as I set my basket on the table. She pulled the tab on a can of beer and handed it to me, then went back to stirring something in a bowl.

"I'm gonna try baking date bread in the coals," she said. "Watch this." She upended the bowl over a fat little pillow made entirely from aluminum foil, and with a wooden spoon guided the gloppy batter into a hole in its top. "It's hollow," she said. "I made it thick so the bread won't burn. It's an experiment that sounded interesting when we

101

thought of it." She did a little pantomime of smoking a joint. The women giggled along with her while she fitted a tinfoil cork into the pillow and gave it a pat. "What do you think?"

I wondered if she'd remembered to grease the inside of the foil pillow. I had become knowledgable about these kinds of things since discovering Betty Crocker and the joys of baking, but I didn't mention it. "I can't wait," I said, looking at the others for agreement. Everyone nodded enthusiastically.

"How's the fire? Are we ready?" Sylvie glanced around the kitchen. One of the women wedged the tray of corn and potatoes against her hip and swished out the door with it, screen slamming behind her. Sandy and the other girl left too, carrying a huge bowl of macaroni salad and four six-packs of beer. "See you down there," she sang over her shoulder.

Sylvie leaned against the refrigerator. "I'm already tired." She lifted her chin in the direction of Martin's house. "I wish I could just have a quiet dinner up there." She ran the backs of her fingernails across the bodice of my dress. "Mm. Is this new? It's very pretty. Don't tell me it's your mother's from the forties."

"No, I bought it in town." She stood with arms akimbo, gazing crookedly at me in a way she had not done before. Her eyes zoomed back and forth over my face, up and down my dress. I could see that she was already a little drunk. It made me want to get out of there, follow the others down to the beach. "What's going on?" I said, but the record ended and Sylvie stomped over to flip it, so she didn't hear. Another tune began. Raspy drum brushes, a saxophone tiptoeing along, coyly doling out the melody. I had to get that album.

Sylvie fiddled with the volume knob. "So, did Martin visit your mother's studio?" she said over her shoulder.

I thought for a moment. What had happened that day? It was still a complete mystery to me. Now here was Sylvie, getting right to it.

"Yeah, he did." Should I tell her what I had seen? Was it even real? When Sandy came to pick me up I decided fate had given me the opportunity to find out what I could this day, since I was in the neighborhood, so to speak. I would walk up the hill and have a look at that Polaroid, maybe ask Martin some questions. "He didn't stay long. I think he had a headache or something."

She stood with her back to me, staring down at the record revolving on the turntable. Did she know something I didn't? "There isn't much to see in there," I added, hoping it would satisfy her.

"Uh huh." She turned to me with a bright, forced smile. "Let's go down, shall we?"

I picked up the basket, shucked off my shoes and followed her along the path to the landing, hoping the tense atmosphere I had sensed was my imagination. She asked nothing else about Martin's visit as we walked along in silence to the beach. More people had arrived and were standing around the fire pit drinking beer and passing joints. I spotted Joyce sitting by the water with some other women. Deep in conversation, they were making a kind of fat obelisk by scooping up handfuls of wet, sloppy sand from the waterline and letting it dribble through fingers onto the tip of the thing where it oozed down like candle wax, adding another layer. I watched as it slumped to one side, then buckled and fell, only to have them begin again on the ruins, dropping sand onto a new tower, neither stopping the construction nor the discussion. Joyce saw me and held up a bottle of Chianti, beckoning. I waved, but I wanted to get rid of the basket of cornbread first, so I headed for the food table.

It looked like everyone had brought their dog. A panting, swaggering band of mongrels ran circles around the guests and chased each other up and down the beach, spraying sand. The fire in the pit was burning down. Ray scooted around the perimeter raking coals flat while Sal tossed armfuls of seaweed on top. A hissing, sea-scented steam rose, and into it they tossed the foil-wrapped potatoes and corn, then another layer of seaweed, then a dozen live claw-clacking lobsters. I looked away as they curled their tails against the blast of heat. More seaweed went on, then a bushel basket of mussels and clams, then the whole thing was covered with yet more rockweed and several wet burlap bags.

"Isn't it beautiful?" Sandy appeared in front of me proffering a joint. I took a puff, distracted by Ray's gosling Bobby, who tottered underfoot very close to the fire, trying to stay close to Ray for protection from the dogs. I went over, grabbed the little bird and took it with me. They'd set up a big table near the dock for food. I put my basket down on one end, then sat with Bobby nestled in the hammock of my skirt. The table was crowded with bowls and platters of various side dishes. A pyramid of bread rolls had been arranged with daisies stuck in the spaces between them. In the center a fondue pot full of butter waited to have its flame lit. A stack of paper plates fluttered in the breeze. I watched as the top three peeled off and went rolling down the beach. I picked up a rock to weigh down the rest, just as an arm reached out beside me and dropped one on.

"Problem solved." A shirtless man in army fatigue pants sat down on the dock. He lifted his shoulders in an aw-shucks gesture and smiled at me. I gathered from the pants he was a Vietnam vet. He had a reddish-blond, bushy mustache which dominated his face. The ends of it were unusually long. The whiskers spiraled down under his chin, terminating in two blue beads which swung crazily with every movement. His eyes matched the color of the beads.

"I'm Leon. Who's this?" he asked, patting Bobby's tiny head and letting his hand linger in my lap. I figured it wasn't the bird's head Leon wanted to touch and, lifting Bobby out of the cradle between my legs, held him up instead for inspection.

"It's Ray's. It's a baby Canada goose."

"What's he gonna do when it grows up, eat it?" He laughed, a wheezing, phlegmy sound. His eyes danced like the beads under his chin, four jiggling blue spots making me dizzy. I pulled away, started to stand up, but Leon put his hand on my arm. "How about I get you a beer?"

"No thanks." I backed away from him but stumbled into the table, toppling the tower of bread rolls. Half of them bounced off the table into the sand and I stooped to pick them up, still holding Bobby. A couple of the dogs spotted the rolls and ran over and a growling, snarling fight over them erupted under the table. Everyone started yelling. Ray rushed over as Leon ducked under the table to try and pull the dogs apart. Almost immediately he screamed and began scrabbling out backwards, holding up his hand. Blood gushed from an inch long tear in the fleshy part of his thumb.

"The fucking things bit me!" he screamed, flapping his hand and flinging blood onto the table as everyone gathered around. The dogs slunk away into the woods. Sylvie marched over and had a look.

"Let's soak it in the water," she said. She took Leon's arm and led him to the dock. He swished his hand around, then held it up. It dripped blood, coloring the water in a widening circle.

"Aaagh!" he wailed. "It's my right hand, goddammit! How am I gonna work?"

"Someone go and get Min," said Sylvie. "She has a good first aid kit. She can tell us if this needs to be stitched up."

Ray shot off up the path to Martin's house while we all stood around listening to Leon curse the dogs, the rolls and life in general. The mustache beads had tangled below his chin, and with increasing frustration he tried to unknot them one-handed until Sandy waltzed over and did it for him while he ogled her cleavage, which calmed him significantly.

Blood had spattered the hem of my dress, so I dunked it in the water. It had only just dried after I'd scrubbed out the bicycle oil. No one else at the party had bothered to put on anything other than the usual cutoff jeans and t-shirts they all wore, and I felt overdressed in something I would have worn on a trip to the bakery in Paris. The gosling paddled around in the water peeping happily, then swam over and hid under the dock. Sylvie and Sandy inspected the table's contents for any offending stray drops of blood. Thankfully, most things had been covered in plastic wrap or foil. They picked through the rest, wiping or discarding here and there. Pretty soon Min came bustling over the sand toward us, followed by Martin, who saw me and smiled sort of shyly, I thought. Min took one look at the wound and nodded to Martin.

"I'll take him over," he said. "I have to go anyway." He beckoned to someone standing at the edge of the fire pit, the man who was sitting with him in the The Foc'sle the day I got my job at the motel. Theo. He had on the same tall black rubber boots. The clambake emitted little eddies of fragrant steam. Theo lifted a corner of the tarp and took a long theatrical sniff. Min wrapped a wide strip of gauze around Leon's hand while he swigged from a bottle of beer.

"We have another passenger," Martin said to Theo when he arrived at the boat. Min got in and settled primly in the stern. She wore her white hair in a classic chignon which the last of the sun's rays highlighted, giving her head a kind of celestial glow. Leon sat in the bow holding the injured hand against his chest, both covered in blood. Min saw me watching and winked.

"Hang on a minute," Martin said, then brought Theo over to me and introduced us. "Theo knew your parents," he added.

Theo took my hand. "I was very fond of your mother," he said. "And you too, when you were little."

What? I was momentarily speechless. "Oh!" I managed to say.

"C'mon, let's go," wailed Leon from the boat.

"Excuse me, I guess I'd better. . ." Theo turned toward the dock.

I wanted to follow Theo as he got into the boat, to pepper him with questions, but Martin took me aside and whispered, "I'll be back, and I'll tell you about it. And the other thing, too. Wait for me, OK?"

"OK." Theo got in, sat next to Min and put his arm around her shoulders. Martin shoved off, jumped aboard and started the engine, ending any chance of further questions. I stood there with about a million of them caroming around in my head.

"So, he invited you up?" Sylvie stood close behind me as I watched the boat leave. Startled, I turned to see her swaying slightly, hanging on to the edge of the table for support.

"I think so," I said. She stared at me again, a look of disapproval in her eyes. "Look," I went on, "Something happened at the studio, and he . . ."

She put her hand in front of my face, an inch from my nose. "Stop," she said, turning away. "I don't want to know." She stomped off across the sand to stand beside Ray.

Baffled, I fished the gosling out from under the dock and began to make my way over to where Joyce sat. She and her friends were gathered around the drip castle as if worshipping some phallic idol, until it fell over again and someone patted it into a little podium for the bottle of Chianti. As I walked I tried to figure out why Sylvie seemed so bothered by the idea of Martin visiting my mother's studio. She had behaved strangely almost from the moment I'd arrived in her house. It made no sense. Yes, she was a little tipsy, but she showed real anger when she put her hand in my face. I glanced at her as I passed. She stood with a boisterous group of people around the clambake pit. They were passing yet another joint, laughing and fake-pushing each other in. It looked dangerous to me, and I cradled Bobby a little tighter in my arms. Suddenly all I wanted was to go home, but I was determined to hear the explanation for Martin's bizarre behavior, and I was not going to pass up the opportunity. I was also more than a little curious about Theo.

"Hey girl," Joyce called out as I got closer. She sat on a yellow blanket woven with a pattern of black birds. I handed her Bobby and she cooed over him, lifting him up

108

to kiss his miniature beak. He cried out, wings flapping wildly, so she dropped him in the sand and he ran the few yards to where Ray sat. Joyce poured me some wine as I settled on the blanket. It was delicious. I realized I was quite hungry, having forgotten to eat in all the flurry of preparation to get to the island. Joyce had been telling the others about a train ride she'd taken through the Alps ten years before.

"It was one of those affairs you read about in Barbara Cartland novels. Sudden. Overwhelming. Such a cliché," she laughed. "Though the love was real, and we both felt it. During the day we had to pretend. We sat looking at the scenery with our secret squirming in the seat between us like a joyful child. But at night we unfolded the seat in my compartment and. . . well."

"Well, what?" one of the women laughed.

"I recommend seeing the Alps by moonlight from a train window," was all she said.

"So, what happened to him?" someone asked.

"We left the train at Naples. His wife met him with a little girl in her arms, and I walked past them into the crowd. The end." Joyce shrugged. "See? I told you it was a stale old script."

"Ingrid Bergman."

"Exactly."

We sat talking about movies for a while, until the bags covering the clambake pit were peeled back and everyone gathered around as Ray lifted out lobsters with the rake. People reached in to snatch hot corn cobs and potatoes from the steaming seaweed. With heaped plates we settled back on Joyce's blanket, broke open lobster claws and dunked the meat into a paper cup of melted butter. When the sky was fully dark, the people over by the still-smoldering pit began rolling things in foil to bake on the glowing coals. I watched some guy carefully wrap an entire bag of Oreo cookies and toss it in, plastic and all. Another person carefully laid on a bunch of bananas, giggling maniacally. Sylvie's date bread pillow was added. Someone emptied a bag of popcorn onto the heap, and soon popped kernels were shooting out of the hole. People tried catching them in their mouths as Bobby ran around plucking them out of the sand. The party seemed to have ratcheted up to a new level of rowdiness. Min appeared on the beach and looked around, spotted Joyce, and waved.

"That's my cue," said Joyce. She picked up her stuff and kissed everyone goodbye. Sal rowed her and Min to the landing. I was beginning to think I ought to have gone with them when I heard the sound of Martin's outboard, a discordant drone against the music and conversation on the beach. I went down to the dock to wait for him. Leon was sitting in the stern, his hand in a fat white bandage. Martin tied up and walked toward me, taking me by the arm as he passed.

"Come on up to my place, all right?" I hesitated, and he let go. I had spotted Sylvie watching us through the crowd. She lifted a bottle of beer to her lips and took a slow, exaggerated sip without taking her gaze off us. Martin looked over. "Oh, for god's sake," he muttered. "Listen, don't worry about her. She has a bit of a thing for me, and now I suppose she's jealous." He beckoned to her, but she shook her head.

"I tried to tell her what it's about," I said. "Maybe I should try again." I started toward her, but Martin stopped me.

"Don't bother," he said. "Come on. We'll go up to the house, we'll talk, and I'll take you home after. All right?

110

She can come if she wants." We set off on the path. I could tell by the brisk way Martin walked, shoving aside stray branches and undergrowth, that he was annoyed. Although I wanted to hear what he had to tell me, I didn't want it like this. I stopped and said, "Are you sure?"

"What? Yes of course," he said. He took a deep breath. "Listen, sorry. The trip to the doctor with that knucklehead was a pain in my ass. I only wanted to get back to speak with you. I'm sorry about the other day, and I've been waiting for an opportunity to make it right. I've got some very good port, and I picked this up while Leon was seen to." He reached into his jacket pocket and held up a small wrapped cheese in the shape of a heart. Neufchatel, by the look of it. "I thought you might like, it, so. . ."

"So, okay," I said. Bring on the French cheese, I thought gleefully. I wondered idly where he might have bought it, especially at that hour. I knew for a fact there was no cheese of that caliber to be found in any store in Orleans. We walked the rest of the way in silence, the occasional peal of laughter or pop of stray corn kernel reaching us through the trees. When we arrived at his door I looked out toward the barrier beach. Though the moon was only half full and high in the sky by then, it lit up waves in long white lines as they collapsed and disappeared behind the dune with a steady susurration.

"Come in, please." Martin held the door for me.

I stood by the kitchen counter while he pulled the cork from a bottle of port and trickled a couple of inches into two glasses.

"*À votre santé.*" He held his up. We clinked.

I sat down in one of the sumptuous white armchairs and looked over at the filing cabinet he'd taken the Polaroids from that evening. "I talked to my mother," I began.

111

"Oh yes?"

"Yes. She remembered the painting from the wall. She told me a story about it. She said some American collector bought it." I thought I might as well get right to the point. Martin brought a cutting board to the table with the Neufchatel and another baguette. Maybe Min makes them, I thought.

"That was me," he said casually, taking a seat. "What's the story?"

"Why don't you get that little picture out?" I felt bold. Probably from too much wine, but I didn't care, it helped. Martin got right up and fetched the photo. The packet was still lying out on the desk. He extracted '*A Swim at Pochet*' and brought it over, placing it in front of me. It showed an off-white ground with slashes of blue, green and black crisscrossing, muddled, jumping off a central area, traced in places by thin yellow lines. I could see how, if you had studied the marks on my mother's studio wall, you'd at least recognize the colors.

"The paint was wet after you left. I touched it."

"What?"

"Yeah. Right here." I put the same finger on a spot on the photo.

"My god, that's extraordinary. Are you sure?" I nodded.

He stared at me in silence, his eyes shooting back and forth between mine, the pupils dilated until his eyes shone black and glittery. The look was almost accusatory, as though I had told a life-threatening lie. He took a large gulp of the port and poured himself more, then leaned against the chair back, breathing heavily as he glared down at me. His cheeks had reddened, his eyebrows lowered to graze the bridge of his nose. I felt a slight tickle of fear stir in my stomach. This was not part of the scenario I'd envisioned.

112

Suddenly he grabbed the bread knife with such swiftness that I jumped up, knocking over my glass. I tried to run toward the door but my foot was caught between the chair and table legs. As I twisted to free it, Martin put down the knife and laid his hand gently on my arm.

"Elli, please don't be afraid," he said calmly. I was only going to slice us some bread. Jesus." I sat uncertainly back down as he went into the kitchen.

"I guess you saw me," he said. He came back with a roll of paper towels and tore off a few while deliberately not looking at me. "Painting, I mean." He used his fingers to make quotes.

"That's what it looked like."

"I did not mean for you to see that. It's a secret. My secret. But it can be explained." He laid the wad of towels on the spill. We watched it blot into a puddle the shape of Italy, then he wadded it up and tossed it toward the kitchen.

"So, why was the paint still wet when I touched it? Did you put some chemical on it?"

"No."

"Then, how –?"

"The short answer is I did it with my mind." He turned to look at the glass wall and the sea beyond in the darkness. "But the long answer needs a little time. Please, sit down with me. I promise I'm not a monster."

I reached over and unwrapped the cheese, sliced off a bit and leaned back against the chair cushion. "Okay," I said, my voice a little squeaky. "Tell me."

"For a number of years I . . ." He shook his head. "No. I have to talk about some science first. What you might call metaphysics, but Einstein, for example, took it seriously."

"The quote on your fridge."

"Yes."

"Do you remember what I talked about, that everything is made of energy, even thoughts?"

Here we go again, I thought. *J'en ai ras-le-bol,* as we say in French. "Yes," I answered. "I was discussing it just the other day, over coffee, with Sylvie. She was saying that thoughts hook up with other matching energy in some big spacey zone of possibility."

"Well, yeah, sort of." He sighed, a quick, exasperated outbreath. "Okay, picture a limitless number of particles zooming around everywhere, even in front of us right now, sort of rippling in wave patterns." He undulated his hands like fish swimming to illustrate. 'Waves of potential."

"Potential what?"

"Things."

"Like paintings?" My foot started to jiggle impatiently, and he noticed.

"Look, this is not some pseudo-science. I'm not talking about anything which has not been tested by physicists, though it still mystifies them. Did they teach you about the Double Slit experiment in high school?"

"No, what is it?"

"Never mind. Let's suffice to say that what it proved, and this is a long time ago incidentally, is that particles, those waves of potential I was telling you about, behave in a certain way. They can be here, there, everywhere. They are everything and nothing, waves of past, present and future, all at the same time."

"Uh huh," I said encouragingly.

"But what they discovered with this experiment is that when the particles are *observed*, in other words, when they are measured by a device or looked at somehow, they coalesce into a pattern. I believe there is a way to match your own wave pattern –your thoughts– to those particles dancing around out there, and when you do, they cannot help but mesh."

"And?"

"And become something. You see, when you have a thought, the thing you imagine, the moment you have it, it exists somewhere, because thoughts are things, too, because they are made of energy. Though that is an extremely simplified version of interacting with the quantum field."

"The what?"

Martin had a squinty, preoccupied look on his face, as if he were trying to summon up the long-forgotten name of an old friend. I felt a little sorry for him, trying to explain esoteric ideas to a semi-stoned naif.

"Look," he said. "How about if I just tell you about what happened with your mother's painting? Then maybe things will be more clear." He chuckled to himself, then added, "Or maybe you'll be running down the path to jump into the nearest rowboat out of here."

"It's really not that funny," I said, impatient and more confused than before. I wanted to hear something I could believe, and not anything to do with magic quantum zones of potential, or whatever he said.

"Now you know, I own this painting of your mother's." He picked up the Polaroid, held it delicately by the wide edge at the bottom, and gazed at it.

"Yes."

"Okay. I didn't want to say it back then, but it's one of the first pieces I ever bought. I had an experience looking at this painting which changed my life, and I have been trying to understand it for all these years. I have kept it secret for obvious reasons, but then seeing the spot where it was made, I . . ." He shook his head as if to clear away some substance clogging its inner workings. "I had the experience again."

"What was it? What happened to you?"

Martin took a deep breath, held it for a second then let it out. "I saw the painting one day in a gallery in Paris. It was 1964. I went to Paris because I wanted to look at art. I had spent the previous ten years studying reproductions in books, reading about painters and buying new work. I walked around for hours and hours in American museums and galleries trying to expand my knowledge, to take in all that was available. I went to Paris as a kind of pilgrimage, to learn even more about the origins of abstract painting." He sighed. "It's a wonderful city, isn't it?"

I nodded, struggling to overcome an instant surge of homesickness.

"Even though I bought many pieces I hadn't yet seen anything that made me feel the way your mother's painting did. It caught my eye one day as I passed on the street. The gallery was full of other pictures but I saw only that one. It was hanging in the back in the semi-dark with a tiny spotlight trained on it." He held up the Polaroid at arm's length as if to recreate the scene.

"I entered, greeted a person behind a desk, and made straight for the back of the gallery. I don't know how to put what happened next into words, the strange physical sensation which overcame me almost immediately, but as I walked toward the painting . . ." He took a sip of port and stared at the window again, recollecting the moment. "As I approached the picture, I saw that it was not a finished composition, but in the process of being painted. I watched, incredulous, as small black lines snaked through blocks of blue and green, and then one of those areas would smear itself, as though someone was passing the heel of an

116

invisible hand over it, blending the colors. At first I thought it was some kind of mechanism, some trick. I checked behind the frame but there was nothing, only unpainted canvas. I glanced over at the owner who was writing something in a notebook, then touched the canvas. It was wet paint."

Martin shifted in his chair to face me, grabbed my hand and said, "Then, a force over which I had no control took my hand, extended its finger, and the painting continued to paint itself, only now it seemed I was doing it."

"I saw you," I said.

"Yes? So you know how it was." I nodded.

"I continued 'painting' your mother's picture until I heard footsteps come up behind me and suddenly the gallery owner was saying something to me and I to him and I don't remember any of it but when I came to my senses I was standing on the street with a wrapped painting under my arm. I went immediately to a cafe, sat down and undid a corner of the package. I recognized it immediately. The paint was perfectly dry, even cracked a little where it had been thickly applied. I ordered a coffee and looked around. The place was half full of customers, but no one was looking at me, so I must have seemed normal. The gallery owner hadn't chased me down the street, so I hadn't stolen the painting. I took my checkbook out of my pocket and opened it. I had written a check, but made no record of it."

"Wow." I sat there otherwise at a loss for words, that one silly one standing in for so many more appropriate responses. It would have been beyond belief, but I had seen it myself. The paint had been wet. Martin and I sipped in silence for a minute, picturing. Then he continued.

"I took the painting back to New York and hung it up. It happened again almost immediately, and this time I was able to stay more conscious, to know better what to expect. The painting repainted itself while I retained an awareness of my surroundings, felt my bare feet on the carpet, a breeze from the open window. By the fourth or fifth time I was able to control the speed of my visualization. I could stop in the middle and take it up again after a few moments, or sweep my hand over the canvas and see it pulsate to life as an entire finished image. I have since acquired many more paintings by some very good artists, and each one I bought gave me the same experience. I can tell which work of art will interact with me as soon as I see it."

"How long does it stay wet?" I remembered running down the driveway after my discovery, wiping my finger on my shorts.

"As long as my attention stays on it. That's the mystery today. Remember, when you came into your mother's studio I took the tray from you, put it down and then ran away because I was so overcome. I never expected to have the experience with mere scraps of paint. I didn't know how to explain my behavior at the time, so I took off. I apologize."

"It's all right." I was relieved to have some kind of story, though it wasn't what I would call coherent information.

Martin sat back and studied my face for a few moments, then said very softly, "So, after I left, you touched the paint, and it was fresh. Right? Your observation collapsed the wave, is all I can think."

"What?"

'Except that I had already done that, hadn't I?"

"Huh?"

"Oh Elli, I am sorry. Part of me wishes you hadn't seen that, but part of me is very happy to have my secret shared. Confirmed, sort of."

"I don't know what I saw, something magic, I guess."

"No, not magic, not hallucination. By collapsing the wave, I mean that those particular particles changed their behavior because they were observed. By you." He rubbed his eyes, looked over at me again. "That is, after me. Ah shit! I don't know . . . attracting the electromagnetic signal from a parallel universe is maybe more accurate, but I don't fully understand it yet, either." Martin stared off into the middle distance again, leaving me to struggle with everything I'd just heard. After a couple more silent minutes went by he said, "What it means is that you have the ability to attract, too."

"I do?"

"Yeah. Well, you saw it, didn't you?"

"I saw you moving your arms around like a mime, and then I touched some wet paint on the wall. So, were we aligning with some kind of supernatural waves of energy by observing them, or whatever it was you said?" His story and the parallel universe stuff didn't add up. From what I understood, he would have had to imagine my mother's painting before it appeared in a gallery in Paris for him to run across by chance. "I thought you said the original time was an accident, a surprise."

"Yes."

"So, you weren't thinking of this painting or one like it before you saw my mother's?"

"Actually I was. I went to Paris not only to run away from the enormous pain of my wife's death six months before, but I was also there to find her, in a way." He leaned back and sipped thoughtfully. "More explanation, bear with me. She died suddenly, a cerebral hemorrhage. I was completely undone by her death. I loved her so deeply that after she was gone I nearly forgot how to speak. I could not comprehend a life without her, and for a while I didn't want to live any longer myself. I didn't know how. Freya, that was her name, so completely possessed me, ordered my time, my tastes, my very existence, that I had lost track of who I was before her. But of course I had to go on, and I found after a while that a way to connect to her was through the visual language of art, the automatic, subconscious marks made by others which speak to a certain part of the viewer's mind and have the power to evoke strong emotions. It was a passion we shared. The feelings I experienced looking at paintings was the closest I could get to being with her. So I spent a good deal of time and emotional energy interacting with this substitution." He rubbed his eyes, sat forward and asked, "Do you understand?"

"Yes, I think so." I pictured my mother painting alone in our apartment full of my father's things. What was she trying to express now?

"I combed through dozens of American museums and galleries we'd visited together, looking to feel that specific emotion. And I did. I felt it very powerfully at times. I began to believe that Freya existed somewhere as dis-integrated matter, and that a portal to her was somehow available through a work of art. I thought that I could eventually either bring her back or go to her, wherever she is. I still do."

Martin looked at the wall of glass again, as though he'd seen her shadow pass by. I thought I saw it too, a wisp of white flitting across, possibly clouds moving past the moon. It was unsettling, but I was starting to believe.

"So then you went to Paris," I prompted him.

"Yes. I deliberately took myself out of my known world to an unfamiliar place in order not to be able to unconsciously control my surroundings, my actions. I was ready to experiment. I read everything I could get my hands on about quantum theory, about entanglement and nonlocality. That's when particles which have interacted become forever linked, and even when separated by great distance –even light years away– instantly know each other's state."

He waved his hand in the air as if to rub out what he'd started to say. "Never mind about that. Technical stuff I'll tell you about later, if you want. What I did was to open my mind and concentrate on being no one and nowhere, in no particular time, so that my desire might be purer and send a stronger signal. And then I went about searching for the creations which would lead me to her."

"And that's when you found 'A Swim at Pochet'?

"Yup. It took a few months, but then it happened, just as I told you."

I didn't know what to say. I would have thought he was nuts except for the fact of that dab of green on my finger. I thought I felt Martin waiting for me to respond, but instead he continued.

"I taught myself to meditate. In my trance I call up those particles which make up Freya, because they are somewhere still in the quantum field. Everything is. Remember what I told you about matter and energy? Freya spent much of her childhood sailing on Pleasant Bay, and this island was her favorite place in the world." He pointed with his thumb at the ocean. "Her family owned a summer camp out there on the barrier beach. She described it to me many times, and about ten years ago we came here to have a look. The camp was washed away years ago, but by coincidence the island happened to be for sale, so I bought it. Freya and I designed this house together and spent five happy summers here. She died over there on the beach one day." Martin waved his hand in the direction of the southern tip, the high, narrow spit that pointed out to sea.

"When I walk around here I try to imagine I am passing through a thicket of atoms, each of these a small part of someone's energy, some puzzle piece of disorganized matter, parts of all previous existence only waiting for my attention. So, if Freya's and my particles are entangled, I believe it's possible that we will find each other again. She is here on this island, I'm sure of it, as are the Sipson brothers of the Nauset Indian tribe and anyone else who lived and died on these shores."

"So, you're trying to re –reconstitute her?" I recalled the word from a box of powdered milk on the shelf in my kitchen.

"Yes. In whatever form I can be with." He winced, ducked his head as if avoiding a blow. "See, the universe isn't just one history. It's all imaginable histories at the same time. We live in one or another based on the choices we make. Does it make any sense?"

"I think so," I mumbled, though my brain was a melange of half-concepts and snippets of science which added up to something I barely hung on to, like a dream fading as you wake. The harder you try to recall it, the more gossamer the images, until finally you retain only meaningless shreds. Some kind of wave I had "collapsed" made me able to see things which existed in the past and were still available to see, but where were they? Martin made it sound like they were undulating right in front of me, waiting for me to match up my wave pattern to theirs.

It was too simple. No one had mentioned this stuff in any science class I had ever taken. From out on the beach came the sound of real waves arriving at the shore, crumpling and sliding into a different form for the trip back out. Their steadfast shushing was a comfort, a subliminal assurance of organization in the natural world, something to be counted on. Yet here was Martin poking a giant hole in nature's perfect design, rearranging things in a way that disconcerted me, and involving my mother to boot. What was the wave I had supposedly collapsed, and what did it mean? What was entanglement? Linked particles? He asked me if it made any sense. It did, but only in that fleeting, dream-memory way I could not retain. Yet, if my father were out there wandering around in the form of a bunch of particles I could unscramble and communicate with, I wanted to know how to do it.

"Theo knows about me trying to find Freya. Min, too. Telling you seems right, and it feels good." Martin sat back and smiled at me. Over his shoulder the Motherwell painting glowed, the pulsating black shapes like doorways into a void. Were they beckoning me?

"I wouldn't mind learning more about all of this." Just in the spirit of information gathering, I thought. The dab of wet green paint on my finger was proof that I had ventured into Martin's world and I was not afraid to go there again, under supervision of course. It occurred to me that the people down on the beach were likely swallowing tabs of LSD and experiencing something akin to watching a painting paint itself.

"I would like that, too," Martin said. "Not that I know how to teach you, but we could try." He drummed his fingers against the table, thinking. "Maybe we should revisit your mother's studio. Go back to the scene of the crime, so to speak."

"Okay." I picked up the Polaroid of *'A Swim at Pochet'* again. We were all connected by this image, I realized. I pictured my father walking down the path to the water, leaving my mother with me while he swam, my mother's quick-painted expression of jealousy over her husband's freedom, the bay, her motherhood, me, I don't know. Something about it sparked a communication between Martin and his dead wife, if he was to be believed. A scrap of thought kept poking its way into my mind during the discussion, a little flutter of unease. Now that I knew some of his story, it was hard to believe Martin did not know years ago that Ria Bang Overton's house was across the bay from his, or who I was the minute I moved in. Why had he pretended to be surprised? I had to know if I was going to get any further involved. I tossed the Polaroid back onto the table. What the hell, I told myself, and dove in.

"You must have known that my mother's studio was over there," I tipped my head at Barley Neck. "And so you must have asked about who had moved in. Sylvie and Ray would have told you." Martin closed his eyes, nodding slowly. "Why did you pretend not to know?" I pictured the little pink wad of While You Were Out messages he'd dropped in front of the The Foc'sle. Had it been a ruse to meet me?

He chuckled to himself, still nodding. "Well, come on, Elli. Now you know my story, do you get why I did it? If you hadn't touched that green paint, would you have believed a word I've said? Would I have said them?"

"You could easily have told me about owning *'A Swim at Pochet'.*"

"Yeah. You're right. But I didn't have any reason to believe I'd meet you, and why would I? You were an interesting tidbit in the story, and, excuse me, a college kid who was here for the summer, like a hundred others."

"Oh." It made sense, I supposed. I felt taken down a peg or two.

"But I'm very glad it worked out differently."

I looked down at the Polaroid lying now among the breadcrumbs and crumpled napkins. It was just a colorful mass of doodles, really. A grouping of strokes made with a loaded brush. I felt momentarily lost. I held out my glass to Martin.

"Another sip, and then maybe I should get going," I said. I needed to go home to think. He upended the port bottle over my glass, but only a drop fell out.

"Damn. I'll get more," he said, getting up. "Oh, and I want to tell you about Theo."

Just then the door behind me opened, wafting in ocean scent. I turned to see Sylvie standing in the doorway, arms crossed on her chest. She stared at Martin but said nothing.

"Hello dear. Come and join us." Martin took another glass from the shelf and held it out to her. She waved it away with such an exaggerated swipe that her hand smacked hard onto the wooden frame. She was clearly drunk, barely able to stand. Martin tried to take her arm, but she dodged him and tottered over to where I sat.

"This looks cozy," she said, heaving herself into Martin's chair. She grabbed the Neufchatel and took a bite. "Yum. Heart-shaped cheese, Martin? You never tried that one on me."

"Sylvie, don't be ridiculous." He stood over her, hands on hips. "Maybe you should go to bed. I think you've had too much to drink."

"I certainly have, and can you guess why?" She sat forward, leaning over the coffee table to leer at me. "You are so pretty, Elli. Sweet, too. And French, that's a bonus. Martin likes your mother's paintings. Did he tell you?"

"Yes, but I. . ."

"Did he try to teach you how to meditate yet? He tried to get me to do it but I found it soporifically boring." Her words were so slurred I could hardly understand those last two. Martin let a small snort slip out, and clapped a hand over his mouth. She glared at him and tossed the cheese back onto the table.

"Yeah, very funny, isn't it. So, is Elli your new pupil, your confidante?" She turned to me again and added, "He used to talk to me, too. I don't know what happened, but I seem to have been shunted aside. Maybe you're the reason."

It took a few moments for me to understand that she was seriously suggesting Martin and I were having some kind of fling. The idea was so preposterous my mouth fell open. I felt my cheeks burn with embarrassment.

"Stop it, goddammit." Martin said. At that moment a gust of wind pried open the screen door and blew it shut again with a violent bang. Sylvie screamed in surprise.

It was an opportunity to make my way out of there. I stood up and sidled toward the door while Martin and Sylvie glared at each other, both breathing hard.

"Thanks, Martin," I said. "See you later." He called out, "Wait!" as I hustled outside and ran over the lawn to the path through the woods. I walked fast, stumbling over exposed roots, wondering if I could find anyone sober enough to row me across to the landing. I thought if I had to swim, I would. I did not know how to drive, but if I couldn't find Sandy I would sit in her car until she showed up. A few yards short of the clearing I paused to survey the scene on the beach, looking for her. Another fire had been built down by the water and there was Sandy in all her glory, stripped of even the scraps of clothing she usually wore. She danced naked at the edge of the narrows, kicking the water into giant sparkling arcs around her body. A crowd stood along the shore, mesmerized as she lifted her arms and spun like a ballerina. The vision was probably greatly enhanced by whatever mescaline or acid had been swallowed. I leaned against a fat maple tree and watched for a while, glad to be on my own to consider what had just happened at Martin's place. The people on the beach seemed to be peaceful enough, some had their arms around each other, others swayed in time to the music. It was Jimi Hendrix, and Sandy personified the song, "Little Wing" perfectly. It almost looked as if she were indeed strolling through the clouds and not salt water at low tide.

"There is charm under this moon." Someone behind me spoke softly. I jumped, turning to see the man from earlier that evening in the woods near my house, just after I sideswiped the mailbox with my bicycle. I had thought he was Sal then, and almost did again except that Sal was down on the beach watching Sandy. The man wore the same dirty white *culotte* and had added a vest done up tightly with brass buttons. He stepped closer. I said hello. He didn't look all that much like Sal, now that I could see him close. Same hair, but darker skin. And twenty years older, I guessed. His shoulders were beautifully sculpted, muscles delineated by firelight playing off a sheen of sweat.

"I have seen you. On the shore of the Neck." He spoke with an accent I couldn't place. It took me a few seconds to understand.

I nodded. "Yes, my family's summer house. I'm Elli," I added, sticking out my hand which he didn't see because he was staring at Sandy, who waded further out and plunged in, kicking up a final spray behind her glorious derriere.

The man turned back to me and smiled, tilting his head toward the scene on the beach."'Tis an awful diversion, that."

I wasn't sure what he meant, so I politely asked, "Do you live here, or are you from off-Cape?" A common question in this tourist town.

After a long pause he said, "I live here indeed. For my life. Just here." He pointed to the ground. He was trying to be charming, I thought. A love-child wood gnome. Next he was going to invite me into his pillow-lined burrow under the maple. I nodded vaguely, took a step toward the beach. "I have to go," I mumbled. "Nice to meet you."

"I bid you welcome to my island."

I stopped. "Oh. I didn't realize. I thought. . ."

"I am John Sipson, madame."

Martin had only half an hour before mentioned the native Sipson brothers, but I assumed he had been talking about people from long ago, not this present-day person. I tried to work out how many generations two hundred years would produce, how many great-greats back to the original would he have? At the same time my mind had already registered details of his appearance that were distinctly old fashioned. The vest, which came down to his upper thigh, had been sewn by hand from patched-together pieces of some kind of leather. The stitches were prominent, almost decorative. It was shiny with grease along the buttons and nicked with tiny scratches, as if he'd been crawling through a briar patch. His hair was pulled back and hung in a shiny braid, a once-white ribbon wound around the ends. The breeches were coarse linen, fastened below the knee. His feet were bare. He could have been any regular hippie, I supposed, but somehow I knew that wasn't what was standing in front of me.

"Are you. . .?" I couldn't think of how to ask if he was an apparition from the previous century or even earlier. Here I was again, semi-drunk and stoned, seeing things which did not exist. I grabbed a branch for balance and closed my eyes, letting the swirl inside my head run down until I thought I could focus again, then slowly lifted my eyelids a crack. John Sipson was still there. He was politely studying me, as if waiting to see what I would do next. Neither of us spoke as he reached out very slowly and swept the back of his hand toward my chest. Transfixed, my heart flopping like a caught fish against my ribs, I watched his hand disappear as it passed through me, then reemerge before dropping to his side.

I lurched backward, frantically pawing my upper torso. "What in hell?" I snarled. "Who are you?"

"Pray pardon me," he said quietly. "I am not afeared." He held his arms out to show me. "I am not."

"How did you do that?" I whispered. I reached for his hand, but he dodged to one side, out of reach.

"You are but a dream." As soon as he said that he started to fade. By that I mean he rapidly became just a transparent outline, and before I could think of how to keep him there, he disappeared altogether.

Chapter Seven

I made it home that night though I don't remember many details of the trip. I know I rode back in Sandy's VW because it was parked in the driveway when I ventured outside the next morning. I found her sleeping in my old child-bed with her legs hanging over the footboard. I rearranged them so her blood could circulate, covered her with a blanket and left her alone. I did not want to think about her driving a car. Before that I'd cowered in bed for an hour, not able to face what might be my new reality. I lay gazing out the window across the Bay, two fingers on my jugular to monitor my pulse which throbbed away at a reassuringly even rate. Fortunately I did not have to go to work because I wasn't sure if I was recovering from an acid trip or dead and in a parallel universe. If so, would it look exactly the same as the one I was seeing, or had I slipped into a backwards-spinning black hole on my way through the woods, been sucked into a space-time warp and been spit out into John Sipson's colonial-era backyard just as he'd stepped out for a pee? If that were the case, how did I return to my bed, which was clearly manufactured by a machine, to stare out the window at a passing aluminum speedboat? I tried to remember if I'd ingested something which might have been spiked with LSD. Surely I would have felt the effects before I followed Martin up the hill to his place, and I was sure he hadn't given me any. I did not consider a third possibility, which was that things were just as they were the day before: I was Elli lying in bed on Cape Cod, Planet Earth in 1968, and last night was stranger than usual, but had an explanation which would soon be revealed to me. This third scenario gradually became more realistic after I made coffee and had a look around the place.

I wanted to approach the John Sipson thing slowly, sidle up to it from an oblique angle. Since waking I had only allowed an occasional flicker of flashback to pass through my brain before shutting it off. The memory was too mind-blowing to let wander around in there unchecked. I sat outside in the wicker chair wearing my father's felt hat and smoked a cigarette as he would have done when considering a weighty issue. When I was little and a nightmare made me run to my parents' bed, my father would guide me through a sort of procedural analysis, going over details one by one to pick apart the story, raise doubt and thereby defuse the fear. So I tried this, letting random images from the party file across my inner vision and organizing them chronologically. Sandy twirling the rock weed above her head; Ray and Sal stoking the fire; Joyce's drip castle; the blue beads swinging from Leon's mustache which led me to the dogfight, the smoking pit, and everything in between until Martin's boat pulled up to the dock and Sylvie gave us the evil eye. Ouch. That stopped my progress, and I spent a long time just sitting there sweating while a little guilt bug stomped around in my chest leaving greasy footprints I could not ignore. But I couldn't rationalize it either so I skipped ahead to settle on Martin's story of Freya, who was far enough removed from my experience to be only a distant, inert player. Or so I thought. After a couple more cigarettes' worth of contemplation I came to realize she was at the center of the whole thing. She was the reason Martin had bought the island. Her death had given him the impetus to give up living normally in favor of searching for her disarranged particles in abstract art and in the very air hanging over Pleasant Bay, but most disconcerting was his discovery of her in a painting made by my mother thirty feet away from where I sat. Freya was not distant at all, but neither was she the link to any logical explanation of what the hell was going on out there on Sipson's.

Just then The Beatles 'Within You Without You' came on the radio. I let the trippy, orchestra-backed sitar pull me along like Mr. Magoo floating on a cloud of shimmering cartoon scent. The sun was hot on my shoulders, but it felt good. At my feet an ant made its way across the parched, unmowed lawn. Under dried grass bowing in the breeze, the ant zigzagged in time to the music, winding through tabla-tapping seed-head fingers while the pulse in my neck joined George Harrison singing "With our love we can save the world, if they only knew . . ."

For those moments I experienced a sensation of pure bliss, of being nothing and everything simultaneously, not an individual conscious person, but all of consciousness. I was the ant, the grass, the sitar, the song, and at the same time none of it, not even myself. It's hard to describe, but I had a flash of understanding what Martin was trying to tell me. This was the alternate state he talked about. If that moment of pure, perfect awareness I felt could be prolonged and explored, I wanted to go back to it. I tried again to lose myself in the music by staring at a patch of sparkles out on the water and blurring my vision, but the song ended and morphed into the extended weather report for Boston and vicinity. I went into the porch and turned the radio off.

I forced myself to think about Sylvie again, seeing her angry hand in my face and the ugly scene at Martin's before I fled. Why had I never before noticed that she and Martin had something going on apart from being friendly neighbors on Sipson's Island? I should have understood the day she took me up to his bedroom and showed me around. She was worried that he would teach me to meditate, which was fishy. Did they meditate together on that tidy bed before balling each other? But if Martin was so desperate to find Freya again, why would he be fooling around with Sylvie?

I recalled one afternoon she and I sat drinking coffee with Joyce at the Turk's Head. Joyce had expounded at length on the joys of meditation. She'd described the state as being in a kind of pleasant void. "But not a dull place at all," she'd said. "It's a place of luminous awareness of a loving consciousness which is present everywhere, always." Gazing into the middle distance, she beamed a beatific smile. At the time I thought the phrase sounded like a well rehearsed pitch. The place she spoke of sounded as though there were someone else present just when you were trying to get away from every annoying thought and person, no matter how loyal or devoted. But I remembered it. Sylvie had commented, "Yeah, if you can ever get your emotions out of the way. I gave up trying. I'm sure I'm a giant disappointment." She and Joyce exchanged solemn looks which at the time I ignored, but must have had something to do with Martin, I was now sure. I pictured him with Sylvie, sitting cross-legged together on his white bedspread, a cone of sandalwood burning on the bedside table, tumbling surf the only sound, Sylvie cracking open an eye to snake-charm his growing erection. I shook my head to erase the mental image and lit another cigarette.

My review and analysis were getting me nowhere. I sat, confused and overheated in my father's hat, while questions begat questions, tangled scraps of insight which amounted to nothing but the beginnings of a headache. Anyway, the image of John Sipson passing his hand through my chest was a constant interruption, nudging at my brain with dogged, irrepressible persistence, so I gave up and let it in.

I relived every moment of the bizarre encounter, trying to catch a glimpse of something that made sense, some evidence of trickery, a natural occurrence of light or wind or shadow which would explain the illusion. But it all seemed quite real, and not only that but deep down I knew what I'd seen, or rather, who, and I was fooling myself trying to come up with a different answer. Meditation and parallel universes aside, what I had seen was a ghost, plain and simple. That was the common name for what Martin was chasing and nothing more. It happened all the time, I supposed, and now it had happened to me. I let that thought puff up and solidify, pushing other explanations aside. It was an enormous relief to come to that conclusion, one I could even talk about with some frame of reference. The world's literary works were full of ghosts. Everyone knew about them. Although it was by no means an ordinary occurrence to claim to have seen one, and though I couldn't say I'd ever heard a report of a bona fide encounter, at least I could count myself among a certain number in the world who could say it out loud.

"Ghost!" I yelled out to the bay as a gust of wind danced across its surface. I heard the rowboat's answering bump against the dock pilings below. I had seen a ghost, a spirit, an apparition –or OK: a reassembled person from Martin's quantum field, where people's disintegrated particles hung around in limbo, doing . . . whatever they did. What had Martin told me about it? I could not recall, but it didn't frighten me. The memory of John Sipson, saying, "I am not afeared," came to me. Was he saying he was not "afeared" of *me*? Had he passed his hand through my chest to prove he wasn't, as if I were the ghost and not he? A cloud of doubt hung around my head for a few moments, but I took off the hat and fanned it away. No, I had not done anything but walked through the woods on Sipson's Island, present day, and by chance met a 250-year-old ghost. Or a person hanging around then who happened to have thought waves that matched mine the night of the clambake. "Arghhh!" I cried out in frustration. It was ridiculous.

I tossed the hat onto the grass, then got up and paced along the row of white rocks marking the edge of the bluff. The one I used that first day to break into the house had still not been replaced. It sat inside on the table, weighing down a few pieces of mail and a couple of sketches I did of some rose hip flowers. I wanted to try my hand, to see if maybe I'd inherited some artistic gene. Moony correctly identified them based on my drawing, so I thought I must be pretty good.

Moony. I stopped abruptly in front of the hollow where the missing stone belonged, picturing him on the night I came home from that first party at Sipson's Island. He had been lounging on the shore below, talking to someone I couldn't see, talking and drawing in the sand. I had not been sober then either, but I clearly remember going down before the tide came in and discovering the remnants of a drawing. A pyramid, maybe.

I stood for a long time looking out across the water, all the way to Sipson's, just a dark, low hump on the horizon. Could it be possible Moony had had a similar experience to mine? If so, how could I find out without asking him directly? If he had simply been lying on the sand talking to himself or performing some ritualistic offering to the fishing god of Pleasant Bay, I didn't want to embarrass him by letting on that I'd seen. I went over the things John Sipson said to me, wishing I'd paid closer attention. I heard his strange accent, each word considered, then spoken. I tried to to recall something I could interject into a sentence, something Moony might notice if I said it just the right way. But then I realized I could ask him outright about the tribe of Nausets who originally lived here. He would know, of course. He had already told me a few things about the area's history. He said the Pilgrims flirted with the idea of settling around the Bay, except they couldn't get the Mayflower over a sandbar to enter, so they had to keep going north along the peninsula to what eventually became Provincetown. He also told me that Sipson's Island was named for John Sipson and his brother Tom, two of the few remaining Nausets who lived here after they had lost most of the surrounding land to settlers. If I could get him talking about the Sipson brothers again, it might lead to an opportunity for me to tell him what I'd seen, and based on his reaction I could either plead intoxication and laugh it off, or tell him what I'd seen that night and possibly get him to admit we'd experienced the same bizarre phenomenon.

I spent another cigarette's worth of time daydreaming about interviewing John Sipson and becoming famous for the revelatory information I would provide scholars of history, but of course the fame would not be about the natives and their lives, but a circus of attention on the fact of John Sipson the celebrity ghost, and that would only be if I could somehow prove it. I flopped back into the chair and fanned myself again with the hat, nicotine-nauseous. First I had to make sure it really happened, and for that I needed to see Moony. I went into the house and took a half-full can of corn out of the fridge, then made my way down the path to the boat to go fishing. If I didn't spot Moony out on the water at least I might get something good for supper.

The fresh air cleared my head as I rowed out to one of my usual spots and dropped anchor. I fiddled with my fishing rig, tying a tiny brass button I found under the sofa to the string to add weight, keep the hook close to the bottom. A delightful breeze danced over the water's surface. Fresh air puffed into the sweaty crevices of my body, making it easy to put off the business of catching fish until I had calmed enough to not scare them away. I have learned that any physical uneasiness can travel the length of a drop line, transmitting waves of warning to anything living in the water. I lay back and watched long lines of wispy mare's tail clouds stripe the sky. Rain coming. I pictured the parched lawn back home and hoped it was true. My hand flopped overboard into the cool water, and I let my mind follow the current flowing past my fingers as it traced the line of the boat, snaked along well-worn channels through eel grass and mussel beds, skirting the shores of islands, curling into tiny whirlpools where it gathered strands of wayward seaweed, then joined other traveling streams and escorted them out to sea. The boat swung in the stream, tethered to the muddy bottom. A fish surfacing nearby reminded me why I was out there, so I stabbed a couple of kernels onto the hook and dropped it overboard, then lay back again. I watched two boys in a sailboat struggling with a flapping jib. Its line had slipped free and danced just out of reach. They were laughing, grabbing for it and not paying attention to the fact that the boat was being blown directly toward shore. When it rushed into the waist-deep grass and threw both kids off with a jolt, they continued to laugh, only harder. I chuckled, too, glad to have my thoughts interrupted. Just then I felt a jiggle on my line and tightened my grip. I peered overboard and the line went slack, probably my head making a shadow. Sighing, I picked up the crossed-stick reel and began to wind. Last night's music came to mind and I hummed a few bars of Mingus which reminded me of Sylvie as she'd been then, clearly troubled, staring down at the turntable. I struggled to recall our conversation. What wrong thing had I said? I baited the hook and tossed it in, picturing her drunken entrance at Martin's, her hand slamming against the doorframe. It must have hurt like hell, but she showed no sign of it sitting in his chair scarfing cheese, demanding to know if he'd taught me to meditate. It sounded like an accusation. Did she know the story of Freya, about Martin's attempts to contact her? Was she part of it? If they were having some kind of sticky affair I did not want to think about it. It made me feel differently about

Martin. I found myself regretting having invited him to my mother's studio, suddenly seeing him as a satyric old man who lured young people to his art-filled island house, stuffed them with French bread and used them for entertainment.

I let that image flit around in my head for a few minutes, but it didn't develop. Having been brought up around gentlemen I had no doubt that Martin was one. His type had trooped through our apartment for my entire childhood. Like him they all had obsessions about beautiful things, but they treated people with courtesy and deference. I needed to believe he was one of them and so I did, because he and I were tied together not only by that damned dab of green paint, but now by the ghost of John Sipson, who was only a few wobbling particles away from Freya, if I understood correctly.

I wiped sweat off my forehead with my t-shirt sleeve and looked around. There were more people on the water now, kids from a nearby sailing camp attempting figure eights between two marker buoys. I could hear their instructors yelling at them to sit down, stop fooling around. But the wind that had pushed the other two kids into shore had died, and boats were barely moving. Everyone on the water seemed to submit to a midday lull, letting the sun's rays press us into lethargy, a state which made me nervous. I felt stupid, passively ineffective about the night's events. I had seen a ghost, for god's sake. I couldn't just sit there, I had to do something about it. I yanked the line out of the water and deftly wound it. Fishing was not the answer. Neither was looking for Moony. I had to take action, force an explanation myself. I would go back to the woods on Sipson's Island and wait for another encounter, or sit in my mother's studio and study the paint on the wall until I willed it to come alive. Or both.

Or I would find Martin, which made the most sense. He was the only person who would believe me, and he had a vested interest in doing so. If John Sipson was there it was possible Freya was hanging around as well. I grabbed the oars and rowed quickly toward home, spraying myself as I slammed them into the water. The noise roused a pack of ducks into a squawking, flapping panic as they hustled away, careening into one another in clumsy haste. It crossed my mind that I ought to have been rowing toward Sipson's if I wanted to see Martin, but it was the last place I wanted to go. There was no question I'd encounter Sylvie if I went there and I was not willing to do that yet. Martin was sure to come to me. I would tell him what I saw, and he'd explain everything. It wasn't much action but it was all I had, so I waited.

A week went by before I saw anyone from Sipson's. Sandy's car was gone when I returned from my fishing trip. She left a note on the porch table: a cartoon heart with arms and legs said, *Where are you? Last nite wuz outasite! Thanks for letting me crash! Luv ya!* I expected Martin to show up at any moment, but he didn't. I went to work the next day and each day after hoping I would return home to find him or at least a message asking to see me but it didn't happen. By the third day I began to feel slightly angry and had to talk myself out of it several times. In the middle of the week I found a bag full of string beans on the table when I got home, *"Enjoy!"* written laboriously on the brown paper. I knew Moony had a big garden. I could picture him taking a pencil from behind his ear, licking the lead and deciding what to write. I was sorry to have missed him. I had put a sketch of a pyramid under the rock with my other drawings in case he came by again and noticed. A little bee in his bonnet, maybe. It was a long shot, but I was too shy to come right out and ask him if he'd seen the ghost of John Sipson and still hadn't thought of any other way into that conversation. I was starting to have my own doubts about what I'd seen, especially after a few sobering days on the job in the real world.

One day I found a child's paintbox and a cheap pad of white construction paper in a box under the bed, and took it out to my mother's studio, where I had begun to spend my evenings. There I passed the time experimenting with color and line, perspective and shadow. Somehow the little building's atmosphere felt conducive to another otherworldly visit, which I hoped would happen. I went there because it was cooler and still smelled faintly of oil paint, which reminded me of home, but also because in the week following the clambake I suddenly began seeing many things I wanted to paint –a slew of images that excited me and drew me to the green chairs in my mother's studio, paintbox in hand. I made four good paintings in four afternoons. There was something going on within my body; an energy I had never felt before surged through me, driving away doubt and compelling me to grab my paintbrush, dip it in water and swirl it in the little pan of pigment, load the bristles until it was heavy, and without hesitation stroke an exquisite, perfect line on the paper, where it soaked into the fibers and spread. I thoroughly lost myself in these movements. I did not think, or plan. I was an automaton completing a program. I painted the place where I had removed the white rock on the edge of the yard, depicting a black-dark recess in a row of white against the dry yellow lawn, with the blue bay in the background. I painted a flounder from memory, showing it lying on the seat of my boat with the sky reflected in its scales. I painted the tips of the cedar trees surrounding my mother's studio, each bending under the weight of a crow. I painted the Egyptian oil lamp from the shelf with a tiny flame and a huge plume of mauve-colored smoke. My hand was a tool to hold the brush, and the brush never seemed to make a wrong move. Every evening at sunset came the plaintive sound of a bugle playing "Taps," at the summer camp over on Namequoit Point. It was my signal to go into the house, eat something, and lie in bed reading until I fell asleep. The song comforted me. *"All is well, safely rest,"* directed the horn to all the children away from home in unfamiliar beds. I included myself among them.

I was in the studio when Martin finally showed up. It was late afternoon on Saturday. I'd been to work and done some shopping before heading home. On the way I made my every-other-week phone call to my mother. Things were better. She was painting again. My sister had gone to stay with friends for a month in Antibes. She had just asked me how I was doing when the line went dead. I had no more change for another call to the operator, and so I rode glumly home, feeling sorry for myself. I considered going back to Paris. I could start school again, do something serious with my life instead of living this frivolous Cape Cod life of tourists, wealthy eccentrics, tripping hippies, and ghosts. I knew that at some point the weather was going to get cold, and my house was only a summer cottage so I'd have to find a place with heat and a job to pay for it. But there I was, riding my bike down one of the loveliest roads I'd ever seen, a week's worth of food strapped to the baggage carrier and warm wind in my face, my only destination a sweet little sanctum overlooking the bay. I could worry next month, I told myself, and then ask my mother to buy me a ticket home. *C'est tout.*

But the nag of responsibility lingered while I put groceries away, tidied up the place and wrote my mother a letter. Even after a few false starts I could not manage to purge the note of angst from my tone. Not wanting to cause her worry, I put it aside, went out to her cool studio and set up in one of the big green chairs. I would paint her old view for her, a tiny triangle of sea glimpsed through a scrim of swaying cedar branches. How does one put life into stationary paint strokes? Concentrating on that question while hypnotically stirring green gouache into blue, I did not hear anyone approach until Martin's voice startled me.

"Hello Elli." He said it softly, contritely, I thought. I quickly covered my painting with another piece of paper and invited him in. He wore a gauzy white shirt over swimming trunks. His bare feet were wet; orange sand stuck to his toes. Stealing a glance at the wall where the painting had been he announced, "I came by boat," and held out a dripping net bag. "I got some mussels along the way. You like mussels?"

"Oh yes. Very much." I felt suddenly shy, as if he were a date showing up to court me. It was the Sylvie thing, the accusation. We would have to talk about it. "Shall we have them now, or –?"

"Yes, if you like." He was shy as well. "I brought white wine to cook them in," he added. I could have kissed him. It broke the tension, and we walked over to the house chatting about mussel recipes as though nothing unpleasant had ever happened. I turned on the radio when we got inside, as had become my habit. *"Ode to Billie Joe"* was playing, the family sitting around the table discussing his jump from the Tallahatchie Bridge. Martin cocked his head and listened to the story, as intrigued by the mystery as the rest of us. I went into the kitchen and took out a huge cooking pot, lit the stove and cut an onion in half. Martin studied the little Ria Bang Overtons again before going downhill to his boat for the wine. He returned with two bottles, one half full which he held up. "This one's for cooking," he said, and set it on the counter. I chopped onions, trying to think of a way to begin telling my story even though I'd been waiting impatiently all week for the opportunity. I decided to just jump right in and mumbled, "I'm sorry I left so quickly," at the same time he said "I brought this for the pot," and pulled a wadded up napkin from his shirt pocket which he unwrapped and held for me to sniff. "Tarragon, from the garden. You were saying?"

"I said I'm sorry I ran away so suddenly."

"I don't blame you. That was awkward, not to mention embarrassing." He picked up the wine bottle, made a corkscrew motion. I fished it out of the drawer. "I should tell you about Sylvie."

"You don't have to." I did not want to hear about their affair. "She was drunk."

"Yes, very. She passed out soon after you left and woke up at dawn with her hand swollen to three times its size. We had to take her to the hospital. She fractured one of her knuckles." He shook his head slowly, holding up the middle finger of his hand to illustrate. "It will take a few weeks to heal, but she's all right." He laid the hand on my shoulder. "Would you like a glass of wine?" The onions sizzled. I added more butter, again seeing Sylvie smash the back of her hand against the doorframe.

"Somehow I feel responsible," I said, though I knew I wasn't. But I did feel terrible for Sylvie. I remembered her spooning date bread batter into the tinfoil pillow for baking in the coals. She was so competent, so maternal. "She was mad at me. Because of you, right?"

Martin dumped the mussels into the sink and ran the tap over them, rinsing off sand. He uncorked the half bottle of wine and tipped it slowly into the pot with the onions, added the sprig of tarragon, then sat down at the table. He twirled the wineglass between his fingers for a few moments, thinking.

"Look, I must tell you that years ago, she and I had a one-night thing. Which was no thing." I felt my cheeks redden as he went on, but I couldn't find polite words to make him stop. "I was completely undone after Freya died, I told you. It was a very dark time for me, and Sylvie was there. One night I took comfort in her."

I hated that expression. "What about Ray?"

"He wasn't there."

The wine boiled up. Martin scooped handfuls of mussels from the sink and dropped them into the pot, then turned down the flame. The kitchen filled with an anise-like scent.

"I see," I said, sounding more prudish than I felt.

"Ray knows. We talked about it. I can't say it hasn't altered our friendship, but we all need each other out there, so we make it work." Martin gave me a brief look of defiance, exactly like the one my sister used to put on when she bit into a second chocolate bar.

"She's a good person, Elli, and I am quite fond of her. Ray and Sal, too. They keep the place running. I couldn't be here without them. And yes, Sylvie and I are good friends, but that's it." He picked up his wine and peered through the glass at me, his eye distorting into a blob of black-brown. "Can we not have an investigation into it?

Yes, it's a bit of a problem for me. I want to be her friend, but she wants more. I have to be aware of every little gesture, every word, so that I don't encourage her. I cannot seem too enthusiastic or too interested in what she says, because she'll take it as a sign of romantic attachment. Nor can I ignore her or block her, because she has a certain control over the brothers, and I could wind up losing them all." He spread his hands wide and gave me an earnest, despairing look, his mouth screwed up to one side. "I'm doing the best I can. Please don't judge me harshly."

I hadn't. I told him I felt a little sorry for him.

"Yeah, well. I'm handling it, but to tell the truth I'm getting fed up." He ran his finger around one of the lemons printed on the tablecloth. "I hope you don't think I'm here on some seduction mission, either. I'm not. I'm an old man, for god's sake. I want to find Freya, that's all."

The mussels were ready. I turned off the flame under the pot and took two wide bowls from the shelf. I felt sticky, as if Martin's confession had been mixed into the tarragon-scented steam billowing around me, creeping into my nostrils, my armpits and under the waistband of my shorts. I spooned a dozen mussels into a bowl and set it in font of him, little orange vulvas in spread-open shells. *Bordel!* The subject was everywhere. I turned away, embarrassed, and nearly burst out laughing as I dished some for myself.

"I didn't think that," I said. "Thank you for telling me about Sylvie, though. It explains other things."

I snuck looks at Martin as we dug into the mussels. He didn't say much, just made a few appreciative sounds. Close up he did look old, and tired, not as well kempt as usual. His snow white hair had greasy yellow streaks running through it, multiple pulled threads marred the perfection of his handmade shirt. I could see that he'd missed a section of chin stubble while shaving. A glisten of butter clung to it, so I passed him a napkin which he tucked into his lap, and the butter remained. I stopped looking, got up and fiddled with the radio dial. WBCN was playing back to back Grateful Dead, which I knew could go on for hours. I lowered the volume and sat back down, rubbing my palms together nervously, ready to announce the news of my John Sipson encounter, but Martin was concentrating on the mussels and didn't notice. He began to talk about a time when he lived in Cambridge studying some type of Buddhism. He listed the favorite foods he denied himself in order to follow the guidelines of a master he and a small group of people lived and studied with. "We ate nothing but sprouted wheat cakes. Live food, it was called. Nothing cooked, certainly no meat. It was supposed to give us a clean body and clear mind for the work of achieving nirvana, and I must say it did make me very healthy, but after a few weeks I found myself using the group meditation hours to fantasize about food. Step by step I would mentally prepare and cook rich, fragrant, mouth-watering, meat-filled dishes, savoring every moment." He chuckled. "I went out to dinner one evening directly from one of our sessions, and never went back." He turned sideways in his chair and leaned against the wall, mussels finished. He sighed, "I really am just a spoiled rich kid, as my mother used to say."

I didn't know how to react. He had never mentioned his parents or his childhood. I forced my mind back to the day Sylvie and I had sat in his bedroom and she'd told me about them. I tried to remember: booze, gas tanks, Nervilex. But I didn't care. There was only one subject I wanted to discuss.

147

"I saw the ghost of John Sipson on my way home the night I left your house." I blurted out.

He turned and stared at me. Then he cocked his head, squinting, his eyebrows lowering to nearly touch the bridge of his nose as they had that evening, when I told him about the dab of wet green paint on my finger. "Come again?" he said.

"When I left your house, just before I came out onto the beach, I was standing by a tree trying to find Sandy in the crowd. He was there, and introduced himself."

Martin leaned in toward me. "What makes you think it was a ghost?"

I described the encounter in detail, every word I could remember, from the comment about Sandy being an 'awful sight' to John Sipson passing the back of his hand through my chest, then spreading his arms out. I stood up to demonstrate. "Pray pardon me," I said, imitating his speech as best I could. "I am not afeared."

"What?"

"Yeah. I think he was telling me he wasn't afraid of me."

Martin sat stunned for minute, the corners of his mouth turned down. He rubbed his jaw between thumb and fingers, unwittingly wiping off the streak of butter. I waited for him to ask more questions, and I was ready. I wanted to go over the whole thing again, to have my experience confirmed and solidified by repetition. But he stood up abruptly and paced around the kitchen floor, picking up the bowls in passing and laying them in the sink, taking the mussel shells outside to toss over the hill. I stayed where I was and poured myself another glass of wine. I had been living with this thing for a week, and I was savoring the moment. I knew I didn't have to figure out what to do by myself.

Martin came back in and ran the water for dishes. He began mechanically washing them, squirting soap onto a sponge and running it blindly over the surfaces of things, doing a really bad job. I wondered if he'd ever done a dish in his life. He used a lot of soap, way too much. I had a pink bottle of Thrill and a yellow one of Joy. I thought it ridiculous and wonderful that American housewives were given these product name choices for the chore. I had thought to do a painting of them side by side, perched on the rim of a sink full of dirty dishes. Martin stood a bowl in the drying rack and turned to me. "So, you are positive he couldn't have been a person from the party? Someone playacting a role for fun? He certainly would have fit into that crowd."

His skepticism echoed mine. It had driven me to relive the event repeatedly over the past week, striving to see and hear every detail. "Except for the fact of his hand passing through my chest, I suppose that could be. I just can't say for certain." I took a sip of wine and added, "And I wasn't drunk, either."

"You sure?" He turned back to the sink.

I saw myself sitting on the bluff that morning in my father's hat, sweating out a mixture of angst and stupefaction, searching through the swirl of images for an anchor, a starting point, anything that could explain what had happened. "No," I admitted. "I don't even remember the ride home. But that was because I was in some kind of shock, not from being drunk." Now that Martin was poking at the details, doubt loomed up again and I was suddenly embarrassed. I didn't know what to believe anymore.

"Sal drove you. He found you asleep in the back seat of Sandy's car. He dropped you both here, then went to the hospital with me and Sylvie."

"Oh."

"He said you looked like you'd seen a ghost." Our eyes met for a brief moment and we laughed. "Don't worry, Elli. I believe you," Martin said. "I don't think you are the type of person to invent something like this."

I hope you aren't, either, I thought. After all, I was not the one recreating works of art with my mind.

He finished washing the dishes and pulled the plug. There was a large puddle of water on the floor under the sink which he dropped the dish towel onto and swabbed around a little before slinging it over the tap. He sat down with his hands folded on the table and stared at me, smiling.

"So, are you saying your impression was that John Sipson thought *you* were the . . .?" He described a human figure with his hands.

"Yeah, a ghost. That's what I think. His last words were 'You are but a dream.'"

"Very interesting. Perhaps you were."

"But we were both watching Sandy prance around in the water."

"I wonder what he was really seeing."

"What do you mean?"

Martin grunted, squirmed in his seat, then let out a long sigh. "Look, it's complicated. I've told you a few pretty crazy-sounding things already, I know, and I don't want you to think I'm some kind of eccentric living out here on my island, another nutty guru with a band of hippie followers. I confided in you because of what happened in your mother's studio, because of what happened to me with your mother's painting, and you, too." He held up a forefinger and wiggled it at me. "Somehow you have access to whatever it is going on around this bay in a . . . parallel universe, or an alternate timeline. And now you have seen a ghost —I suppose that's what we have to call him— which is precisely what I have been trying to do for years. What are ghosts but brain waves, energy which has no material form?" He bored his eyes into mine, earnestly looking for something, an answer to his rhetorical question, or the reason it had happened to me and not him.

"I don't know," I said. I was trying to stick with him. I remembered his description of walks around his island through a 'thicket of atoms' still hanging around, tiny parts of all the people who had lived and died there. At the time I'd pictured a swarm of gnats which, Walt Disney-style, coalesced into the form of a person, and I admit I found Martin's imagery to be about as believable as a cartoon. Yet from that particle swamp on Sipson's Island the former owner had emerged, and I had seen him.

"When you and the ghost of John Sipson were standing there in the woods watching Sandy dance around in the water, I'm just trying to imagine what he was looking at in his version of the world."

"I don't know, but he said it was awful."

"Maybe he said 'awe-ful,' as in old-style English. Full of awe."

"I suppose so, yeah." It had not occurred to me. We combed through the conversation, picking it apart for more information. Martin agreed with me that John Sipson must have thought me a ghost, and he spent some more time ruminating aloud about the multiverse, more wave-collapsing and other abstract jargon I could not follow, trying to prove the event scientifically. I had so many questions about parallel universes, about particles and entanglement and ghosts. I needed a concrete explanation but I could tell Martin was too keyed up to stop and give me one.

He proposed we return immediately to the tree and wait for a reappearance. If it happened once it could happen again, he said, and this time it could be Freya showing up. I wanted to understand how going back or forward in time could be part of a parallel universe, but I could tell he had no patience for more talk. It was nearly seven o'clock and in an hour there would be little light for the boat ride across the Bay to the island.

"Why don't you grab a sweater and come back with me? Min is there, and Theo will be along shortly, if I know him. We could wait until dark and then go and stand in the woods." He got up and started looking around for his shoes, forgetting that he'd arrived barefoot. I did not want to go to Sipson's. We would have to walk past Ray and Sylvie's house to get to Martin's, and it would be strange for me to do that and not stop in. I was not willing to sneak past, either.

"What about Sylvie"? I said.

"What about her?" Martin walked from the kitchen to the porch and back, scanning the floor.

"I feel uncomfortable. She's my friend. I can't just ignore her." Especially if I'm lurking in the woods near her house, I thought. How would I explain it? I didn't want to lie, but neither could I tell her I was there to reunite with a ghost I'd met at her party. I could feel myself getting worked up about being put in that position. Martin could look forever for his damn shoes, I was not going to tell him.

"She's not there," he said, still distracted. He lifted the skirt on the sofa and bent down to peer underneath.

"What?"

"Yeah. She's staying with her sister in Boston. Seeing a therapist for the hand. Saves driving back and forth." He let out a sigh as he straightened up. "Come on, Elli. Everything's fine. Let's just go and find Mr. Sipson." He edged over to the porch door. "We can talk on the way."

It still felt vaguely duplicitous, but I could deal with that later. I wanted to see the ghost again. I went into the bedroom for my flannel shirt, pausing at the closet door to check myself for any sense of foreboding, a hunch that this was not a good idea, but all I felt was a calm determination to act and glad for the partnership with Martin. I tied the shirt around my waist, shoved my feet into the old espadrilles, and left.

Chapter Eight

That night we waited until it was fully dark, then settled in under the big maple to wait. Martin insisted we sit in a silent, thought-free trance so that we would be able to accommodate what energy from the other side was ready to enter our minds. It wasn't exactly a re-creation of my experience, but I deferred to his greater knowledge and sat still while he fidgeted beside me, changing position and location, trying to produce the perfect ambience for a visit. I leaned against the trunk with my eyes slightly open, watching ripples of reflected starlight rushing by in the narrows. After an hour or so it was difficult to keep them open, and I think we both may have drifted off, because suddenly the glowing face of Martin's watch was in front of my face with Martin's finger tapping on it. "It's one in the morning," he whispered. "Let's give up for tonight."

I was happy to do that. Earlier that evening while we waited for darkness, we sat around the table with Min and Theo eating onion soup and drinking more wine. "Just one glass," Martin directed. "We don't want to fall asleep."

I took the opportunity to ask Theo about my parents' life on the Bay when my sister and I were little. He had been close with them both. "Your mother mostly. She and I met here at summer camp when we were fourteen, just down the shore there," he said, waving his hand at the other end of the bay. "We stayed friends until you all moved to France." He described various cookouts and car trips and recounted a few funny childlike things I'd said, though I cannot remember any of them. He said that after they had children my parents bought the house on Barley Neck and drove here from New York at the beginning of each summer. My father would deposit us and go off on his art-dealing missions. He had another place in Provincetown, where he had met my mother when she was a student at Hans Hofmann's famous art school. My father spent part of the summer there on his own. I thought it was a little strange but I didn't want to ask Theo, whom I hardly knew, to talk about my parents' living arrangements.

I woke up in Martin's guest bedroom the next morning wishing I were home lying on my parents' sagging mattress and gazing out across the Bay. The room was quite plush, with deep pile carpeting, works of art and a private bath, but didn't fit what I had begun to love about this part of Cape Cod. Here opulence was out of place. The land was soft, barely there, consisting of sand and weeds. Trees had shallow roots, marshes were washed through twice a day. There were no boulders, only occasional large rocks; no majestic oaks and pines, only windblown scrub versions; no stately brick chateaus, just wood-shingled houses which looked like they could be blown down by a blast from the Big Bad Wolf. People dressed in work clothes, drove rusty cars, ate simply and drank beer. I liked it. Martin's handmade shirts and the raw silk coverlet I lay under that morning were more familiar to me than any of the world I now lived in, yet I felt out of place in that room. When I emerged from it I found Martin sitting at the kitchen counter buttering a piece of toast.

"We have to go out again tonight," he said, handing it to me.

Min stood at the sink with her back to us. She turned to say good morning, then went back to it, holding the soup pot under the tap. I tilted my head toward her and shrugged at Martin. Could we talk about it with her there?

"It's all right. Can you come back tonight?"

I had to work the next morning at eight, and said so.

"I'll give you a ride whenever you want. Middle of the night, morning, just tell me," Martin said, nodding eagerly. His foot jiggled against the leg of his stool, a crazy staccato to Min's dish-clattering. I wanted to please him, to help him, and naturally I wanted to see John Sipson again. But I was also relying on Martin to ease an uncertainty I secretly felt about the encounter. During the past week skeptical thoughts had been flitting through my mind about what I'd really seen and heard that night. Telling him about it had been a way to confirm that it had happened, but I admit there was also a part of me that wanted to unload it, to be free of the obligation to prove it, to find the ghost again. Because in that week something almost equally compelling had distracted me. My sudden ability to paint, to experience the sensation of another power taking over my eyes and hands almost transcended my desire to find John Sipson, and so I had begun to tell myself that maybe meeting him had never happened, that it had been a dream, an hallucination. I only wanted to go home, sit in my mother's studio with the paint box and lose myself to the divine magic I'd found there. I'm sure the sensation was akin to what happened to Martin when he first came across 'A Swim at Pochet', and I ought to have told him about it but I wanted to keep it to myself for a while. Things seemed to be happening too fast. I was losing my ability to manage and I wanted to stop, just for a few days. Stop and paint.

But instead I said, "Pick me up after dinner. We can try again in the same spot. I should leave in time to get some sleep, though."

"Done." Martin slapped the countertop, causing Min to jump. "Now, let's get you home." He thrust another piece of toast at me and spun around, heading for the door. Min stared at me. I shrugged, rolled my eyes, and followed him.

In the car I asked about Min. What did she think we were doing? Did she know about my encounter?

"She knows I go out looking for Freya," he said, keeping his eyes on the road. "I told her."

"Does she believe Freya is out there?"

"I don't know what she believes, but she doesn't question it, and that's how a housekeeper should behave."

I glanced over expecting to see him grinning, but he was intent on driving and serious about Min, I guess. "What about Theo, what does he think?"

"Well that's a different story. He thinks I'm nuts."

I laughed. "So, I take it you haven't told him about your painting adventures." I waggled the finger which had touched the wet green paint.

"No. I only told you because of what you saw." He turned onto Barley Neck Road, swerving to avoid a Jeep full of surfers heading toward the ocean. Radio playing at top volume, stacked boards jutting out like a giant bluejay's tail, the Jeep skidded around the corner and slotted into beach traffic, leaving Martin stalled on the verge.

"Jesus!" Martin shouted after them. He honked the horn but they were long gone, Mick Jagger singing '*Brown Sugar*' after them down the street.

In front of us a field of wildflowers waved. Over a short hill the land sloped to another of the bay's many inlets, where I knew Moony kept his boat, a wooden dory from Newfoundland with a proud, upthrust prow. I had a sudden idea to go down and see if he was there. I knew he liked to fiddle with it on his day off, and it was Sunday so I turned to Martin and said, "I'll get off here, okay? I feel like walking."

"Oh." He looked pained, laid a hand on my arm. "I hope that didn't put you off riding with me. I swear I'm a good driver."

"No, not at all. I want to visit a friend."

He started the car. "Okay. I'll pick you up tonight, right?"

"Tonight." I thanked him for the ride and started down the hill. I'm pretty sure he sat there until I was out of sight. It was the start of a period of clinginess for Martin which went against the other impressions I'd formed of him, and was frankly a little unnerving. He was desperate to keep me close because I had the key to the world where Freya lived, or so he thought. I understood, but my enthusiasm of a week ago for ghost-chasing with Martin had cooled somewhat. The whole Sylvie/Martin thing made me feel stuck into a snarl of past events having nothing to do with me but which were now dictating my actions. I wanted my discovery of John Sipson to be free of complication, which was a ridiculous thought that made me laugh aloud just as I spotted Moony. Bent over the boat with his back to me, he turned when he heard my laugh and I saw that he was not alone. Joyce sat nestled into the bow, her loose hair a froth of black and gray, strands streaming from her temples and disappearing into her armpits. Her eyes were hidden under dark glasses. Sun glinted off a tangle of silver bracelets as she waved me over.

"Hi honey," she sang out. "Come join us. We have snacks." She sat up, gripping the gunwales to haul herself forward. Moony stood working a rope around a nosegay of wire scraps. He lifted his chin and smiled. "Hey," he said. "Everything all right?"

I was so surprised to see them together I had a temporary loss of momentum, forgetting completely what I was doing there. I mumbled hello and stopped walking, just stood staring at them. Joyce reached into a paper bag, pulled out a fat string bean and dipped it into a bowl of something pink, then held it up to me. I recognized the robust color of the bean, an almost day-glo green particular to Moony's garden. I stepped closer, took it, had a bite and another surprise. I was eating a favorite food my father had introduced to the family. Made from fish roe and mashed potatoes, it was something he liked to whip up for us now and then. He said it brought him back to the neighborhood in Smyrna, Turkey, where he grew up.

"*Taramosalata.*" I chewed with delight. "I can't believe it,"

"Is it French?" Mooney asked.

"No dear, it's Greek." Joyce handed him one. He bit into it, cocked his head, nodded approval. "What you up to?" he asked me.

That was certainly the question I wanted to ask them. Joyce had her legs slung over the boat's seat. She wore one of her usual long colorful skirts which made a natural tablecloth for the food arranged between her knees. I had no idea they knew each other, let alone had picnics together. I feigned nonchalance as I re-dipped my bean. Why had I wanted to see Moony? I had nearly forgotten.

"I was walking," I began. Joyce took off her sunglasses and examined one of the earpieces. She wriggled it back and forth, frowning at the hinge. "I thought you might be here," I said to Moony. Joyce put her hands up in her hair, pulled out a little barrette.

"I was thinking about Indians," I said. "The Sipson brothers out on the island." I looked sharply at Moony to spot any flinching, but he dipped his bean into the *taramosalata,* expression unchanged, waiting for me to continue. Joyce inserted the flat metal band of the barrette into the tiny screw of her sunglasses and began to twist it.

"I was wondering if anyone had ever reported having seen a ghost out there." I ducked my head. It was more direct than I had planned, but what the hell.

"Ghost?" Moony looked at Joyce, she at me.

She put her glasses on, jabbed the barrette back into the thickest part of her hair and said, "Why do you ask? Have you seen something?"

"Ha, no," I lied, still keeping an eye on Moony. "Someone at the party mentioned it. It may have been a different island, now I think of it."

"Well, what do you expect from that crowd." Joyce clicked her tongue and leaned back in the prow. "Ghosts, magic, witches. The Hierophant, The High Priestess. They love to discuss the supernatural, especially after a few joints. That kind of thing?"

"Well . . ."

"Oh, wait a sec. I know. Ray and Sal talk about it sometimes. Sal insists that their garden is suffused with old magic. They think it used to be exactly the spot the natives used, and the souls of those old gardeners are helping out. They say the soil has a quality to it which is nowhere else on the island."

She looked at Moony, fished around in the bag for another bean, held it up to the light, then tucked it into her mouth. "Probably like the soil this grew in," she said, munching. "Do you have otherworldly help at your place, too?" she said, playfully.

Moony just smiled. "I don't think so, but maybe," he mumbled. "Anyhow, about that, people used to keep sheep out there. No need to fence, and plenty to graze on." He scratched his head, looking at me from under his hand. "I bet it's why the soil's good, I mean."

"Why don't you ask Martin about it?" Joyce said. "I think he's done a lot of research into the history of that island. He found an Indian skull over there which is pretty impressive. You should get him to show it to you." She and Moony exchanged a look. Moony's face revealed nothing.

I was not going to tell them what had happened to it. Maybe they already knew, and were keeping it secret, like me. It confused me. There were far too many secret things to keep track of. I had given Moony an opening, but perhaps with Joyce there he couldn't say anything. Hopefully he'd suspect that I knew something and show up later at my house to discuss.

I could easily have stayed there with them passing a tranquil Sunday afternoon, but I felt I was intruding. Come to think of it, did Moony even have a wife? I didn't know. I had assumed their picnic was a secret tryst, when perhaps they were an established couple. They certainly weren't trying to hide anything. I was happy for them. But still, it was something I needed to think about, another piece to fit into the story.

"Thank you for the *taramosalata*, Joyce," I gave her a little bow, and mock-saluted Moony as I turned to leave. "I've got to get home. See you soon, I hope," I added, and started up the hill to the road.

"You can walk all the way to your place along the water from here, if you like," said Moony. He pointed to a path tramped into the grass. "It might take longer, but it's a nice way to go. And you've got the tide just right."

"Thanks. I think I will," I said, reversing my steps. I could see the trail's white line snaking around the inlet and I stepped onto it, waving back at them.

It was indeed a lovely walk. I had to cross someone's lawn at one point but the rest was obviously a route many feet had tramped over the years. Even so, it was only a little wider than my hand. There were many child size foot prints along the way, shooting off the path to where boats had been pulled up onto the sand, or where a rickety dock listed in the shallows. In a couple of places the path veered off to higher ground when the land turned marshy. Thick wooden planks had been laid in the mud to walk on. I savored the peace and quiet, the smell of low tide heated by warm sun, little sounds made by foraging crabs, and the trickle of fresh water seeping from the upland. A lone kildeer called its name out across the still water, announcing my presence to others. I strolled along surveying this unfamiliar part of the bay, close to my house but behind it so I couldn't see it from my parents bedroom. I pictured John Sipson walking barefoot along this same path, some sort of Indian fishing gear dangling from his hand, a canoe parked nearby, though I had no idea what kind of boats the natives of this bay had used. I came upon our dock, almost a surprise when approached from this new direction, and heaved myself up on its weathered boards, sighing. Though I had promised Martin we'd go out again that night to wait, the thought made me tired. Of course I would help him, and had my own curiosity about our little project. I wanted badly to have my encounter confirmed.

"Why don't you come over to Barley Neck and make it easier for me?" I said to the ghost of John Sipson, then climbed the hill.

Five days later I was muttering much the same as I tossed a wet towel into the hamper of my cart at the Governor Hancock. I wheeled it along to the next room and pushed the door open. The place was a shambles of discarded food wrappers, pizza boxes, and potato chip bags. Beer cans dribbled wet blotches on the rug and the bedspread lay wadded up by the bathroom door.

"I hate to imagine what they wiped up with that," said Becca, coming up behind me. She laid her chin on my shoulder and added, "I quit."

"Me too," I said, sighing again. I seemed to be doing a lot of that. I was dead tired. "I sleep like a brick and wake up like one too" –another of my father's Greek expressions which summed up perfectly my state of mind. Martin and I had waited every night for John Sipson, but he had not appeared. I wondered if it wouldn't be better for me to sit under the maple alone, but that was not something I was willing to do.

I was being well-fed though, by Min, in the hour or two before we went out. Martin would fetch me at suppertime and bring me home with him, and twice we picked up Theo on the way. Those were enjoyable evenings. I heard more about my parents' lives in their younger days, which was quite compelling. Listening to Theo's stories, seeing the change in his eyes as he talked, gave me the idea that he might have been one of my mother's suitors but was bumped aside by my father and demoted to the role of friend. "Were those your mother's?" he asked me on the second evening, eyeing my espadrilles.

"Well, yes," I answered, looking down at them. They were faded pink and dotted with grease stains. "How did you know?"

"I just remember," he said.

Even so he made sure to tell me how happy my parents were together.

Theo worked as a reporter for The Cape Codder, so he knew everything about the goings-on around town. Min would pry all kinds of gossip out of him while he protested but eventually told us some pretty unsavory yet hilarious stories. I suppose they were the usual kind of small-town secrets everyone knew about: the Catholic priest who was in love with the paperboy, the family with twin boys who were replicas of the man next door, the selectman with the new car who signed off on the mini-golf course built on a cranberry bog, et cetera. Back then I was shocked and fascinated.

Theo and Martin would discuss quantum theory, energy in many forms, and things like the possibility of a fourth dimension and what it would look like as a modified cube. While Min and I did dishes they did umpteen geometric sketches on a fat block of drawing paper, passing it back and forth as they debated. Theo said the shape would have to be animated for anyone to illustrate four dimensions, but Martin would insist it could be drawn and go at it again.

"It's out there," he'd say, "but we just can't see it with our three-dimension brains." I could tell both Theo and Min were skeptical but they were polite about our "project," as we referred to our night watches. As far as I knew they had no idea we were out there waiting for the ghost of John Sipson to reappear; they thought we were testing energy fields or something. I heard Min ask Martin once how our "affirmations" were going. Maybe she assumed we were praying to the moon or a sea goddess. The subject was never discussed directly and I went along with Martin's vague references to our experiment in the woods, not adding anything.

On a few occasions Theo tried to temper my confidence in Martin's theories and beliefs. He would say things about his particle wave statements when Martin was out of the room. "Elli, don't take this stuff too literally. Remember, "collapsing the wave" is only a hypothesis, not a theory. Because it cannot be tested."

"Well, we're about to test it in a little while." I barely knew what I was saying but I jumped in anyway, though I could not elaborate. Out of politeness Theo did not press me for more. I'm sure he knew I was out of my league, and he was right, but I knew about Martin's experience with "painting" works of art, and about my own brief encounter with it. Theo and Min did not. Martin had told me I'd collapsed the wave then, and I had believed him.

But I was beginning to have my doubts, as I said. I had gone over every inch of the wall where *'A Swim at Pochet'* had been painted –and repainted– and I had not found even a tiny hint of disturbance in the wall or its skim of dust. The scraps of green paint under it were bone-dry. So I didn't know how Martin could have fooled me, or why he would bother. If the whole thing was an elaborate trick I didn't understand why I had been selected as the victim. I was also beginning to feel a little silly sitting under the elm tree every night, waiting for something I suspected was not going to happen. What I did think, though, was that any night now Sylvie was going to show up, stand there with her arms assertively crossed, and condemn us both to hell.

I plowed through the motel room chaos and gave the rolled-up bedspread a kick. "No dead bodies at least," I said as Becca snorted. I mentally counted the number of rooms left to clean. I was working about six hours a day then, the height of summer. Because we had to be done by one o'clock for the new check-ins, we started earlier, at seven. Martin and I usually gave up waiting for John Sipson well after midnight, so I was getting home around two. I suppose I could have taken an afternoon nap, but the minute I got off work I'd take a quick swim to wash off the sweat, then go directly to my mother's studio and pick up where I'd left off, not stopping until I heard Martin's car in the driveway at dinner time.

The previous evening I'd been in the studio painting, contemplating begging off for a night. I was happy to be so wholly absorbed in my near-silent world, the only sound my brush tinkling against the glass as I rinsed. But then I pictured Martin's eager face holding the car door for me, recalled his enthusiastic small talk as we drove to the landing, and admired his quiet, prayerful devotion as he sat cross legged under the tree while I struggled to stay awake. So I went with him again. I wanted badly to please him, to make possible this gift so that he could go off to look for Freya with more than just hope. But I also wanted to ask him: Did he think John Sipson was going to give Freya a message of some kind, a While You Were Out note in the

166

afterlife? That sarcastic thought and others like it were no doubt creating the kind of energy field around me that sent the wrong message. Again I concentrated on reproducing my state of mind on the night of the clambake, when I had fled Martin's house after Sylvie's drunken visit. Were they the thought waves that had attracted John Sipson? Or had he already been standing there, watching the awe-full spectacle of naked Sandy frolicking in the narrows? I wasn't about to reenact her dance to attract attention from a ghost, or for any other reason.

While we sat there trying to direct our thoughts mine drifted frequently to the paintings I was making in the studio. My mind's eye would correct a line, deepen a shadow, or swirl the brush around in a pot of imagined color, the brilliant blue-green of a tropical butterfly's wings, turning it into a luscious glistening soup from which I would sneak a taste. I could understand why Van Gogh was said to have eaten yellow paint. I meant to ask Martin if it was true. I was feeling some thrilling little zings of passion myself those afternoons in the studio. I wanted bigger paper and better brushes, and I wanted to paint right on the wall as my mother had. There was an art supply store in the middle of town and I stopped in occasionally to drool over the fat tubes of acrylic. One night I was busy mentally multiplying my hourly wage, figuring how long it would take to afford them, when Martin spoke up.

"Do you hear anything?"

"Uh, no. What?"

"Listen."

"Do ghosts make sounds when they walk, or do they float?" I whispered. Sarcasm again.

Martin sighed. "Maybe it's time to call it," he said, peering at his watch in the darkness.

"Let's give it another half an hour," I said, guiltily, then snuggled deeper against the elm trunk.

Remembering that little exchange as I pulled hot towels out of the dryer, I promised myself I would not let Martin down. I would hang in there until he gave up, or at least for another few days. I had the next day off, so I would have plenty of time to sleep, or paint.

But that night as we sat in our spot, Martin was not at his usual ease. Instead of adopting a meditative demeanor he rubbed his eyes, digging his fingers in so deep I thought his eyeballs might pop out from between them. He was wearing the same shirt as I'd seen him in the day before, and it showed. He may have slept in it; twisted wrinkles were set in the linen. He was unshaven and his feet were filthy, shoved into cheap rubber flip-flops which I knew belonged to Min. After half an hour he was still fidgeting, running his hands through his hair or cleaning out his fingernails with a broken-off twig.

"I think we need to take a break, maybe think of a different approach," he said abruptly.

"Okay." I expected him to suggest that I stay out there alone, or walk around on the shore so I could be spotted in the moonlight.

"Look, I have to be absolutely certain about what you saw out here," he said instead. "Maybe you could describe it to me just one more time."

I couldn't immediately respond. I had made it clear that I wasn't entirely sure myself. I'd said it more than a few times. "There's nothing else to add," I said slowly.

"Because. . . well, I'm beginning to wonder if maybe you had a little too much to drink that night. And maybe –I mean, I did pour you an awful lot of port, so perhaps you. . ." He did not continue, but I got his drift. He was starting to doubt, too. But I needed him to believe in what I saw so that I could be sure myself. It was pretty much what I was going on, at that point.

"You don't believe me anymore?"

"Well, yes, I want to, Elli. But let's face it, you are still almost a girl, a, –at an impressionable age. Maybe he was just a regular old hippie from the party and, I don't know, being a foreigner, maybe you misinterpreted what was really happening. I mean, maybe he tried to touch your, your chest, and you. . ."

"What?" I was stunned.

"I talked it over with Sylvie, and she thinks–"

"Sylvie! You told her?"

Martin shifted around to face me. Dappled moonlight danced around on his hair, made his eyes look blacker than usual. "I had to, Elli. Sal saw us out here together and mentioned it to her. She wanted to know what we were doing. She didn't believe any of the fibs I told her, so I finally just said it."

My heart pounded. I was aghast. It was our secret, a very delicate one at that, not something to be used to quell a jealous lover's interrogation.

"Sylvie is so much better, Ellie. It was good to see her. She knows I want to find Freya, and she wants to help. All she did was suggest we be a little more certain about this before we spend any more time out here waiting."

I looked toward Ray and Sylvie's house, just a hundred feet away through the trees. Was she there now?

"She said the party was fairly out of control that night. Lots of people were hallucinating, seeing all kinds of things. Maybe your encounter was not what you thought it was, is all I'm suggesting." He smiled at me, a kindly-father face full of compassion for a child.

"And now you think I turned a simple grope attempt into a ghost story so my mind could accept it?" He didn't answer, just sat there hanging his head and picking at his cuticles.

I was not angry but I felt betrayed, and that hurt. I got up, walked swiftly over to the narrows and jumped in, aiming for the other shore, feeling the current pull me. I swam strongly toward a little chevron of moonlit sand, sure I could make it. Martin shouted at me a few times, then I heard the sound of a boat engine. We reached the landing at the same time, but I was determined not to acknowledge him.

"C'mon, Ellie," he said. "Please." I heard the boat bump against the dock as I stomped off down the road. "Ellie!" he called again, then was silent.

The woods were denser on that side and much darker. If the moon had not been almost full I doubt I would have found my way. Willing myself to be unafraid, I walked along nursing my hurt and swearing silently at Martin, my stupidity, my gullibility. I got about half a mile down the road before I heard the car behind me. I briefly contemplated hiding from him, but I didn't want to make things any worse. That truly would have been childish.

"C'mon, get in." Martin leaned across and opened the door for me. I sat down, hoping my wet, salt-soaked clothes would permanently stain the leather seats. We rode in silence. Martin noticed me shivering and turned on the heater, but said nothing. The longer he says nothing, I thought, the more it confirms that he thinks I'm an idiot girl who makes up stories for attention. I prayed fervently that John Sipson would decide to appear on the road standing under a streetlight in his breeches and vest, holding up a hand to stop us. But of course he did not, and by the time we were headed down Barley Neck Road I had all but stopped believing in him, anyway. Martin was probably right. My meeting with the ghost of John Sipson had been a trick, or I had dreamed it, or had drunk too much port, smoked too much dope. It was a relief in a way, to give up on him. Life would be much simpler. I did not want to think about the other stuff, the finger full of green paint, *'A Swim at Pochet'* or any of the quantum baloney I had taken seriously. No more, I told myself as we pulled up next to the house. I got out and walked to the door without looking back. I heard the crunch of the car's tires slowly backing down the shell driveway, and then nothing. I started to cry.

Chapter Nine

The thing about Van Gogh eating yellow paint to feel happy is apparently untrue, I found out. Instead of riding past the town library every day I decided to stop in and discovered in the main reading room a large collection of art books just lying around waiting to be borrowed. So I got myself a card and took a few home. In a fat volume called *Lives of the Painters,* which judging by the charge record inside the back cover I was the first to read, I found: *"The medical notes of Vincent's physician, Dr. Peyron, state that he was not allowed into his studio while suffering attacks, as he had tried to poison himself by drinking turpentine and eating cadmium yellow paint."* But maybe at that point he thought death would make him happy, not the color.

I dragged the coffee table from the house into the studio, laid a piece of the window plywood on top and spread out books with double page reproductions so I could look at them while I painted. I loved Georges Braque landscapes, especially the ones leading up to his exploration into Cubism. And Paul Cezanne. I was seeing everything in a new and different light. My scrubby, sunburned hill and gray-green water below suddenly looked like the south of France, the stunted cedars like poetic Mediterranean cypresses. I asked my mother to advise me but she said, "For now honey, just paint. Get to know the stuff. I'll think about specifics, OK?" When I pressed her she added, "One thing you need to know right off: shadows never involve black paint. Look at them. They are full of color, and light. Use black for drawing." Invaluable info which at the time I thought stingy, but I took it and used it, and with my mysterious newfound power still driving me, managed to make some pretty astute observations and turn them into quite delicious pictures.

I was still using the child's gouache set but had splurged on some actual watercolor paper, a pad of thick, absorbent white with visible cotton fibers. Twice the size of some typing paper I'd swiped from the office at the Governor Hancock, the stuff gave me leeway to try things I had not been able to before. I quickly covered three sheets painting huge wide bands of brilliant red, just to watch, mesmerized, as the paint soaked into the surface. Then I got down to business —or I should say my hand did, because I seemed to have very little to do with directing things after an idea for an image came into my mind. The red was briskly transformed into a line of trees by adding white and varying shades of yellow ochre. I made all three red pages into tree portraits just by painting the negative space and leaving the red to glow as if illuminated from behind. As my hand, just barely under my control, began to loosen up,

173

wet lines trailed after my brush suggesting forms in the landscape, not needing to delineate anything. Yellow burst forth from the surface, held in place by green and purple shadow. Hovering above, orange sky bled into the blue-green of moments before sunset. It was not a frenzied outburst, but an evenly paced, steady flow. I was not aware of time; three hours could pass in a few minutes. It completely threw me off my cooking and eating schedule, which had been loose anyway. Now I stood in front of the fridge at midnight and shoveled whatever I could find into my mouth before forcing myself to get into bed. There I'd sit, still chewing, reliving my paintings stroke by stroke. I hadn't been fishing in two weeks or making cornbread. I lived off Ritz crackers and peanut butter. I fretted that my paint supply was getting down to brown, black and purple, having used up most of the other colors in the tray. I had to wait until payday to buy more, but I told myself I'd buy some food, too. And an extension cord for the radio.

I got through my days at the motel in good spirits, considering. I was happy. The crazy things people did to their vacation nests no longer annoyed me, I just plowed through and put things back in order without analysis or judgment. We had it down to a system which almost nothing could buck off course. Becca kept up a steady flow of hilarious underbreath commentary that sped us guffawing down the line of rooms and into the laundry, where we could laugh freely as we washed the food, booze and sex from those sturdy yellow sheets and towels. I'd normally rush home after work to paint, but one day Sandy waylaid me at the intersection in town.

"What happened to you, girl? You split like that, it seems." She snapped her fingers and gave me a searching, empathetic look. "Everything cool?"

I didn't want to sound as if I had a problem with anyone out on the island, or seem ungracious after all they'd done to welcome me. I hadn't heard a word from Martin. He had not visited, nor left a note on my door, hadn't sent anyone over with a message. Maybe he went back to New York, I don't know. I was sure he owed me an apology, and I was not going to go to him for it. Sylvie was also missing from my life and I didn't want to assume –but I did– that she'd successfully gotten rid of me. I had not seen her or Ray in those weeks. I was baffled, but not sad. I had my painting, and it was almost all I cared about then, because it made me more than happy; it gave me desire and fulfillment at the same time. *Je donne ma langue au chat,* I mumbled to myself when the matter passed through my mind. The French expression seemed suitable, and comforting. Literally to give your tongue to the cat, to not know the answer and to stop guessing.

"I've started to paint, and it seems to take up all my spare time, is all," I said, smiling serenely. "How are you, how's Sal?"

"We're good. Summer, y'know?" She did a little squirmy, joyful undulation, then hugged herself, squeezing the silver fairy charm between her breasts. It was hard not to stare as the little head sunk lower, drowning in lush lobes of bosom. The image of John Sipson passing the back of his hand through mine flickered to life but I deleted it with a hard blink.

"How about a coffee?" Sandy pointed her chin at the Turk's Head.

"All right, sure," I said, not sure at all.

The place was half full, a scattering of tourists among the regular hippie types who spent hours in there, tapping their feet to folk music and sipping a single cup of coffee.

175

Joyce didn't seem to mind. I suppose they rounded out the room's atmosphere of poetic haven. She liked them, and so did I. Downtown Orleans stomped its foot, demanding attention, conformity. Make money! it screamed in that seasonal economy, three months of beach weather, but in the half-dark of the Turk's Head the push for advance did not exist. The greater outside world didn't penetrate into my life much, either. Snatches of Vietnam war reporting would blare forth from TVs left on at the motel, but Becca would snap them off as soon as we entered. Her older brother had returned from the war with both legs amputated above the knee. He sat in his wheelchair all day smoking pot and watching TV. At three o'clock he'd get himself outside and sit in the driveway waiting for his friend, another vet, to deliver a bottle of Applejack whiskey which he'd drink over the course of the evening, then pass out.

"They killed him," Becca said, "but it's a slow death."

Sandy and I sat down as Joyce appeared from the kitchen with a pot of coffee. Her face lit up when she saw me, and after she'd poured at another table she came over to us. She filled our cups, then sat down.

"Haven't seen you around for a while. Moony says you don't fish anymore. What's up?" She got right to it.

"She's an artist now," Sandy announced, beaming proudly.

"Oh? I didn't know. What are you doing?"

"Painting like crazy." It felt good to say it. "I found some old watercolors in the house I think must have belonged to me when I was a kid. I've nearly used them up." It wasn't much of a report, but I didn't know how to talk about what went on my mother's studio, how to describe the dazzling visceral imagery spilling from my

176

brush. "Trees and landscapes, just stuff around the property."

"That's wonderful," she said, smiling maternally.

I was waiting for one of them to mention Sylvie or Martin, which would have been natural. I gulped my coffee, trying to think of a good excuse to leave before it happened. Two evenings before, Taj Mahal had played there on the little stage, and Sandy had held back long enough to be polite before gushing her excitement over the event, giving me a long description including the touching of his guitar when he went for a bathroom break. It was quite a coup and I wished I'd known. I might well have ridden into town for it. Maybe. Joyce wandered off to serve her clientele saying "Don't go away without saying goodbye," and winking meaningfully.

When Sandy leapt up to greet a couple coming in the door I saw my chance. The woman was wearing coveralls with the sleeves cut off, and had embroidered crude flowers over the rest. The pant legs were shredded below the knee to make long fringes, each strand with a knot at the bottom. The knots bounced joyfully with every step. Sandy bent to admire them as I made my getaway, but not before stopping at the kitchen door.

"Leaving now," I called to Joyce, who was taking something from the oven. It smelled heavenly and my mouth instantly watered. I really needed to get some food.

"So, everything all right with you and Martin?"

Damn. Instead of answering I said, "How is Sylvie's hand? I haven't seen her since that night."

"It's fine. Slow to heal. Tiny fractures, you know?" She held up her hand, still in an oven mitt, and pointed to the knuckle area. "Here, here and here."

177

"Ouch. I hope she heals." I began to back away. "Thanks for the coffee. See you soon, maybe. Tell Moony I said hi," I added, then turned and hurried away. It wasn't very polite, I knew, but it was all I could manage. Besides, I wanted to get home to paint. I stopped at the art supply store and bought two tiny tubes of watercolor. One red, one yellow. That left me with 70 cents, 4 cents short of the price for a box of Ritz crackers. I bought some Saltines instead, and half a dozen eggs, then rode home. The sight of Sandy and Joyce, the mention of Sylvie, Martin and Moony had punctured the bubble of my retreat, and now I had to figure out how to think about the whole thing, which I had not yet allowed myself. But that's what I did for the entire ride home.

I arrived in a sweat not only from riding a bike in the July heat but added to significantly by anguished thoughts of Martin and Sylvie. I wanted to ride more, ride away from them, but I knew I had something better waiting. After I put the eggs in the fridge I hurried out to the studio to reconnect with my little world, my haven. I unscrewed the cap from the tube of yellow and squeezed a blob onto my fingertip. No, I didn't eat it, but I confess it was my instinct, at least to lick it. Instead I wiped my finger in a long streak across a fresh piece of paper, dipped it in water and went over the yellow again and again, spreading it. That biographer had to be wrong about Vincent. A certain level of artistic fervor could make one want to behave almost sexually toward the material. From my forehead fat drops of perspiration splashed onto the widening stripe, washing spots of yellow momentarily back to white. Then my hand took over. I can only offer here an imperfect description of the sensation, because words are an inadequate mode of expression for what was happening to

178

me back then. It felt as if another entity had taken over my body —my right arm, specifically— but not my mind. My heart did not beat faster, my breath went calmly in and out. I was me, except that while creating a picture, watching it come to life, each tiny thought, idea, every instinctual eye movement was spontaneously realized by the brush, or rejected by it. My hand made no mistakes, did not experiment or discard. The time I imagined it would take for a normal painter to think through a concept or visualization was condensed to the point of instantaneousness. The power which took over operated like a high-speed computer, leaping ahead of my thoughts and carrying out the business of choosing colors, making brush strokes form images, shadows, background, then examined the result with a swift sureness that had me sitting there, mesmerized by my own handiwork yet knowing full well what I was doing. It was no one's creation but mine. It wasn't fast, but efficient. Even normal intervals of hesitation and study were included. I'd stand up and take a drag off my cigarette, scrutinize the piece and know exactly what was needed next without doubt or reworking.

I did not allow myself to think that I was under any influence connecting me to Martin; I rebuffed any memory that appeared of seeing him in that very room, going over my mother's work with a finger. What I believed was happening to me was a separate thing, a product of DNA coding now expressing in me, triggered by being in my mother's environment.

I painted like that in complete absorption and concentration for two hours before I became aware that the force was slowing down, disengaging. My hand cleaned the brush, then laid it on the table. At that very moment I heard Moony talking to someone out on the water.

When the tide is low in Pleasant Bay there are vast areas where one can walk around in knee-deep water. Most of those places are covered in marsh grass, which looks like a lush lawn but dips below the surface when the tide comes in. The grass provides shelter and food to many species of marine life as well as birds and even some upland animals. I'd often see people out there shuffling with their feet to locate the hinge of a fat quahog poking out of the mud, or kids catching crabs with a dip net and a chicken leg on a piece of string. When I heard Moony's voice and went to the edge of the hill to investigate, I spotted him about a quarter of a mile out, lolling in the stern of his boat which drifted slowly in the grass, untethered. He had one arm in the water, raking his fingers through the mud. Every now and then he'd pull something out and toss it on board. Another man sat in the bow with his back to me. I wasn't close enough to see who it was but I couldn't deny significant details of his appearance: a black braid, a leather vest over dark brown shoulders, white trousers. He sat leaning over, resting his forearms on his knees. Every now and then he'd pick up something, fiddle with it, then toss it overboard, or he'd reach across and pass it to Moony. Probably they were digging up baby quahogs —or cherrystones as they're called— and having a snack. I knew who Moony's partner was, and felt a shiver pass through me as I said his name out loud. "Mister Sipson, I presume." I squinted, shading my eyes as I watched Moony grab handfulls of grass to pull the boat along to another spot, where he resumed clamming, listening to his partner chatter

180

away as if he were reciting the plot of a complicated novel. I desperately wished for a pair of binoculars. I lay on my stomach at the edge if the bluff and watched the scene for half an hour more. Low rays of afternoon sun shone intermittently from behind the treetops behind me as it sank in the sky; the dancing, dappled light made it more difficult to focus on the two men. Neither made any sign of getting ready to leave, yet I felt I had to do something before they rowed off. I needed a better viewpoint. After a few minutes hesitation I slunk down the steps to the little dock, crawled on hands and knees over the boards, and rolled off into the water with a little splash. Then I started half swimming, half running, pushing myself off the bottom and breast-stroking toward the patch of marsh grass, keeping my head low with just my eyes above the water. It wasn't the wisest decision I'd ever made, I could feel the incoming tidewater beginning to move me sideways, but I needed to get closer without being seen. I had time before the current was too strong to swim against. If worse came to worst, I said to myself, I'd be pushed toward shore, anyway. I swam until I reached the grass, then crept like a crocodile through it, pushing along with my toes, parting the swath of green like a curtain. A hundred feet away from the boat I stopped. A kingfisher flew low over me, investigating, its black eye trying to warn me off. At the sound of its call, more like a rattle than a chirp, John Sipson turned his face my way for a second, then he looked at the sky, following the retreating bird. I sat as still as possible, holding onto tufts of grass to stay in one place. Bits of conversation from the boat, a few words here and there, reached me across the water. Moony chuckled, said, "Hell yeah," before a long interval of silence. And then I clearly heard John Sipson say, "If the worst come to the worst . . ." and then whatever came after was literally drowned out by my immediate plunge completely underwater. My heart pounded. Had I not just thought that very phrase to myself when I felt the incoming tide tugging at my legs? I crouched under the waist-deep water, holding on to plant roots, digging my toes into the mud to keep my head under. I heard only the sound of my heartbeat and the usual gurgle of saltwater life. My lungs began to protest, but I stayed perfectly still for several more seconds, until I could not hold out any longer and rolled my head to the side, sticking my lips out to suck air from the surface. Unfortunately I also breathed in a good amount of water and began to choke, which is impossible to do underwater. I covered my mouth as I lifted my head for air, coughing and sputtering and thrashing as I tried to stay hidden.

"Elli?" Mooney called out. "Is that you?"

I heard oars clattering into oarlocks, and then the rhythmic knock and splash of rowing. I continued to cough and hack, now freely since I'd been discovered.

"What are you doing out here?" Moony took the last stroke and shipped the oars, gliding near. I glanced up, but couldn't see over the high bow of the Newfoundland hull. Moony leaned over the side and stretched out an arm.

"C'mere, honey. The tide's on it's way in. Hop on."

I pulled myself up to standing and managed a fake smile through the last bit of coughing. Moony sat on the middle seat, quite alone. The floor of the boat was scattered with cherrystones. I grabbed the gunwale and swung a leg over, then settled where John Sipson had just been, not two minutes before.

"Whatcha been up to?" Moony said, once again fitting the oars and turning the boat. "I haven't seen you since . ." He paused, thinking. I shivered, though the temperature was around 80. My heart was still banging away. I put my hand on the seat and brushed my fingers across the smooth boards. Would a ghost warm a seat? I coughed again, and said, "It was when we ate *taramosalata*, with Joyce."

"Oh yeah."

We were both silent for a few moments as the boat reached my dock. Moony expertly swung the boat around to lie alongside, then held on.

"I saw him," I said.

Moony's eyebrows went up. He looked out to where he and John Sipson had just been clamming, then back at me. He shipped the oars again and sat watching the blades dribble, an orange-tinted sparkle in the lowering light. "Who?" he said finally.

"You know who." I stared at him.

Moony picked up a cherrystone and cupped it in his palm. He reached into a pocket, took out a knife, and in one alchemical motion managed to flip out the blade, open the clam and present it to me, dripping, on his fingertips.

I slid the meat onto my tongue –heaven!– without taking my eyes away. I had him there, the proof I needed that I was not insane, nor had consumed too much wine, nor was I too innocent to understand a murmuration of particles hanging around waiting to coalesce into someone again, given the right circumstances.

"John Sipson. I've met him before," I said, defiantly.

Moony had picked up another cherrystone and performed another sleight of hand for himself. "Oh?" he said just after he'd tossed the clam into his mouth, so it came out gargled, then it was his turn to choke.

"He introduced himself to me one night. Over on his island," I added.

Moony coughed and spat and looked at me through watering eyes while he considered this. He raked his hair back a few times, not minding his hands wetting it with clam juice. It took him a while to recover, but when he did he smiled at me, tipping his head to one side. "Want another?" he said.

"Of course."

He picked up a couple more clams and opened them, while I pushed the rest toward him with my foot. I guess neither of us knew where to begin, but I think we both felt a fresh camaraderie in our shared secret, and for me the relief of knowing I was not crazy. We sat in silence as more clams were opened and enjoyed. Finally he asked me, "So, just the once, or . . .?"

"Yeah. That was it. I tried to find him again, but no luck. I think he was afraid of me." How I wish I had been able to talk with him there in the boat, to show him I was normal, and that I was a friend of Moony's, although approaching as a wild animal creeping through the marsh grass would possibly not give the desired impression. I suddenly remembered what I'd overheard.

"Today, did he say, 'If the worst come to the worst'?" I asked Moony.

"Yeah. He's worried about —well, I'll tell you later. It's complicated. Why?"

I told Moony about having that thought only minutes before, about the tide pulling me.

"Yup. He does that."

I had so many questions, but oddly enough I resisted asking any. I glanced up at the bluff, at the space where the rock was missing, and thought of my paintings in the studio, the cans of Campbell's mushroom soup lined up in the kitchen cabinet, my father's hat, the collection of objects on the bookshelf, my bike. I was reluctant to let anything or anyone intrude into my little haven again, to take over my attention as Martin had.

Moony must have felt my reticence, and asked, "Does he frighten you?"

"No," I said, although if I woke up in the middle of the night and found him standing at the foot of my bed I would probably have a heart attack.

"I'm surprised he talked to you. He's quite skeptical about females." Moony opened the last of the cherrystones and passed it to me. I thought of standing with John Sipson, watching Sandy dance in the narrows.

"How long have you two been, uh . . ." I wasn't sure what to call it.

"Friends? Let's see, about twenty years, now. But I saw him long before that, the first time, when I was sixteen. It was over on Sipson's. I was keeping track of an eagle nest in the cliffside. I thought the little ones were about ready to fly and I wanted to see it. I skipped out of school as usual, took my dad's binoculars, and rowed over there." Moony shook his head. "He was standing under the nest, like he was waiting for me to show up. Back then we knew everyone around here, so he was definitely strange-looking." He laughed, and flashed me another smile. "I guess these days he wouldn't be."

"No, I thought he looked fairly normal."

"Ha! Well, he came over to me and said hello. I pointed to the eagle nest and he told me they'd already hatched, and that anyway, the eggs were not good to eat. He has an old-fashioned way of speaking, I'm sure you noticed. He said 'eyern" instead of eggs, so I didn't understand. I lifted the binoculars to have a look and he disappeared." Moony leaned back and looked at the sky. "It was ten years later that I saw him again, and I had all but talked myself out of believing what I'd seen. Except that between those two meetings I started to notice a certain change in me, especially in the beginning. I was able, effortlessly, to make things I wanted happen. Suddenly things came to me easily. The first time it was a car. I loved cars, and knew all the models, makes, horsepower, all that stuff. I would go to the drugstore to look at pictures in the one magazine available in Orleans back then. Of course, around here were very few modern cars, but in summer one or two might pass through. That year my father got a subscription to Popular Mechanics, and I used to cut out the car ads. I worshipped a car called a Cord Phaeton. Man, it was beautiful. Big front fenders, like giant lion's paws. I wanted badly see one but they were very rare, especially around here. Lots of people still had a horse in the barn." He puffed out a little breath, remembering. "The company only lasted a couple of years, but those cars were really something." He stopped, glanced up from his reverie. I leaned forward, gave him an enthusiastic nod, and he went on. "One day I was coming through the woods on the way home from Camp Viking. I'd been sent to fetch my dad's toolbox which he'd left behind after a plumbing repair. Someone invited him sailing and he just took off. Anyhow, I rode our horse out to get it, and there I was plodding along, daydreaming about a red Cord Phaeton, and what do you know, down that dusty dirt road came one, a red one to boot, going slowly so as not to scratch the paint job on the bushes. I was stunned! I sat there with my mouth hanging open as it passed. It was some kid's father, coming to pick him up."

"Wow. What a coincidence."

"I thought so, too. But then it kept happening. In school, for example. I was always what they called

186

'detached' during classes, either looking out the window or watching the clock, waiting for it to be over."

"Oh yes. That's how you got your nickname. I remember."

"Yup. I barely scraped by with my grades. But that year, after I saw the Cord Phaeton, I began to see all kinds of things with ease. My imagination, the movie playing behind my eyes, often became real and, like the car, appeared before me. Answers to questions clicked into my mind, no figuring needed. In school my hazy interest in the animals and birds around the bay was transformed into a clear knowledge of biology. Solutions to math problems were there at the end of my pencil. I could spell, something which had always given me problems, and I wrote essays on all kinds of subjects with absolutely no effort. I started to get nothing but high marks. My teacher was astounded, and my parents were over the moon, and for all that winter and spring I had an awful lot of fun being smart and having my little desires satisfied." He laughed, smoothed his hair back again, and added, "Girls were interested in me for the first time, and at age sixteen that was a pretty big deal." He gazed off into the middle distance, remembering. I sat still and let him have his moment. I thought he was quite desirable for an old guy, in his tshirt and jeans and blue eyes sparkling, the long hair only just under control. I called up a little mental snapshot of him and Joyce at the landing, the picnic spread out between her thighs on the boat seat. I was thinking about what he'd said about math solutions, essays flowing from the tip of his pencil. I wanted to tell him about my sudden gift for making artworks.

"It didn't last, however," he said. "Not like that anyway."

187

"What happened?"

"Hard to say, exactly. I started to be used to it, this ability, and I forgot how I was before. It wasn't that I was a magician making things appear, or that a supernatural power had suddenly transformed me into a genius. I guess you could say I just started to feel normal. I thought about it. The stuff I knew about the natural world was actually pretty comprehensive. I had done a lot of observing. And so I knew the answers to the questions on the biology tests, for example, all along, or I could logically figure them out. I realized I had knowledge of history from reading. I could do the math if only I decided to apply myself. There was no magic; it was always there. I learned easily, once I decided to. While I was staring out the window, some part of my brain was paying attention. I only had to want it to access it."

"Hm. So, what made you change?"

"I think somehow, believing that I had manifested the Phaeton woke up a power which had been in a kind of dormant state, is all I can figure. Desire to know, to see, to be, to have —was all that I needed."

"Desire."

"Yeah, or maybe expectation is a better word. As if it's been there all along, hidden in plain sight, and suddenly you can see it."

"Do you mean like John Sipson?"

He laughed again. "I think so."

The tide had risen half a foot in the time we sat there. Its current moved fast along the side of the boat and curled into little eddies off the stern. They swirled, thrusting out bubbles into the passing stream. I looked through to the bottom where the empty cherrystone shells lay, their edges just beginning to lift in the rush of water shooting past. A crab sidled over to investigate a scrap of meat as both were whisked away in the flow. I looked up at Moony. He shrugged, opening his hands.

"Elli, you're the only person I know who has seen him. I have to tell you I'm glad there is someone else."

I wanted to ask if John Sipson had mentioned me to Moony but it felt awfully silly, as if we were talking about an old acquaintance and not a being from another dimension.

"So when you saw him again . . ?" I prompted.

"The second time was here, close by." He pointed beyond the dock to the shore, where I'd walked along the path. "Just over there. He was standing, looking right at me. I was out in my boat fishing for flounder. Something made me look up, and he smiled at me. He put his hand up, clearly a greeting, and I waved back. Then he was gone again. Just, poof! So then I was sure of what I'd seen all those years before." Moony rubbed his palm over one of the crooked pilings. "That evening I walked over here to find him sitting on this dock, leaning against this post and swishing his feet in the water. Your parents were up on the lawn, talking. I could hear every word. I smelled meat cooking on the grill. Your father wanted lemon, she did not. I could tell John Sipson didn't know they were there. He said 'Good morrow' to me although it was evening, and he said it so loudly that I thought they would come running down the steps."

I was having a hard time with the time frame. "My parents?"

"Yeah. That was around 1947. I was 28."

And I was a baby. My mother painted *'A Swim at Pochet'* that year. I closed my eyes, trying to picture it. "So, what happened?"

"I whispered good morning back to him and walked past. I pointed to some imaginary thing along the path, hoping he would follow, and he did." Moony tilted his head in that direction. "By the way, that's why I showed it to you the day Joyce and I were having our picnic. You were asking about the Sipson brothers and I thought, well, that's a good place to find John. He goes along there to look for whelk, which are his favorite and because 'water swims to this place'—he says— from a sweeter stream than where he lives."

"Is it sweeter?"

"I don't know. I've never found a whelk there." He shrugged. "I think he's talking about conditions a couple centuries ago."

"Oh, right."

"We went around the shore. I was several paces ahead and never sure if he was following, but each time I turned there he was, grinning at me. Finally I sat down in a clump of grass and he joined me."

"Wow."

"He introduced himself. His body seemed as solid as yours, not diaphanous as I expected. He wore pieces of deerskin fitted from knee to ankle, and a knife in a sheath on a belt, with a white shirt tucked in. His shoes were handmade —cobbled, I guess. I was fascinated, but I didn't want to stare, y'know? He was looking me over, too, as we made our greetings. He asked me if I knew of him. I pointed to Sipson's Island and said 'That is your island,' and he smiled as if it was great news to him. We talked a little more. I don't remember the exchange exactly, but from it I gradually got the idea that he also thought I was a ghost, or a spirit, except that I was in *his* time."

"That's what I thought, too!" I told Moony about John Sipson passing his hand through me and telling me he wasn't 'afeared.' Moony considered that for a moment while he smoothed his hair.

"Yes. And what's more, he thinks he's dreaming. It makes for confusing conversation at times, and also because he is not able to conceive of a future as far away as this, or one at all, really. For him the past, present and future are all happening at the same time."

"What?"

"Yeah. Think about it. He's in our past, his present and his future."

What Moony was saying stirred some memory in me, a thing Martin had said when trying to explain the way particles behaved. I had a vague leftover mental image of them, a buzzing incoherent mass waiting to be some thing, in some time. Waves of past, present and future time all together, was how he described it. And what was it he'd said about certain particles being connected for all time, even if light years away from each other? It was his reason for believing Freya would show up on Sipson's island. Like John Sipson himself? I blinked hard to cancel those Martin-connected thoughts. I told myself I would think about it later.

"So, when you're together, what do you talk about?"

"He asks questions, but he also behaves as you do in a dream, where you're just watching, reacting, going along. I don't always understand what he's saying because of his slang. It's a lot of Wampanoag, I think, but it's English too. Only it's very old English, spoken with an accent, because it's not his native language."

"Does he understand you?"

"Oh yes, he seems to. Sometimes he looks at me as if I am a nutcase, but he lets it go. Other times he simply disappears in the middle of a sentence, maybe when he can't figure it out. I ask him about his life, mostly. He's told me some very interesting things."

Moony described John Sipson's life as best he could while the tide came in, slowing as it filled estuaries and ponds poking into higher ground, then flooded the sea of marsh grass where they'd gathered the clams. Its motion gently bumped the boat against the boards of the dock. Like the tide filling, twilight diffused through late afternoon sun.

"From what I know researching the man's actual history, he and his brother were the last ancestral sachems of the Nauset tribe, a subset of the Wampanoags who inhabited all of Cape Cod back when the Pilgrims showed up. The Sipson brothers owned hundreds of acres in South Orleans before they sold most of it. They kept only a little to live on, and the island was the last of it."

"Did he talk about it?"

"No, but he does mention the colonists. He never includes me in that company, though. He talks about smaller issues, mainly. He thinks I'm able to give him wise direction, as if I were a god of some sort. He has squabbles with his neighbors, his family, his wife. It's normal stuff, believe it or not. Sometimes he asks for advice, and I try to give it. The third time I met him he was angry because a cow from an English farm got loose and swam across to the island, where it ate most of his pumpkins. '*Pon-pu-kun,*' he said, over and over. Finally he drew one in the sand. 'I will cut away his tong!' he said. He was really angry."

"What did you tell him?"

"What could I say? I said I hoped the owner of the cow would compensate him, and tie a bell around the cow's neck from then on. I think he worked out what I said because he smiled at me and said, 'I watched the oxbeast heave its gore on the other side, for no enjoyment.' At least that's what I think he said."

I tried to picture the two of them sitting just yards away on the pebbly shore. It reminded me of the morning I returned from that first dinner party on Sipson's, when I saw Moony talking to someone who wasn't there. Another drawing in the sand.

"Were you discussing pyramids one night a couple of months ago, right after I got here? You were down here on the shore, talking."

Moony scratched his head. "You saw us?"

"No, just you. I saw the drawing after you left."

"Yeah, I remember. He kept saying a word that sounded like pyramid, so I drew one. He had no idea what it was."

I laughed, remembering all the brainstorming I'd dedicated to that little three-line drawing. I imagined wide-ranging discussions about history, architecture, pharaohs and buried treasure. "Oh wow. I thought you were talking to some sort of god, yourself."

"Nope, a sachem, a chief. But a guy like me, with ordinary problems, it seems. Knowing what I know from my research, in the early 1700s he had just sold off more than a thousand acres of his tribal land. He must have been pretty bitter."

"Did he ever talk about it?"

"Not directly, but there was lots of reference to his loss. Remember, he thinks he's dreaming, so in his dream-logic it would follow that I already know everything. He just wants to talk. It's like being his psychiatrist, sometimes."

"Has he ever said anything about what's going on over there now?" It was hard to think about the island as anything but what I knew, to juxtapose it with this new picture of John Sipson living in a bark-covered hut with his wife, tending his pumpkin patch, governing a band of Nausets. The present island with . . . the counterpart struck me suddenly: Martin, leader of his tribe of hippies, and John Sipson, sachem of his, two hundred and fifty years apart on one 20-acre island. *Mon dieu!* Talk about a parallel universe.

"He has. I have a story to tell you, and I know you'll be interested because it concerns your friend Martin. But Elli, I have to go. I was supposed to bring those cherrystones to Joyce's place. We have a . . . a date tonight." He smiled sheepishly.

"Oh, of course. Sorry." I scrambled to get out of the boat.

"When shall we meet again?"

"Tomorrow. After work. All right?"

"Perfect." We both smiled excitedly, a conspiratorial look passed between us. It felt very good. I turned and walked up the steps to the bluff, hearing the splash of his oars as he rounded the point toward home.

I didn't get far. Just as I hit the top a flash of headlights blinded me momentarily before they were shut off. It was Sandy again, stepping out of the car, shoving the door closed with a hip. She was wearing a flower-print dress with shoulder straps tied in tiny bows.

"Hey girl." She strolled over, stood beside me and looked out over the water. There wasn't much light left, just the final glow of the sun setting behind us.

"Hi. This is a nice surprise." I felt cautious, guarded. I glanced to my left, hoping Moony was out of sight. Though I had nothing to hide, I did not want any more supposition going on about me and another old man. Fortunately he was gone. "Come with me out to the studio," I said, and turned toward the path. "I need to clean up, then we can have a coffee."

"I brought wine," Sandy grinned.

"Even better," I said, though I would have preferred to sit in the studio for an hour or so and mull over what had just happened. I wanted to jot down some of John Sipson's words. I wanted to think about Moony's description of his sudden 'ability' to excel in school. It sounded very much like what was going on with me and my paintbrush. And I wanted to remember what Martin had said about connected particles. I promised myself to do it the moment Sandy left.

Once inside the studio, I went right over to the painting table to make sure the caps were screwed tightly onto my brand new tubes of paint. I had to search around for one of them, and when I looked up there stood Sandy, hands clasping the sides of her head, swiveling from wall to wall to look at the work I'd taped up.

"Oh my god! Holy excrement!" she squealed. "You did this?"

The paintings really did glow with a kind of voluptuousness, as if they had been painted with colored light in dense, saturated layers. Of course I had stood in the same spot many times surveying my output, proud and amazed by my little collection, but just as surprised, almost, as Sandy. Now for the first time seeing them through someone else's eyes the images were even more arresting.

"Thank you," I said. "I'm just learning how to do it. It's fun." It was so much more than mere fun but I didn't know how to describe the phantom power aspect. "Let's go into the house." I tugged on her sleeve so I wouldn't have to explain it further.

195

Sandy pranced ahead of me, reached into her car and plucked a bottle of Chianti from the back seat. She hung the straw covering from a finger and waited, leaning against the the door, looking like an ad for an Italian pensione.

We settled in front of the fireplace, she on the sofa, me on the chair. "I don't think I've ever been here," she said, looking around. "It's nice."

"Remember the clambake? You slept in there." I pointed to the bedroom.

"Oh wow, right. I forgot." She giggled. "How could I forget?" She shook her head. "What a night."

"Yup." I poured wine, we sipped. I waited for what I suspected was to come. Something about Sylvie, I was sure. "Sorry I left so quickly earlier," I said. It seemed like days ago.

Sandy cleared her throat. "Yeah, that's why I'm here. I wanted to ask you," she began, then stopped.

"What."

"No. Wait. First I have to tell you what's been happening over on the island."

"Oh?"

"It's Martin. He's . . . acting weird. Ray and Sal are, like, freaking out. They don't know what to do. He won't talk much, and Sylvie says he started to lock the door, which he's never done before. I mean, who is gonna rob him out there?"

"Hm. Where's Min?"

"She's there. When I take her shopping I ask about Martin, but she doesn't say much, just that he's feeling emotional and missing Freya. That's his . . ."

"Yeah, I know."

"Min doesn't seem to notice much, or maybe she doesn't want to."

"Maybe." Martin had said as much, I remembered.

"But there's more. He's been digging this hole up on the high side of the island. Like, a big, deep square thing right on the edge. Sal took me up there a couple of nights ago, and it's really creepy looking. It looks like a grave, Elli. That's what I thought."

"A grave?"

"Well, it could be. He had Ray and Sal cut down two pines to make room. They had to wrestle out these big roots. Martin told them to throw everything in the water so the tide would take it, but most of it is still there. It looks terrible. He said he'd have it removed later."

"Weird."

"I know!"

"What could it be?" Of course I thought of Martin's search for Freya and my part in it. Could he be so distraught that he would decide to end his life because he failed to find John Sipson and therefore Freya? Did he want to be buried there to be closer to her so their entangled particles could reunite? I wondered if Freya was buried on the island. Was that something people did in these parts?

Sandy took a gulp of wine and set her glass down carefully, twisting its base on the boards of an old wooden crate I'd dragged in to substitute for the coffee table.

"So, I was wondering," she began, interrupting my inner speculation.

"Yes?"

"Sylvie and I were wondering, actually." She glanced at me out of the corner of her eye, I guess to gauge whether she was safe asking what was coming.

"All right." I tried to sound encouraging.

She spat it out in a run-on sentence. "Well, what were you two were doing out in the woods for five nights? Ray said you were on a watch, or some kind of stakeout. That's what it looked like, he said. He saw you. We thought maybe that had something to do with Martin's behavior, since we haven't seen you since." She sat back with her wine glass and waited.

Obviously I couldn't tell her the truth, because the truth was not believable. But I had to say something. "I was helping him look for the ghost of Freya," I said. It was close to the truth, at least.

"Oh wow. Okay. But, why you? I mean, do you know how to do that kind of thing?"

"No!" I said. "He wanted me to keep him company. We were doing research, about, um, energy." I struggled to remember some of the jargon associated with Martin's theories, stuff Sylvie, Sandy and I had been over several times, trying to make sense of it. But it was still such a mystery to me that I couldn't come up with a persuasive enough sentence to convince her I knew what I was talking about. Plus, the events of the afternoon were still swirling around in my mind. I didn't think I would be able to keep any of it straight or separate, or even lie convincingly, which I did not want to do in the first place. "Look, I don't really understand all of what he says, but I felt sorry for him, so I said I'd help."

"So, were you two having a fling?" My immediate appalled expression must have looked real, because she added, "Sorry. I didn't think so. That's Sylvie's idea."

"No. No fling, no affair, no nothing. He's older than my father, for chrissake." I snorted at the absurdity of it, but at the same time I suppose I could understand why they thought that. I was French. We had a reputation, thanks to Anais Nin, Colette and company. "So, Sylvie thinks I left him and he's falling apart?"

"Sort of, yeah."

"And . . . what? –digging his own grave so he can shoot himself and fall into it dramatically?" I held the back of my hand to my forehead and swooned.

Sandy's shocked expression turned into laughter as she thought it through. "I guess so."

"Sylvie sent you over here to ask me that?"

"Well, everyone did. Sorry."

"Jesus."

"Sorry," she said again.

"Me too. It's not funny."

We sipped in silence. I lit two cigarettes and passed one over. Then I got up, went over to the radio and switched it on. I hit it just right, because after two seconds of silence, Paul McCartney sang the opening words, *'Hey Jude,'* and his accompanying piano chords gushed out from the speakers. I turned it up. The song is an old standard now, but that August it was brand new, and it was an immediate anthem, a goosebump-raiser. It made people cry, then bray exuberantly along with the five minute chorus of na-na-nas. WBCN played it several times a day. Sandy stood up and hugged me and we swayed there together, singing along at the top of our lungs. It was a perfect interlude. When the song faded out I lowered the volume again, and we flung ourselves down, sighing. Sandy picked up her burnt-down cigarette and took a final puff before smashing it into the ashtray.

"Oh, Elli. I am so stupid. I see what you've been doing out there in your studio, and I get it. You have more important things going on."

"I guess so." I was still feeling stung. But now I was worried about Martin, too. If he'd unhooked himself from reality and was involved in some precarious activity, the right thing to do would be to go over there and help him.

"I should go," I said. "Maybe he'll talk to me."

"That's what we were hoping. All of us, Elli. Sylvie feels awful about the way she treated you. She really wants to apologize, but you know her. It might take a while."

"I can't go there now, or tomorrow." Moony was coming tomorrow. "How about a day next week?" I said, not wanting to jump so fast.

"That's great, Elli. Thanks. I'll bring you over. Just stop by the bar." Sandy got up and headed for the door, mission accomplished. I followed, emerging into the cricket-song, starlit night, a sliver of moon reflected in the water. We hugged goodbye. The thought of seeing Martin again did not bother me, I missed him, to be honest. All his talk of invisible events in plain sight provoked and inspired me to look at everything differently even if I did not fully understand the science. Chanting crickets rubbing their back legs together in perfect unison was more than just a phenomenon of nature, it was linked synchronously to twinkling stars, the sough of wavelets hitting the shore and the beating of my heart. Martin had given me the notion of much more going on than merely what was in front of me, and now my paintings did the same.

Sylvie on the other hand was a different story. As Sandy backed down the driveway a little flutter of foreboding passed through me. I would stand up to Sylvie if I had to, and concentrate on Martin. I would go and see this hole of his, hopefully discover the reason for his odd behavior, make my report to Sandy, then get right home again to the studio.

Chapter Ten

It didn't quite go as planned. When I finished work the next day I found Moony waiting next to my bike. He leaned against the wall outside the laundry room rooting around in a paper bag from the hardware store. His white shirt was smeared with rust and his pants and sneakers were wet. I was surprised to see him there, completely out of place in my routine orbit. He lifted something from the bag and studied the label.

"Hey," I said, making him jump. "What are you doing here?"

He dropped what he was holding back into the bag. "I just came to tell you I won't be able to make it. The water heater at the Turk's Head let go, and there was somewhat of a flood. I gotta fix it before tonight. Some blues musician is coming to play. Eric Von Schmidt. Ever heard of him?"

"Nope."

"Apparently he's a big deal, because Joyce is running around worried as hell that she won't be able to use the kitchen, and she's expecting a crowd."

"Is there anything I can do to help?"

"I don't know. Maybe. Why don't you come over?"

We put my bike in the back of Moony's truck and drove over. Afternoon sun baked the town center. Exhaust fumes mixed with the smell of melting pavement, burnt sugar from the candy store, deep-fried clams scent wafted out of the The Foc'sle door and mixed with Mobil station gas fumes across the street. Pastel-clad tourists sat on the benches in front of the cemetery licking ice cream. Kids ran around the headstones playing tag and dropping candy wrappers. Moony pulled the truck around the back of the coffeehouse and cut the engine.

"She's in a frenzy, so don't mind if she snaps at you. Just a warning."

We entered the kitchen, passing the broken heater which lay next to the door dribbling a rust colored puddle. A new one was on the way, Moony told me, but wouldn't get there until 5 o'clock, which was three hours before the show.

"Plenty of time, but she doesn't think so," he said, nodding into the main room at Joyce, who was on her hands and knees sweeping a giant sponge across the floor in muddy arcs, then wringing it out into a bucket. Behind her one of the Oriental rugs was heaped up on a chair, dripping. I went over and grabbed it, threw it over my shoulder and headed for the kitchen.

"Oh, Elli!" Joyce wailed. "Can you believe it?"

I took the rug outside and draped it over the bed of Moony's truck where it would get a full blast of baking sun, then went back in. Over the next two hours we managed to mop up under all the tables and put the room back in order. Certain electrical connections had been damaged, and those Moony worked on, getting the stereo up and running and seeing to the microphone on stage. In the kitchen, while we waited for a huge pot of water to heat on the stove, Joyce, considerably calmer, made us coffee.

"Thank god you came. Do you know who's coming tonight?"

"Eric Von Schmidt, yeah. Except I don't know who he is."

Joyce got up and flipped through the record shelf, pulled one out and brought it over to me. It wasn't Von Schmidt, but a Bob Dylan album, *'Bringin' it all Back Home.'* The cover showed Dylan and his girlfriend lounging in front of a fireplace on a velvet chaise, she in a red dress looking serious and holding a cigarette, he in the foreground amid a scattering of magazines and record albums. The album on top of the pile showed a black and white photo of a man with a guitar who is tipping his hat to the viewer. Joyce laid her finger on it.

"See that?" I looked closely Across the top of the album cover, on a bright pink banner it said, *'The Folk Blues of Eric Von Schmidt.'*

"He was one of the first. Dylan learned a handful of songs from him. I remember them together back then, in Club 47, in Cambridge. Oh, wow. That was a scene. Have you ever been to Boston?"

I said I had never.

"Joan Baez was there in the beginning. Do you know her music?"

I did. My mother often listened to her in the early morning, Baez's pure, clear soprano told stories of impossible love, lords and ladies, entwined thorns and roses, all mysterious subjects I longed to understand. I used to stare at Joan's picture on the album cover, wanting to be her, though I knew I'd never come close. I hummed a little from one of her songs, and Joyce joined in, pretending to guitar-strum, imitating Baez's distinctive tremolo. She asked about French music –who did I like? Without waiting for an answer she got up and did a little swaying dance, twirling slowly, clicking her bracelets together and singing phonetically a few lines of 'Le Méteque,' a song my father had a 45 of. I knew it well. He used to tell me it was about his kind. I joined in, singing the poignant lament of the foreigner who has suffered to get by, to fit in. My father never gave any indication of having experienced that, but he understood. Joyce hugged me when the song ended, and we went back to cleaning up.

A couple of hours later the coffeehouse doors reopened, and the room started filling immediately. The new water heater was silently doing its job in the corner of the kitchen. Moony gave me a ride home so I could change out of my stinking uniform and come back for the show. As we passed the Methodist church at the edge of town and slid into the tunnel of overhanging trees along the road to the beach, Moony said, "So. Getting back to John Sipson."

I laughed. Our secret was so unbelievable, so literally out of this world, that we had not even shared a conspiratorial wink all afternoon. I don't know why Moony and I weren't jumping up and down with mind-blown enthusiasm about our discovery. Instead, there we were driving along on a summer's eve, bringing up the subject of a real ghost in our lives as though discussing an old friend who showed up unexpectedly. But something about the phenomenon dictated that behavior. It was somehow clear to me that having John Sipson in my life was a normal part of it.

"Yes. What was the story? You said it had to do with Martin."

"It does. John Sipson told me about it a long time ago, and I only recently began to understand what he was saying. Do you remember that I told you he had a brother, Tom?"

"Yes. They were the last of the tribe's sachems, right?"

"Uh huh. They lived out on the island with their families. It seems from John's stories that Tom was maybe the less responsible brother. John says things about him which make me think he was a little resentful, that Tom didn't pull his weight in the tribe. He left the planting, fishing, hunting to others, for example. John said often, *'My brother work not, yet he make a fine appearance,'* which I take to mean that he got away with it. Lots of John's dream stories feature his brother's escapades. He did little acts of sabotage on the colonists like breaking apart fences or knocking over a rain barrel. And he collected things, apparently, which he found lying around."

"He was a thief?"

"No, I think he had different ideas about ownership, is all. Mind you, it's often hard to tell what's going on in John's stories, or get what he's talking about at all. He'll explain in great detail the chimney of a house he saw in Wellfleet, stone by stone, then skip to a story from his childhood, or tell me with genuine horror that 'Hobbomock,' which I believe is their devil, in the form of a snake with horns, pulled his boat under the waves and spilled everything."

"Jesus."

"Yeah, it can be baffling sometimes, just trying to make sense of it. Then, poof! he's gone.

"Maybe that's when he wakes up."

"Funny, I never thought of that." He scratched his head pensively for a bit, then went on. "Sometimes he states very seriously things like, '*A fish is naught but the sea.*' or he will go on a long ramble about trees, birds and animals being "*naught but the sun.*'"

"What does he mean?"

"I don't know." Moony giggled. "Maybe he's the original hippie."

"Oh, come on!"

"Well, think about it. Once, he drew a picture in the sand for me. First he made a lot of long, wavy lines. '*This is wind,*' he said. Then he made some of the lines curl into spirals, and pointed to one, said '*This is storm. Storm is a man, wind is god,*' he said. Then he erased the swirls –the storms– and redrew the wind lines where they had been, and drew storms in other places."

"Cycle of life? Birth and rebirth?" It was meant tongue-in-cheek.

"That's what I thought. But so much of what he says is open to interpretation."

"I can see that, though, yeah. What do you say to him?"

"I don't say much, to tell the truth. He talks a lot. And, as I said, much of it is lost to me because of mixing in Wampanoag. He also has a hard time pronouncing L and R, so words come out sounding like none I know. I listen and nod, try to fill in between words I can understand."

I laughed. "Sounds like quite a puzzle, but absolutely fascinating. Have you never told anyone?"

"Nope. Can you imagine what it would do to my life – or the Cape? If anyone actually believed me, and I could come up with the goods, there'd be an invasion of media, scientists, movie people, you name it. The whole bay cordoned off. No one would ever see it again. My life would be hell."

"OK, I get it. Don't worry, I won't say a word." I wouldn't. I could see that everything he imagined would happen, and worse. "Now, tell me the story having to do with Martin," I said, as we took the turn onto Barley Neck.

"Right. Let's see. Around the Sipson brothers' time, a lot of ships were coming across the Atlantic, and whaling was a full-blown industry." Moony pointed toward the ocean. "Big ships sailing along out there were a common sight." I recalled the decor of whale ribs in the restaurant in New Bedford.

"This coastline is a ship graveyard," he continued. "Hundreds of them are buried out there. See, the sand is constantly shifting around, so they could never be sure of where the deep ended. If a storm was blowing onshore, and if a ship were perhaps too near the coast, they were in for it. Done. After a ship foundered all kinds of stuff would wash up on shore. People would go out to the beach and drag off whatever they could get, from lumber to teacups. If you look closely, you can see houses in town with parts made from shipwrecks. The timber was great stuff, indestructible."

"Did anyone survive?"

"Not many. Lots of people died out there."

I tried to imagine combing the beach for people's belongings after they'd perished in a storm at sea. It sounded heartless, but I suppose in a pioneering situation one didn't have much choice.

"I'm guessing Tom Sipson collected things from them."

"Yes. John told me they used to go out to look for stuff after a ship went down, and that Tom loved finding anything feminine '*of a lady's locker.*'"

"What? You're joking." Moony's imitation of John Sipson's guttural Ls sounded like a character in a tv cartoon. In all my childhood stories of ghosts I had never read about one with a fetish for women's undergarments. It was getting more bizarre by the minute.

"One night after a fierce storm he dragged home a figurehead. He installed it at the door to his wigwam.'*She'd yellow hair and rose bosom,*' John said."

"A figurehead?"

"The carving on the bow of a boat, under the bowsprit. You know, like a busty woman pointing ahead. Onward!" Moony imitated the pose, then pulled into the driveway. We sat there listening to the truck's engine cooling, a slow and gentle tick-tick. "John said after his wife died Tom brought it into the wigwam."

I laughed again. These were not the usual American Indian stories we'd been told, even by Disney. "But what's it all got to do with Martin?"

"Oh, right. The story I wanted to tell you." He shifted to face me. "When Tom died he was buried in traditional Indian fashion, knees drawn up with the head resting on them, then lowered into a deep hole, as if going back into the womb of Mother Earth, you know? But before that, while he was dying, he insisted he be buried with the figurehead, and John refused. Tom was so angry that he would not speak to or look at his brother from that point on. He died that way. I figure John can't sleep because of it, which is why he appears in our time."

"You mean in his dreams."

"I guess so, yeah. Hard to say. Anyhow, what happened is that when Martin was building his house, they came across Tom Sipson's grave, and Martin took Tom's skull. John Sipson is very bothered by it. He must have told me fifty times about that skull, and how it needs to go back in the ground. He says he used to sleep next to the skull but then suddenly it was gone."

I knew where it was. Crushed into the paving of Sandy's one-eyed friend's driveway. *La vache!*

"Did he ever show it to you?" When I shook my head Moony sighed. "See, I was thinking that if he has it he should put it in the cellar. Or better yet re-bury it."

"That would be good."

"And I was also thinking that you could get him to do that, or maybe you could do it, if you know where the skull is kept."

I grabbed the door handle. "I'll be back in ten minutes." I needed to think about whether it was a good idea to tell Moony about Tom Sipson's shattered skull, or that Martin already knew about the ghost of John. Inside, I filled the bathroom sink with water, stripped off my sweaty uniform and flung it into the corner where it promptly began to sprout mildew. If I didn't tell Moony about the crushed skull, if I simply pretended I hadn't heard that little tidbit of gossip I could go about my business, which was painting, and leave those details to others. As I sloshed water over my face and pawed some into my armpits, I added the secret to my already barely manageable pile to see how it felt. Not good. If Moony knew and didn't tell John Sipson, he –and I– might be the cause of his prolonged state of in between-ness, if that's what was happening. I pulled the little blue dress off a hanger, thrust my head in and pulled it over the rest of me. John Sipson didn't seem so unhappy being a ghost, but who was I to say? I finger-combed my hair, clipped it behind my neck and shoved my feet into the espadrilles. Great, I thought. French girl on the town. I didn't even own a lipstick.

"I know where it is," I said as I got back into the car.

"Oh, that's good."

"No, it's not."

Moony started the truck, wrestled the gearstick into reverse and twisted around to look out the back window. "Because . . .?"

The truck stopped abruptly when I told him. "Oh, shit," he said.

We drove in silence for most of the way back to the Turk's Head. I spent most of it with my mind a labyrinth of various strategies for getting the skull back to Martin in whatever shape possible without revealing why I knew, or cared. I didn't want to tell Moony that Martin knew about my John Sipson meeting, or that we'd been on a five-day mission to lure him out of the past, but I think I know why he never reappeared. He was mad at Martin for losing his brother's skull.

I also entertained myself with a little mental scene featuring Moony and John Sipson once again reclining on the little shingle of beach. Moony explaining, drawing a car tire in the sand as John Sipson looked on, a dignified yet curious look on his face. I stifled a giggle, but not completely.

"What?" Moony said, rolling to a stop across the street from the coffeehouse.

"Nothing. What a day it's been, that's all. Let's go in."

The room was full, though not packed. Thankfully Joyce had saved us a seat along the back wall, a padded bench under the Ganesh poster. She and Moony kissed lightly in the kitchen before she ushered us in. "Don't tell anyone, but here's thanks for this afternoon." She set a little coffeepot on the table with two espresso cups. I had not seen so many people in one place since I came to Orleans, and I admit it was exciting, like being in the city again. Both doors were wide open to let a steady draft from the southwest waft through the room, taking with it the lowest layer of cigarette smoke. Even with the breeze everyone glistened with happy, caffeinated perspiration, and the gabble of excited vacationers was steady. Joyce had set up more tiny tables and some spindly stools to accommodate the extra people. I spotted Becca and waved her over, but she nodded toward a nice looking man sitting next to her, and shrugged hopefully. The wall behind the stage was hung with some kind of sparkly fabric, a rich blue with tassels along the edge, which made a regal backdrop. Moony got up to do a last minute wiring check while I poured a cup of coffee for myself. I took a sip, and cool, sweet espresso ran over my tongue, but alcohol-enhanced, spiced with something else. Licorice? I looked up at Joyce and she winked, then turned to another task. Moony came back to the table and I poured him some. "Ah, I do love her," he said, elbowing me.

Eric Von Schmidt emerged from the kitchen and strode toward the stage. The crowd parted reverently to make room for his passage, but he didn't seem to notice. Tall and thin with black hair and beard, he stepped up on the carpet, the one I'd slung over Moony's truck tailgate only hours before, and strummed an opening chord to enthusiastic yet tempered applause, appropriate for folk music. He started

211

right in on a song about not needing any whisky or rum, just you baby, etc., in a slurry, easy, hypnotic cadence, his gravelly voice breaking, hesitating, then filling in. Every now and then he'd throw out an inventive, melodic little ditty from his guitar while he closed his eyes and enjoyed the audience's attention. Someone got up on stage with him for the next number and played a mournful harmonica in the background, a story of a sugarcane worker strike on Barbados. I snuck a look at Moony to see what he thought. He sat leaning his chin on his hand, tapping one finger against his cheek. He caught my eye and we exchanged the goofy grin of a fabulous shared secret. As I watched Joyce snake her way through the sea of knees with a tray of heaped-up ashtrays and rattling mugs, I wondered why Moony hadn't told her about the ghost. Maybe he knew of some protocol for preposterous yet true events, one which dictates wise silence until undeniable facts are declared. If that were the case I had violated it almost immediately by telling Martin, which I didn't want to think about. To change my mental subject I took a sip from my espresso cup and tuned to Von Schmidt. I cringed inwardly as I watched him lay his expensive-looking acoustic guitar on the still-damp rug and pick up a mandolin. He started in on a melodic, high-voice love song about watching the way his lover stands. Something simple like that is what love is really about, I thought, though I had very little experience to judge by. I had only had friendships with men –boys, really, until Bard and Don's rubbery lips. *Beurk!* I took another sip and paid attention to the music through a few more songs. The guy was pretty good, I thought, but it was clear why Dylan had left him in the dust. I was working on my third cup of espresso flavored booze around then, and quite happy, high beyond the drink and feeling at home among the cozy crowd of folkies in that little tourist town. I began to create a fantasy scenario of living there permanently, then modified it to attending college in Boston –if they had an art school, and otherwise living on Barley Neck where I would paint all summer and . . .

"Elli! Hi!" Sandy stood in front of me, whispering loudly and waving her hand in my face. I motioned for her to sit beside me and squeezed closer to Moony to make room. Of course Sandy was sheathed in one of her bust-featuring blouses, so several men in the vicinity felt the need to turn around to look at the Ganesh poster as she sat down beside me.

"Who's he?" she whispered, indicating Moony with googly-eyes.

"My date," I decided to say, which got me another nudge from him.

"Far out," she said, covertly checking him out. Moony smoothed his side hair and re-crossed his legs. Von Schmidt began a song about cocaine 'running 'round in my brain,' He informed us the song was written by a Reverend Something. I was sure that was a member of the clergy, which intrigued me, but I missed the rest of what he said because Sandy was whispering in my ear.

"I saw Martin today. He came into the bar with Theo and the two of them sat poring over an art book. Pictures of big metal sculptures, I think. Then they spent about two hours drawing diagrams on a pad of paper. Cubes and squares and adding up figures. Weird."

"Good to know he's talking to someone, though, right?" I said, and Sandy nodded enthusiastically. Likely they were discussing the fourth dimension again, I thought, which was an indication that Martin was talking about Freya. For all I knew, he'd finally made contact and was getting ready to announce it to the world via The Cape Codder.

I glanced at Moony, who was talking to a man on his other side, and whispered, "By the way, did your friend ever tell Martin what happened to the skull?"

Sandy gave me a puzzled look. "How did you know about that?"

"You told me."

"Oh yeah? No, I don't think so."

"Because Martin mentioned it to me," I lied. "He feels bad about digging it up, and wants to put it back." I figured I might as well get to the point.

Sandy gave me a wide-eyed, cogitative stare. Her lips parted and her jaw dropped. "Oh, wow," she said. "That's heavy. I thought the same thing! I mean, it's not right, y'know, especially after what happened." She paused, running her hand up the back of her own skull as if making sure it was still in one piece.

Eric Von Schmidt wound down the cocaine song with fading chords, and announced a short break. He stepped off the platform and disappeared into the kitchen. Joyce was ready at the stereo, pulling a record out of its paper sleeve. Moony got up and went to join her. I liked seeing them together, and hoped he wasn't married to someone else. A minute later Bob Dylan singing *Rainy Day Woman #12 & 35* came blaring out of the speaker above my head. Once upon a time I had that album, I thought, and I will again.

"I love this song," said Sandy. "Want to dance?"

"No thanks," I said. How anyone could dance to Bob Dylan was beyond me. It just wasn't that kind of music, or that kind of place. But it didn't stop others from frugging away in the aisles between tables. I don't think they knew what they were listening to, though half the room joined in

214

on the refrain about getting stoned. Just then a rowdy group arrived at the front door and stood packed into the opening, discussing whether to stay or find a different place. As I watched I saw Sylvie pass behind them and look in, giving the place a good once over, scanning the crowd for someone. I hoped it wasn't me, because I was not in a state to have that confrontation. I silently willed Moony to come back and sit down, but he was in the kitchen fiddling with the new water heater.

"I gotta go outside for a sec," I said to Sandy. "Get some air."

"OK. I'll come with you." She cleared the way through to the door easily enough. Everyone reared back to stare as she passed, making plenty of room. When we got outside she ran over to the benches in front of the cemetery and flung herself down on the nearest one. "Whew! It sure is hot in there," she said, swiping her hand across her forehead. "So, is that guy really your date?"

"Moony?" I laughed. "No, he's Joyce's boyfriend. You didn't know?"

"Nope." She gazed up at the underside of the elm hanging over the street. Its leaves fluttered in the wake of a passing truck. I heard clapping coming from the Turk's Head as Von Schmidt took the stage for his second set. Sandy sat up.

"I think I might as well go," she said. I could tell she was thinking about Sal, and their complicated, risky situation, which could end at any time, abruptly and with much pain and ugliness if he were carted off to jail. And now, when Martin's behavior was jeopardizing what little security they had, she must have felt caught between loyalty to their plight and her own freedom. She could not fully enjoy either situation, or choose between them without enormous loss.

"Want to give me a ride?" We could talk on the way. I could listen, the only thing I had to offer. I wanted to go home anyway, if Sylvie was lurking. I stuck my head in the back door of the Turk's Head and told Moony, who was doing dishes, that I was leaving.

"OK honey." He gave my shoulder a squeeze. "I'll be around." We grinned again, a mutual, silent acknowledgement of a subject for which there was no small talk.

We drove through town in silence, and out past the church. Sandy heaved a long sigh. "It must be hard for you sometimes," I said. "To be with Sal when he can't come out in public."

"It's a drag, definitely," she said quietly. "But most of the time I don't care. It's only at times like tonight, when I want to show him off, that I get lonely." I was sure he felt the same, and said it.

"Of course, it's also pretty good to always know where he is," she turned to me and we laughed. "To come home to the little woman after a hard day," she hooted.

"Barefoot and pregnant, that's how I like 'em." I added. "Home cooked meals."

"Fuckin' A!" We laughed, stuck our arms out the windows and flew down the road to the beach. After a few moments Sandy's laugh died, and she became quiet again. "It does make it kind of impossible for us to settle down. Y'know, actually have kids, be normal. I want that, and so does Sal."

"It can't go on forever."

"Yeah, but I'm getting sick of living in fear."

We'd turned down Barley Neck Road, passing a turnip field on the right. Their leaves were lit up by the moon, resembling a vast, green quilted duvet covering the gently rolling hill all the way to the bay. As I scanned the soft-looking landscape I spotted a figure standing out in the middle, with one hand raised. It was John Sipson.

"If worse comes to worst we could go to Canada," said Sandy at that exact moment.

My head whipped around in astonishment. That phrase again. "If worse comes to worst." I turned back to the field, but John Sipson was gone.

"What?" Sandy said. "You don't like that idea?"

Her hand was draped over the gearshift knob. I covered it with mine and said, "I'm sure everything will work out long before then."

Chapter Eleven

I knew I promised Sandy I'd go over to Sipson's island to talk to Martin and Sylvie, but as each day came that next week I told myself that tomorrow, yes, definitely tomorrow I would go, and then I'd get home from work, go directly out to the studio and emerge five hours later, elated, starving, and in a daze of absent-mindedness about what it was I was supposed to do. Something I didn't want. Oh yeah. That. Then I'd go inside, take some food out of the fridge, anything that was edible without preparation, stuff it directly into my mouth and fall onto the bed, chewing and reviewing what I'd created. Then I slept.

My uniform was disgusting. On the third day, at Becca's insistence, I took it off and tossed it in with a load of pillowcases on my lunch break and hid in my underwear for the duration, then wore it wet for the next hour. Luckily rayon dries quickly with a little body heat.

In the studio I ran out of red and yellow again because I mixed up a bucket of viscous orange and coated most of the sheets of cheap watercolor paper I had with it so I could continue making my negative space tree paintings. I used a fat crayon made of solid pencil lead that I found in a box of children's toys under the bed. The black it made was hugely satisfying because the line was thick and dark and gave off a slight sheen. After I'd used up all the orange paper and added detail with dabs of red and yellow from the squeezed-out watercolor tubes I realized that it wasn't necessary to get any more because my graphite crayon was all that was needed to make art. And since I hadn't bothered to buy more paper I started to draw directly on the plaster walls. As I had done with the red and orange paint, I resolved that the negative space around an object was more interesting than the solid form, and so I began to scribble that on the wall, gradually revealing a vast network of things –yes, objects, but also some previous states of those objects as well as the hands or minds or serendipitous chain of events that created them. I know that sounds a bit vague, and again, it was mostly my hand doing it. However, I understood perfectly what I was making, and why. For instance, when I drew the area around my feet standing in water; the water itself was a dimension which was encompassed by space. That space revealed not only the outline of a pair of feet but also held the imprint of those feet before they were born, so a darker layer of crayon peeked through the one over it, through layers of water displaced and arranged by any bits of matter floating in it. All these things along with their past iterations had the interweaving thread of black crayon, which could reveal any number of additional objects, and they in turn were linked to the things still uncovered. The whole looked to me like a limitless deep macrocosm containing every organism of existence. I started in on another wall, making a picture in the same kind of descriptive way of the natural world outside my door. The cedar trees were rendered only by the air around them, and because they are living, evolving things, their surrounding space was constantly changing as the wind changes the configuration of leaves or branches or the location of small animals, birds and insects, seeds and flowers living on and among them. I saw very clearly that all things were unfixed, expanding and contracting, influenced and connected by the flow around them, which was my crayon, and I tried to draw those variables.

I know that might sound like nonsense, but it was perfectly clear to me. I was astounded by the ability of my hand to portray something so elaborate and inexplicable as life, and though I admit I had a niggling doubt as to the value of my output in the greater art world, I was having so much fun producing such magic with nothing but a cheap hunk of graphite, that I continued.

On Monday, my day off, I took my bike into town to do some grocery shopping. For once I had plenty of cash, and my intention was to buy something exotic and expensive, like olives, to celebrate my creative success. I vowed I'd stop by the The Foc'sle and ask Sandy to pick me up that afternoon when she got off work, and bring me out to Sipson's as I'd promised. At the store I bought a load of staples: cans of my beloved Campbell's mushroom soup, cans of corn, a block of butter and a big bag of rice, plus vegetables, oranges, and a jar of big green olives from California. It was more than I could carry, so I located

Sandy's car parked behind the bar and dumped the heaviest bag in the back seat.

When I stepped inside the cool, dark room she saw me right away and came over. "Hi!" she sang out, hugging me. "You finally came. Do you want a ride with me?"

"Yes, if that's all right," I said. "Sorry it's taken me so long." I told her about the bags in the back seat of her car.

"Cool."

"How are things on the island?"

"About the same. Still weird, y'know? Martin stopped digging his hole though, so that's a relief. At least he and Sylvie are talking. She says only just barely, but it's something. If you come maybe he'll tell you what's going on with him. Man, the vibe out there is heavy."

She had to attend to a couple tables so I sat at the bar to wait. The place was full of tourists, but I spotted several local boys drinking mugs of beer in the back corner. One of them I recognized because he sometimes came to the motel to fix broken plumbing. He waved at me and motioned with his head for me to come and join them. I shrugged, and walked my fingers out the door, but smiled too, so he might ask me again. I liked him. Maybe I'd ask him to the next show at the Turk's Head. Sandy grabbed my hand as she passed.

"Let's go," she said. She flipped the strap to a suede handbag with foot-long fringe over her shoulder. "I just have to stop for some beer on the way."

As we passed the turnip field on Barley Neck road I looked for John Sipson, as I had every day that week when passing on my bike, but he was not there. I hadn't seen Moony in all that time either, so he didn't know about my sighting. He had been to the house twice with little offerings from his vegetable patch, but so far we'd missed

221

each other. Had I been in the studio when he came around it was highly likely that if he took one look through the screen door and saw me in my drawing frenzy, he would not have interrupted.

When we got to the house I hauled the bag out of the back seat and went in to put the groceries away. Sandy walked over to the bluff, sat down on the wicker chair and lit a cigarette. "Your view is outta sight!" she squealed.

After I put my perishables in the fridge I grabbed a sweater off the arm of the sofa and turned on the bedside light for when I came home in the dark. Then I stood just inside the door taking a few deep breaths, telling myself I was doing the right thing getting involved with the gang on Sipson's again just when I was making headway at being independent. I could hear Sandy humming to herself between puffs, something that sounded like the jingle for Oscar Meyer Wieners, or the marching band music our boss played in the laundry room –a motivational, fortitude-inspiring tune, and yes, I thought, I definitely had it. I owed it to them to help if I could, and if I had something to offer I would certainly give it.

When we arrived at the landing, Sandy cut the engine and coasted to a stop. The little wooden rowboat they used to get back and forth was tied to the dock, rocking gently in the passing current. Martin's boat was on the other side. Sandy slung a duffel bag onto the seat and went back for the two six-packs of Rolling Rock beer we'd bought along the way. She said that Ray and Sal drank the stuff because their father did, and he did because it came from his home state of Pennsylvania.

"How does it taste?" I asked. I was dying for one at that point.

"Like fermented pee," she laughed. "But don't try to tell them that."

We'd only rowed a few yards across the narrows when Rollo, Roxie and Bobby burst out of the trees and ran down the beach to greet us. Bobby was much bigger; the fuzz on his back had turned brown though his head was still baby yellow. He staggered across the sand peeping and flapping and making such a huge fuss that the dogs gave up and lay down quietly until we swung alongside the dock. Sandy greeted them, then knelt down as Bobby threw himself open-winged into her arms, making a soft whistle-honk and pecking her hair as she giggled.

"Oh yes I do love you, you little rascal," she baby-talked to the bird, then gave the dogs a round of kisses, hugs and head scratching before extracting herself to stand. Her hair was a mess and she had wet smudges across her blouse. "Whew!" she said, laughing. "We're flying the freak flag as usual on Sipson's."

Sal appeared, gave her what was by comparison a fairly chaste peck on the cheek, then picked up the beer. "Nice to see your face again," he said to me, beaming. "C'mon up."

Ray and Sylvie were on the deck when we rounded the corner. Ray's pants were rolled up and he sat with his feet in a bucket of water. He was reading aloud from a copy of Vonnegut's *Welcome to the Monkey House.*

"Here's to the re-emergence of Elli. Dig it!" he said, toasting me with a can of beer. Sylvie sat cross-legged on the floor doodling designs with a pink marker on a cast that enveloped her hand, wrist and half her forearm. She leapt to her feet when she saw me and rushed over to give me an awkward, hardly-touching hug. "Oh wow. I'm so glad you came," she said, holding the cast behind her back.

"Let me see." I reached out and gently pulled it toward me. It was substantially heavy and covered with writing, flower-power, hearts and peace signs. "I'm so sorry," I said solemnly. "I didn't realize you'd been wounded this badly."

"It's fine. But it makes cooking difficult, and writing, and driving and tying shoes and doing up buttons and a million other things," she laughed. "But I'm getting pretty good at being a lefty." She handed me the marker. "Want to sign it?" I made the same four-line drawing of a flounder that Moony had done in the sand when he instructed me about fishing, and wrote my name in the middle.

"Nice." She smiled at me. "Come sit. Someone, give her a beer, willya?"

After Sandy's quip about its taste I was about to turn down the offer, but with a wink she passed me a can of something else.

"I thought he knew better but somehow Ray walked through a patch of poison ivy," Sylvie said, rolling her eyes at him. "I've got him soaking in baking soda."

"You two make quite a pair," I said.

We sat in the sun for an hour, talking about various things and getting comfortable with each other again. They wanted to know what I thought of the Eric Von Schmidt show, and I said, "I liked the cocaine song." I don't know why I said that. Maybe it was the only one I could remember. I had never tried cocaine, but for some stupid reason I thought it sounded hip. It wasn't a drug I'd seen making the rounds at Bard so I didn't even know if it was smoked or injected or what.

"Oh ho, that's too expensive for me," Ray said. "I'll stick to this." He held up his bottle of Rolling Rock and swigged. Sylvie disappeared into the house and after a minute I heard the song's opening guitar refrain plinking from the outdoor speakers, then the growly voice of Von Schmidt. Ray and Sal got into an involved discussion about his music and the folk music scene in general. They had been at Newport together a few years before when Dylan got up and sang *'Maggie's Farm'* and a couple of other songs backed by electric guitars at the all-acoustic festival, forever changing music history. Von Schmidt had been there too, and they had wanted to talk to him about it and had actually sent Sandy to invite him out to the island for a 'true Cape Cod vacation,' but he had other gigs.

"Apparently," said Sal.

I glanced at Sandy when I heard this but she put a discreet finger against her lips, and I said nothing. They continued a passionate discussion of all the folk musicians who had followed the electric lead of Dylan while Sandy, Sylvie and I wandered into the kitchen.

"We came to your place yesterday. Martin and I." Sylvie said abruptly, as Otis Redding began to sing *'My Lover's Prayer,'* the epitome of a soul song performed by a master. I loved Otis, but I was so startled by what Sylvie said I couldn't savor his vocal emoting. "What?"

"Yesterday. In the afternoon."

Had they seen me in a crayon frenzy and gone away? What a mortifying thought. "I was at work." I hoped.

"Martin peeked in the studio, but no one was home, so we left."

As Otis' saxophone backup slid into the second verse I tried to picture the state of the place as I'd left it. I know the tree paintings were spread out on the floor where I put them to dry. But if anyone opened the door and looked in they'd certainly not miss the giant drawing on the wall opposite and likely withdraw quickly. I wanted to ask if he'd had any remarks, but pride stopped me and I said nothing. Sandy looked at the ceiling. After a half a minute of uncomfortable silence Sylvie said, "Hey, would you like to see the day lilies? They're blooming right now in the garden."

"Sure," I said, and stood up.

"Back in a flash," she said to Sandy, who winked at me again.

We walked through the still woods to the garden in silence. Our footfalls were a raspy rhythm through the sandy soil. We passed through a stretch of sweet- smelling forest grass as chickadees called to each other overhead. The drone of an outboard motor faded as it cleared the narrows, leaving us with the muted shouts of campers taking sailing lessons over by Namequoit Point. Not far from the cottage was the elm where Martin and I had held vigil, but Sylvie strode by as if she didn't know. When we arrived at the clearing a wide swath of orange lilies nodded lazily to us on long stalks. I had never seen flowers of that size or color in a natural landscape, and said so. It was quite stunning.

"They're called day lilies because the bloom only lasts that long, then another one comes along, and the patch will go for about a week or so." Sylvie murmured, gazing at them lovingly.

"Very beautiful," I said. Sylvie put her hand on my shoulder and I turned. She stared intensely into my eyes and shook her head.

"Listen, Elli. I wanted to apologize for that night. I feel horrible. I was an asshole," she said softly. She looked steadily at me as her eyes began to glisten, then fill with tears.

"Don't worry. You had too much to drink, like the rest of us."

"Maybe, but the rest of you didn't alienate a friend or stupidly crush a knuckle joint." She wiped under her eyes with the side of the cast, smearing a line of tiny pink hearts. "I am truly sorry that I thought anything was going on between you and Martin."

"Nothing but friendship."

"I know. That's what he said, too. But . . ."

"But?"

"About this ghost thing."

"Yes?"

"C'mon. What was that? I don't understand why you'd want to get him all jazzed about something we all know is never going to happen." She was still speaking in a gentle, intimate tone, but the waver in her voice sounded barely under control.

I wanted to say that it was none of her business, but I was too polite. I understood that they were all concerned about their hideaway's security if Martin was acting crazy, and I reminded myself that I had come to the island to see about that, not to quibble with Sylvie about ghosts.

"I know what I saw, and that's all I'll say. But I will tell you that I only went with him to look for Freya out of sympathy. The other was supposed to be a private matter. I don't know why he told you." I backed away from her, stepping onto the path to Martin's house. "Sandy tells me you want me to try and help with him. That's why I came. I'm going up there now and I think I should go alone," I said over my shoulder as I started up the hill.

"Good luck," Sylvie called after me. I rolled my eyes.

As I approached the house I noticed that the big sliding doors over the second story entrance were closed, the two x-braces looking like a blockade, a stop sign that left the little spiral staircase leading to nowhere. I rounded the corner of the house and ducked under the willow. I gathered several long fronds around me and peered at the wall of windows, trying to see if Martin was inside. All I saw was the white-line strip of outer beach and the cloudless, saturated blue of late afternoon sky reflected and refracted in all those panes of glass.

The screen door opened, and Martin's head emerged. "Come on in, Elli," he said, calm as anything. "Nice to see you again." He held the door open for me as I let go of the branches, slightly reluctant to lose the cloak of protection they provided at that awkward moment. I walked past him into the house and sat on one of the barstools at the kitchen counter. He stood opposite, nodding and smiling at me. He looked even more disheveled than the last time I'd seen him. He was unshaven and his hair hung greasily in front of his eyes. His clothes looked as if he'd been wearing them for a few days. Gone were the pressed slacks and linen shirt. He had on a pair of cutoffs and a threadbare, once white t-shirt with a wide smear of dirt near the bottom.

"Something cool to drink?"

"Sure," I said. He took a pitcher of lemonade out of the fridge and poured two glasses, then yanked the freezer door open and extracted an ice tray. I have to admit it felt good to sit there again in the refined atmosphere of his opulent refuge, and though he was definitely not relaxed, he still gave the impression of amicable, paternal attention.

"How is Min?" I asked, wondering if we were alone.

"Fine. Gone shopping. How are you?" He dropped ice into the glasses and tossed the tray back in the freezer. "Let's go over and sit."

I sank into one of the sumptuous white chairs. The carved reclining horse was splayed in front of me, and I reached out to touch the burl of its flank as I had done the

228

first time I saw it. Martin settled on the edge of his chair with his long legs crossed, sipping lemonade, watching. He seemed a little twitchy; the ice rattled in his glass and he jiggled a foot against the table leg. "So?" he prompted.

"Im fine," I said. "Busy, but all right."

He got right to it. "I was at your house yesterday, did you know?"

"I didn't, no. Until just now, when Sylvie told me. Sorry I missed you."

"Yeah. I was . . ." He reached across the table and grabbed my hand, which was holding my drink. A little lemonade sloshed on the horse's neck. I started to wipe it off but Martin said, "Elli, stop. Listen – I went into the studio. Don't get mad at me, I was just looking for you, but my god, what I saw in there! Is that you? Did you make that drawing? Did you paint those gorgeous red trees?"

"I –"

"Because if you did you have made some of the most exciting work I have ever seen."

"Really?"

"Yes! It's breathtaking, it's stunning. It's . . . have you always made these kinds of pictures? Why didn't you tell me?"

"I didn't know. It just started to happen." I struggled with my answer, deciding whether to tell him the truth. Though he had experienced something very similar, I felt protective about my newfound ability, and didn't want to share it with him. I didn't want him to turn it into something about entangled particles or wave collapsing, or another reason to go searching for Freya.

Martin let go of my hand and gazed at me, slowly shaking his head. "The drawing on the wall –what is it to you?"

"I think it's, um, everything," I said, for lack of a more literate symbolic interpretation. "While I was drawing it was clear to me that I was illustrating the connecting thread of all things, even in the past and future. In my mind I saw one huge moving mass and, well, I just kept copying those lines." I squeezed my eyes shut, willing a broader explanation to come to me, but saw again that it was simply as I'd said. I glanced up to see if he understood. His head bobbed up and down in agreement, waiting for me to say more. "The trees came first. I was playing around, trying to draw the space between them with this crayon I found, and they were moving in the breeze so of course I had to include that."

"I love the patina. What is it?"

I told him about finding the stick of graphite and discarding paint in favor of its soft, black marks.

"You said you merely drew what you saw, the huge moving mass?"

"Sort of," I lied.

At that Martin got up and began to pace around the room, talking and gesturing with his glass, launching lemonade droplets into the air. I began to see the slightly manic behavior Sandy had described. He talked about the first time he had the experience of 'painting' with his finger, but in a rambling, disjointed way and I wondered if he forgot that he'd already told me the story. He recounted a sequence of events that was screwy, altered from his previous description, and he talked in terms of 'we' at the Paris gallery. Was he including Freya? I was sure she was dead at that point in his life.

"When we stepped out onto the street I knew we had purchased the tool we needed to communicate," he concluded. Was he still talking about my mother's painting? I was about to ask him when he spun around and added, "And now I must show you the next phase of our reunion." He rushed over to the desk where he kept the Polaroids of his art collection and plucked a folder from the filing cabinet. He sat on one of the arms of my chair, just as he had the first time he showed me the picture of *'A Swim at Pochet'.'*

"Look at this," he said, his voice trembling with excitement. He held out a large color photo of a metal sculpture. On a long black pole a flat, triangular slice of red was attached. At the base of the pole another, larger triangle was stuck to the pole at a different angle, painted black. The pole and its appendages were set into a block of granite. Martin slapped his forefinger on the red triangle. "See how it's a sail on a mast and also the shape of this island?"

"Ye-es," I answered hesitantly. I had thought it looked more like a windsock or a megaphone, proportion-wise. It certainly had the shape of Sipson's, though.

"It's a Calder. I commissioned it years ago when we bought this place, for the lawn. Somehow I never got around to installing it, and now I am going to. The thing is huge, maybe fifteen feet tall, so you'll be able to spot it from far away."

"Alexander Calder?"

"Yes. The very one." He pointed to the lower triangle. "You can't see it from the photo, but this is a hollow box. I'm going to inter Freya's bones in there."

"What?"

"Yes. I've already requested a removal from the family plot back home, and they are getting the paperwork together. This town is being quite fussy about burial on personal property, bla bla bla, but I'll get around that." This last was brushed aside with the back of his hand as a minor triviality.

"It's quite unusual," I said weakly.

"But here's the best part," he announced, leaping up again. "An item I found years ago when we were building this house, and which has significance to this island and me, and even to you, Elli." He went back to the desk, pulled open a drawer and removed a shoe box with 'Jeepers Sneakers' printed on the side. He cradled it in one arm and took off the lid, then laid it in my lap. Inside was something unrecognizable at first, just a jumble of ivory-colored pieces, but when I saw the teeth I knew what it was, and stared into the box, astonished.

"It has just been returned to me, though when I lent it it was whole. No matter –can you guess? I'm positive it's the skull of John Sipson!"

"John Sipson?" I squeaked, as I put the box on the coffee table.

"Yes, your old friend, remember?"

"How can you be sure it's. . ." I started to say, but he waved the question away.

"I know. I found it in a grave when we dug the foundation here. It was an Indian grave, I could tell. I've always felt guilty for taking it, but now I'm going to put it back, only in a slightly different place. I'm going to bury it with the sculpture on top."

"What?" I said, thinking of what Moony had told me. "Not back under the house?"

"No, this is better. It's a brilliant idea, if I do say so myself. Both people died on this island, and if they're together as part of a work of art they will connect over the centuries, the bones will become entangled, their particles will be permanently merged and so lose their individuality and behave as a solo entity."

"I didn't know that was possible."

"Nobody does, but here we have a situation where we could prove it is. You see, if I'm right, when John Sipson appears again, so will Freya."

Thank god I was able to stop myself from laughing out loud at my mental image of Freya/John –or rather Freya/ Tom, which would be more accurate– appearing in the woods at night and scaring the shit out of Martin. No, it was not a laughing matter. Except that then I thought of Tom Sipson's penchant for women's underthings and I had to take a swift sip of lemonade to control myself.

"I see," I managed to say, as I tried to look pensive. I was fervently hoping he wasn't going to ask me to be in on it with him again, not only because I was otherwise involved, but the plan sounded nutty, to say the least.

"What do you think?"

This was the moment that I had to admit I had not taken the situation very seriously because I had been so distracted by what was happening to me at home. Until that moment I had never really considered that my mature, erudite friend would ever need advice from me. Now, as I got my sniggering under control and saw what was really going on, I knew that I couldn't just take the passive route, tell him it was brilliant and report back to Ray and his household that all was fine. Because it wasn't, and I could not bring myself to lie about it, either to them or him. I needed some time to think so I said, "Where are you going to put it?"

"Come on, I'll show you." He leapt up and hastened over to the door, beckoning to me and practically skipping with excitement. I followed him, mincing across the prickly, dried-out lawn which he crunched over in his bare feet. We sped along a path heading toward the highest point of the island, along the cliff overlooking the narrows, then across to the eastern side. Martin talked steadily even though he was out of breath by the time we got to the trees at the edge of his yard.

"I've got a team coming over next month who will bring the Calder piece and install it. Before that I have to have a foundation poured, a plinth to bolt the thing to. I have to organize a load of cement and stone and then I'll get the guys to put it together but of course they need to be a little creative about it since it's the only material I could get around here and it won't look as elegant as I'd envisioned." He went on and on about the base and what kind of stone he would have had if he had time for the quarry to cut it and how long that would take and so on, until, panting, we reached a clearing near the point of the island at its headland, overlooking the barrier beach and the Atlantic beyond. It was a serenely quiet, commanding spot.

"Right here," Martin said. I looked over to see him pointing to a large square pit in the sand, and I realized it was what Sandy had been talking about, the grave she hinted at, a hole a little larger than the one they'd lowered my father into only a few months ago. It made me want to cry. I looked around and saw the smaller cavities where Ray and Sal had taken down the pines and dug up their roots. I glanced at the shore below and there they lay half in the water, the root balls looking like giant octopuses.

"This is where they'll pour the plinth," he said, jumping down into the hole. "And here," he added, stomping his heel down in its center, "is where John Sipson will go. In a proper burial container, naturally." He beamed up at me and spread his hands. "Back to the earth where he belongs, and seven feet away from Freya."

It was a ludicrous plan, but what did I know? Maybe Martin had come up with the perfect situation to put his theories to the test, now even more loaded with possibility since there were bones involved, DNA, particles, cells, all that. I really had no idea anymore. What would John Sipson's ghost think about it? I had to say something.

"I'm speechless," I whispered honestly.

"Yes! So was I when I first thought of it. I didn't tell Ray and the others because I wanted to surprise them, but I think it's time they know the plan, now that I'm ready."

"Oh yes, you should." I wondered how Sylvie would react to my ghost story resurfacing. "But I wouldn't mention John Sipson, if I were you. Too complicated. Too impossible."

Martin stared up at me from the hole, and nodded thoughtfully. "Hm, yes, you're right."

"You only need to say that it's a memorial to Freya."

"Right. They don't need to know what it's really for, do they?"

"Nope."

Martin folded his arms on the edge of the hole and leaned his chin on them, thinking. "I did mention it to Sylvie," he muttered. "Didn't I." His eyes skittered up to mine and back down.

"You did," I said softly.

"Oh dear, I remember now." He smacked his hand onto the top of his head. "Of course! Oh, Elli, what an idiot I am. Somehow I find myself confiding in her because she is so capable, so benevolent. She takes care of us all in her way, that's why I told her. I wanted her approval and support."

"I get it."

"But I owe you an apology. I should never have told your secret –our secret. I am truly sorry for that. It ruined our friendship, didn't it."

"For a while." It hadn't, but almost.

"Yet here you are. Why?"

"Because they're all worried about you, and asked me to come out to investigate." I thought the truth might be effective. There really was no problem as far as I could tell, and if Martin knew the others were concerned about him, he might want to ask them why.

"Why?" he said, holding out his hand for me to help him out of the hole. I gripped his palm as he jammed his foot into the dirt and used it to lever himself up. "Whatever is the problem?"

"Maybe you ought to tell them why you're digging a hole that looks very much like a grave."

Martin glanced at the hole, raked his whiskers and sighed. "Oh dear," he mumbled. "I should have told them sooner. Since Sylvie came back we've all been fairly reclusive."

"She says you've been locking your door at night."

He looked perplexed for a moment, then said, "Once or twice, yes. I saw someone pull a boat up onto the beach one evening, quite late. Two men, in fact, and I didn't want to go down to shoo them away. I was tired, and when I went to bed I locked the doors. I do have a valuable art collection here, you know."

"Right."

"But what was she doing, I wonder, checking on me so late?" he muttered to himself. He shook his head again slowly, and gazed across the water to the barrier beach dunes. The ocean beyond was a steady pattern of waves breaking in long white low-tide lines. "I never thought of it," he said. "I've been a little obsessed, I suppose. All right. I'll go down and talk to them tonight."

I felt instantly liberated from the role of island envoy, and as we walked back to the house I mused about the ironic simplicity of my findings. I could get along not saying any more to anyone about any of it. Martin could erect his memorial unaware that he was re-interring Tom and not John Sipson, and the others on the island need not know what the thing was really for. It wasn't necessary for Moony to know that I told Martin about the ghost, and John Sipson could find his brother's skull again by whatever methods they used in the parallel universe, or wherever he was. I dusted my hands against each other, job done.

"There is another matter I want to discuss," said Martin, walking ahead of me through the trees. He stopped and turned around to face me. "About your paintings."

"Oh?"

"Yes. I want to buy one, if that's possible."

Astonished at this declaration, I stood there feeling a mixture of elation and embarrassment. He had seen my intimate scratchings and wanted a part of them, which felt slightly intrusive, but flattering. I stuttered, "B-but, I'm not –I don't . . ."

"What do you say to selling me one of those red tree pictures?" When I didn't answer immediately, just stood there with my mouth hanging open, he turned and started walking again. "Well, think about it," he added.

"I would like it very much," I said after following him silently along the trail for a while, deep in thought. When we arrived in his yard I added, "It would be an honor. Are you serious?"

"Yes, of course." He stood still in the waning sunlight, the house behind him with its panorama of reflected sea and sky. It would make a good portrait, I thought.

"All right, come over and pick one out. But you don't have to buy it, I'll . . ."

"No," he interrupted me. "I want to. I insist. How about I visit sometime in the next few days to choose one?"

We made a date for Friday after work, then said goodbye. As I walked down the path cricket-song, a mellow bass line from Sylvie's stereo, and the swoosh of tumbling waves accompanied me, providing music for my elated mood. I jumped up to tag an oak branch, then skipped the rest of the way through the pine needles. I found Sandy lounging in the doorway of the house, tapping her foot and humming along to a song I didn't know.

"Hey," she smiled, beckoning me up to the deck. "So," she glanced over her shoulder into the house. "How did it go?"

"Well," I began, climbing the steps. I said that Martin would be visiting them that evening to tell them what was going on up the hill. "Could you give me a ride home before, though?" I said. I thought it would be better without me there and besides, I wanted to sit in the studio, look at my stuff and have a private little jubilation session. And for once a proper, cooked supper.

We went inside and I hugged brief goodbyes. I told them I'd be back soon, figuring I'd leave the explaining to Martin. Sylvie asked with a shrugging, hands up pantomime what had happened and I answered it with a thumbs-up, then blew her a kiss, and left.

Chapter Twelve

You might think that my story ends there, and it would have been a good place to do so, with all loose ends tied up in a neat bow and a benefactor on the way with a big check. I passed the following few days in a state of tranquility, enjoying the camaraderie of Becca and her hilarious stories of attempts at finding true love and a decent living, and later the hours on my own with the graphite crayon. However, on Thursday when I returned home from work and leaned my bike up against the house I spotted an unfamiliar sweater draped over the back of the wicker chair on the bluff. I went over to investigate. It was light green, cashmere, and when I picked it up the unmistakable bouquet of cigarette smoke and Shalimar surrounded me: my mother.

And there she was, bursting out of the door, yelling "Surprise!" She threw her arms around me, pinning mine to my sticky uniform, and kissed my cheek. "Elli, honey," she pulled away to survey the post-work mess. It was very good to see her face, hear her again, but I was in a kind of shock, truly at a loss for words. Finally I stuttered out, "Mom, wow. How did you . . . I mean, where did . . .?"

"I told Moony to keep it secret. He didn't want to, but I insisted. You look wonderful –so tan, so healthy. Is this your work uniform? I hope so, ha ha. I stopped on the way and bought some food because I didn't think you'd have any, and I was right." She tugged me along into the house, chattering all the way, while I struggled to answer her dozen questions and come to grips with the fact of her presence. In a daze, I let her sit me at the table while she punched holes in two cans of Schlitz beer and handed me one.

"Ahh," she sighed, after taking a giant gulp. "So, what's going on?"

"I can't believe you're –" I started, but she interrupted me.

"I had to get out." She looked around at the kitchen and through the doorway to the living room, then sighed again, a long, moaning exhale. "Oh honey." She covered her face with her hands, covertly wiping at tears. "This place, everywhere I look, he's here. We were so happy back then. God, I miss him." She took another swig of beer and lit a cigarette, blew a cloud of smoke at the ceiling and wiped carefully under her eyes with the side of her thumb, a mascara-preserving gesture so familiar my heart almost burst.

"I'm really glad you're here, Mom," I said, though I wasn't entirely sure about it. "How are things back home?"

240

She told me about my sister Charlotte, who had managed to persuade our mother to let her stay alone in the apartment for the last week before school started up again. The show which she'd so casually mentioned back in June had been a major retrospective of three French painters, one of whom was my mother, and the weeks leading up to it had been a stress of re-framing, paperwork, and "about a million phone calls," right up to the day of the event. In addition, my father's business dealings had been left in a somewhat disorganized state owing to his habit of making deals with a handshake or the trust of old friendship.

"Luckily Christos (that was my father's accountant, lawyer, sometime collaborator and best friend) took care of most of it. He was in and out of the apartment packing things and rooting around for paperwork while I was doing the same with my own stuff. We would sometimes meet in the kitchen to have a good cry before going back to it." She laughed a little, but teared up again. "He was the one who suggested I come here. But he didn't know what a museum it is, and neither did I." She reached across the table and took my hand. "I love that you thought of it, Elli. The house feels alive again, though it's a little painful for me right now." She talked about the summers when Charlotte and I were little, how we spent evenings out on the bluff, my father barbecuing on a grill he'd made from piled up stones; and the map in the bedroom, which made her eyes fill again as she recited the islands' names from memory, ticking them off on her fingers. She remarked on the dock, the boat tied to it and the fact that everywhere had so many more trees. "My god, the shady streets now! It used to be a dry, almost treeless farmland around Barley Neck, and so quiet. Lots more tourists now, I see."

"When did you get here?"

241

"About half an hour before you," she said, wiping under her eyes again. "I told Moony to just drop me off. He said you'd be along fairly soon. I've been sitting on the sofa, remembering. Did you notice it still smells like your father?"

I nodded, remembering my first night there, curled up under a dusty sheet with my nose jammed into the crevice of arm and cushion. How miserable I had been then, so freshly wounded, a helpless little girl who didn't even know how to use a can opener. I snorted at the memory, and lit a cigarette.

"You smoke," my mother remarked.

"Yep."

"And drink," she added, taking another sip of her beer.

"I do now," I said, toasting her with my can. She smiled, and we had a good little moment.

"So, what about you? Moony says you're doing very well. He says you're a competent fisherman, and that you've made friends with some people on Sipson's Island." She craned her neck so she could get a glimpse of the bay through the tiny kitchen window.

"I have, and I am, sort of. Flounder is my speciality." I smiled.

"He says you've been painting, too."

I was hoping it wouldn't come up just yet, that I'd have time to scramble out to the studio and turn over the tree paintings, cover up the wall drawing somehow. I wasn't at all ready to let my accomplished mother see my naive scratchings, no matter what Martin said. "Yes, I have," I said, hoping she wouldn't pursue the subject, at least until I could do some sorting and fine-tuning.

"I noticed a well-worn path to the studio. You out there?"

242

"Yeah."

"Oh Elli, that's wonderful. I'm glad the place is getting used. I designed it myself, you know. I was very sad to leave."

She must have sensed that I was reluctant to talk about what I was doing; it was likely a feeling she was quite familiar with. She asked about the owner of Sipson's, the man with the Motherwell, and *'A Swim at Pochet'*.

"What's his name, Meyer?"

"Yes. Martin Meyer." I did not want to go into that story, particularly right then, when my stinking uniform was beginning to chafe at the waist and under my arms. I needed a swim.

"Mom, I have to change out of this horrible dress. I'm just going to go jump in the water for a few minutes to wash off the sweat, OK? I'll be right back."

"Of course honey. I'll watch from the bluff."

When at last I dove into the water, savoring the high tide and my ability to flap around without hitting bottom, I waved to my mother and settled in for a few minutes of peaceful water-treading. I told myself not to panic, that her presence was a good thing. I was proud of my work in the studio, and my mother would react as she felt and the worst would be that I'd learn something from her critique. I don't know how I would explain my 'process' to her if it came up, because I certainly was not going to say anything about the virtually independent behavior of my hand. My most anxious thought was that the next day was Friday, and Martin was due at four o'clock as we'd arranged. Now it would be a momentous meeting between him and the creator of the painting which started him on his metaphysical quest, and not just a simple visit to pick out a picture to buy. I dove under, wishing I could stay there for much longer than a breath's worth of time. I reached out and held on to some eelgrass fronds to keep from floating up, and let myself undulate as their extension in the water washing over us. That's how I would take tomorrow, I decided, I would go with the flow, as the saying goes. I had my secret power, and I would soon discover where it had taken me.

That evening was a memorable one, not because anything momentous happened, or involved anyone other than the two of us, but it was the first time my mother and I spent time together as adults, a rite of passage for everyone if they are fortunate. As afternoon waned my mother suggested we collect some mussels for supper. She had surprised me with a small *flamiche*, a leek pie from the bakery near our apartment, a treat she knew was a favorite of mine. She brought it in her purse all the way from Paris in a little lacquered box my father used to have on his desk. We rowed across the channel to a place she remembered off Namequoit Point. I was skeptical about finding them in the same spot after all that time but apparently, like all of us, mussels stay put if provided with everything they need. We gathered enough for a feast, then jumped into the boat which she insisted on rowing and did so expertly despite not having touched an oar in sixteen years. We steamed them in beer and brought the pot outside with the flamiche, and ate at the bluff's edge as my parents had done in the old days. We talked for hours about my father, telling stories and laughing at his eccentric business model yet admiring his dextrous bargaining style, and we agreed that above all his open curiosity and love for handmade things had brought much beauty into our lives. After a few beers I told her about sitting out there in his hat and moth-eaten suit until it fell apart, and she told me that she had not been able to get rid of a single article of his clothing. "Even his undershorts," she laughed.

Eventually we got around to discussing the owner of Sipson's Island, since we'd been looking over at it all evening. She had asked me long before if *'A Swim at Pochet'* was hanging there, so she knew it was somewhere in New York, but she wanted to know more about this 'mysterious collector," as she called Martin.

"I don't know him that well," I lied. I was not about to describe the hours we'd spent sitting in the dark woods under a tree together, waiting for a ghost and discussing life. She'd told me that she was only staying for a week, and I decided immediately that I would try to keep all mention of anything supernatural out of our conversations.

"There were no houses on the island, last I remember," she said. "What's out there now?"

I briefly described the two buildings, Ray and Sal's handmade cabin with its cascade of indoor plants and oil drum woodstove, Martin's wall of windows, the spiral staircase and the big willow in the front yard. "Do you remember my telling you about about the Motherwell painting?"

"Oh yes, *Afternoon in Barcelona.* To think of it hanging in the middle of Pleasant Bay! Your father would have been flabbergasted." I told her the story of my first visit, describing to Martin the water stain on our little post card version, and his asking if it improved the image, which she loved. Soon after that she yawned, and stood up.

"I think it might be time for me to go to bed," she mumbled. "Suddenly I'm done."

Earlier in the evening while she cooked I had made up my childhood bed and cleaned up her bedroom so she could wake up to the view and, after a pass through the house touching things and poking around the book shelves for something to read, she wandered in there. Then, with a peck on my cheek, she shut the door and retired.

After I cleaned the supper dishes I went out to the studio. I was aware that my mother had diplomatically avoided asking to see what I'd been working on, or going out to her old place there in the cedars, which must have taken considerable self-control. As an artist she must know how sensitive these matters were, and she allowed me time to arrange things as I wanted them. I stood in the doorway surveying my work, trying to see it not only through my mother's eyes, but through Martin's. I started to line up the tree paintings against the wall in a pleasing order, but there were three in particular I thought excellent, and those I taped up on the one wall I hadn't covered with graphite. I started to make little corrections on them, but stopped abruptly, remembering my underwater decision to let things stand as they were. Besides, I was exhausted. I turned out the lights and left, thinking only of the uniform I had yet to rinse out for the next day.

In the morning I left my mother sleeping soundly and rode off to work. I was distracted all day by thoughts of the momentous meeting about to take place that afternoon between Martin and my mother, and moved through the day in a kind of stupor, letting Becca nudge me forward, room by room. As we pulled sheets from the big industrial dryers and folded them into sharp-creased bundles I talked a little about it, which helped, until she said "Jesus, Elli. This is like the most important day of your life so far, huh?"

Maybe so, I thought on the ride home, but here we go. I hoped Martin would show up with some wine, at least, to ease things along. When I coasted to a stop at the house there was no sign of life. The two chairs were still parked on the bluff with a full ashtray on the ground between them, but when I opened the screen door I found a note on the table weighed down by a quahog shell:

Hi honey
I forgot to tell you –I'm visiting an old friend and I won't be back for supper. Hope that's OK!
Love, Mom

ps: Peeked in the studio. All I can say is, Wow!

Well, I thought, my life just got easier by about a hundred percent. I amended that by subtracting thirty because I had yet to get through someone seeing, judging and buying a piece of my artwork, but that I could handle. I climbed down to the dock, stripped off my uniform and dove in. As I rubbed cool saltwater into my skin I wondered who my mother might be seeing, but I couldn't think of a single person. I ran back up, hosed off the salt with fresh, and went inside to change. The place had obviously been cleaned, and looked the picture of a summer cottage waiting for tenants. On the table sat a jar of black-eyed susans perfectly centered on a doily I'd never seen before. The floorboards in the living room had a sheen that looked like wax, though I didn't have any that I knew of. The kitchen was spotless, even the windowpanes were missing their scrim of dried salt spray. I had no idea I had been so slovenly, and silently thanked my mother for bringing the place back to life. I snapped on the radio and rifled through the closet for something clean, pulling out the white linen shorts and pink blouse I'd bought all those weeks ago and never had occasion to wear. A minute later, not wanting to

247

suggest pecuniary motives, I changed into the graphite-and-paint smeared cutoffs and tshirt I usually had on out in the studio. But then I looked at myself in the bathroom mirror and changed again. Finally I went out to the bluff, sat down and lit a cigarette.

Twenty minutes later I heard the distinct purr of Martin's Mercedes as it pulled into the driveway. He got out holding a single blue hydrangea and a bottle of white wine.

"Nice to be here again," he said, holding out the flower.

He too had been cleaned up from the last time I saw him. Gone were the streaks of greasy yellow in his hair, and he was freshly shaven. He was wearing one of his beautiful linen shirts and a pair of huaraches. We were a little shy with each other, and a few moments went by in silence.

"Come inside with me while I get some water for this," I said, twirling the hydrangea. He followed me into the house and stood looking at the little Ria Bang Overtons when I went into the kitchen for a vase and glasses for the wine.

"I met her earlier," he called out, casually.

I shot to the doorway. "What? How did you . . .?"

"On the way here I stopped to drop something at Theo's place and there she was, sitting on his deck with a cup of coffee. He introduced us." Martin smiled enigmatically, lifted a trinket from the bookshelf and pretended to study it.

Of course. I had forgotten about my mother's friendship with Theo. I started to laugh. "So, did you freak out?"

"No, I did not do that," he chuckled. "But nearly."

He went on to tell me about the meeting, which was brief and a little formal because, he said, he thought gushing was undignified, and because the surprise made him suffer a temporary tongue-tie. She recognized his name as the owner of one of her pieces and they had a brief exchange about the painting, but of course my mother could not know of its significance and besides, Martin said, Theo was giving him 'get lost' looks.

"But you didn't tell me she was coming," he said, leaning against the back of the sofa.

"I didn't know. She was here when I got off work yesterday."

"It was an honor to meet her. She is a great artist." He stared off into space for a few moments, then said, "And now, you. May I have a tour of your work?"

I dipped back into the kitchen for a corkscrew, then we went outside, around the corner and down the path to the studio. Inside, I busied myself with the wine, dribbled some into a glass and handed it to Martin, who stood in front of the wall by the door, the first one I had covered with graphite marks. I perched on the arm of one of the green chairs, smoking and watching as he scanned the surface, first closely, then from a step or two back. Finally I sat down and willed myself to stop sucking nervously on my cigarette.

"Truly remarkable," Martin mumbled. "How long have you been at it?"

I thought back. I told him about the first paintings, the child's watercolor set and my naive attempts, a month or so before, at portrayal. I pulled a picture from the pile on the table, one of a fish with the sky reflected in its scales, and gazed at it a moment, remembering. I handed it to him. He looked at it for an instant, then at me. It was a penetrating, almost accusatory stare. He held up the paper.

"You went from this," he said, "to this" he gestured at the wall, "in a month?"

I shrugged. "Yes."

Martin resumed his tour of the studio walls, then stepped over to where I'd taped up the red tree paintings. He stood for a long time with arms crossed high on his chest, hands in his armpits, as if he were watching a high-stakes poker game or a close horse race. He jiggled a little on his heels, a trace of the jazzed behavior from before. "God, they're beautiful," he said softly.

"Thank you." I wanted to say more, to admit that an automaton guided my hand, which he would understand perfectly, but I did not. If it constituted a lie or deception I wasn't sure. I had already suffered a nagging round of moral self examination that day at work over whether it was ethical to claim a work of art as my own when it had seemingly been done almost solely by my hand, but I settled on the fact of indisputable ownership of that hand. Another reason for not going into it was that I was still so reluctant to stir up any talk of wave collapsing or alternate universes during this visit that I kept my mouth shut. Instead I described my observations about negative space and experimenting to capture its fleeting element, and so Martin did, too.

"I feel a kind of mysticism in the red, a passion of course, but the language you have found here to express the essence, the dynamism out there . . ." He looked through the big window. The cedars practically crowded the little building, as if leaning in to eavesdrop. "It hardly seems the product of a mammalian mind. They are speaking and you have translated for us. I don't know how to put it any better than that. I don't think I'll ever look at a cedar in the same way again."

"Thanks," I said again, lamely. I hadn't been thinking along the same lines, but no matter. He didn't ask me to tell him more about how I did it or what I saw that gave me the impetus in the first place. He picked up the rest of the paintings from the floor and sat down in the other green chair, studying them one by one, sipping wine and making little delighted grunts. I looked at them over his shoulder and, maybe because I was seeing the work through someone else's eyes, a third truth occurred to me: what if the power I thought of as a foreign entity operating my hand was actually my very own mind, and that this was a bona fide gift? Because it came so easily to me I had assumed my skill was magic, supernatural, like my seeing John Sipson. But now, as I looked at each painting with different eyes, I recalled my vision, the conception of threads connecting everything. Maybe it really was my own, like Moony's realization that his scholastic abilities were not magic, simply dormant intelligence brought to life.

After a while Martin laid the paintings on the coffee table and raised his glass to me. "Congratulations," he said. Did I see a tiny edge of incredulity in his face, or had I read it wrong?

"I'm so happy you like them."

"Now," he said, turning in his chair and pointing to one of the three taped to the wall. "I would like to buy that one, if I may. What do you say to five hundred dollars?"

I knew he wasn't joking but I suggested it anyway. I was truly overcome, and tried to stall by making light.

"No, I'm quite serious," he said, looking over at the painting. "And I hope you can use some of it to buy materials for when you run out of walls." He smiled.

"Thank you very much," I said. "I'm honored."

"What does your mother think of this?" He waved his hand at the room.

"I don't know. We haven't had a chance to talk about it yet."

Martin said he had to go to town to make arrangements for storing the Calder sculpture which had arrived and was lying wrapped up on the back of a flatbed truck. The local boatyard was going to get it out to the island on a barge along with the materials for its erection. I followed him to his car, where he pulled his checkbook from the glove compartment. We sat at the porch table in the late afternoon stillness while he wrote. From inside the radio began to play one of my favorites, Bob Dylan singing the beautiful *To Ramona.* I will never forget those two minutes sitting there listening, watching as the late-day orange light traced the contours of the porch, the rocks lined up on the bluff, the chairs, the dry grass. And closer, to illumine the froth of white hair on the crown of Martin's head as he neatly signed his name.

"There," he said, ripping out the check and handing it to me. "May I be the first in a long line of your collectors." I bowed my head and thanked him again, mumbling embarrassment into my blouse. On the radio the host said, "Let's have a little more of that," followed by the call letters.

"Hey," Martin said, pointing into the house. "That radio station –I forgot to tell you. During Sylvie's stay in Boston they offered her a job, and she took it. She starts the middle of next month."

"That's wonderful," I said, not at all surprised. "She'll be so good there." What a perfect match, I thought. Lucky woman. "But, what about Ray, and . . .?"

"Remains to be seen, doesn't it. The war –it's ruining lives in so many ways we don't think about. But life goes

252

on, is what Ray said about it." He shook his head. "I don't know how to feel."

Nothing stays the same, so follow your instincts and change, too –wasn't that the essence of what we'd just heard at the end of *To Ramona*?

"Anyhow, there's going to be a goodbye party this weekend. Monday, to be precise. It's Labor Day, the end of summer. Do you have the day off?"

"Yup." Sunday was my last day.

"So, come. And by all means, bring your mother," he said, grinning as he opened the car door and got in. I waved him off down the driveway and went back to the studio. I was glowing with joy, the five hundred dollar check still in my hand. I laid it on the table and went over to stand in front of the painting Martin had bought. How would he frame it, I wondered. It would be a shame to put it under glass and lose some of the immediate surface luminosity. In that light it looked so fresh I had to touch it, and pressed my finger against a patch of saturated red. The memory of Martin's first studio visit came flooding back to me in an instant and I turned over my finger. Sure enough, the tip was red.

This time I didn't run down the road in panic, but slowly lowered myself into one of the green chairs, wiped my finger off on the wine bottle's label, and poured myself another glass. I lit a cigarette and stared at the little smear for a while, then started to laugh.

Chapter Thirteen

That night my mother arrived home late. I was lying in bed reading when I heard a car pull into the driveway, then a giggling goodbye from her, and the front door latch as it hit the plate. She came tiptoeing into my room and sat on the end of my bed.

"Oh, Elli. What a day I had. Theo and I have just gone over the last sixteen years of our lives. Did you know we met when we were only fourteen?"

"Yes. He told me. Summer camp, right?"

"That's right." She smiled. A dreamy, wine-infused look settled on her face, one I'd never seen before. It was a little unsettling, but I said, "Tell me about it."

"I will, but not right now, all right? I'm exhausted. I'm going to wash my face and fall onto that swaybacked mattress." She pulled herself up by gripping the bed's footboard and added, "I promise I'll tell you the whole story tomorrow." She dipped low to give me a kiss goodnight, then turned to go.

"Goodnight," I said, and closed my book. I lay there listening to her splashing around in the bathroom. My feet hung over the sides of the too-small kid's bed, and I could tell one of them was asleep, so I pulled it to me. Just then she came back into the room.

"I forgot to say the most important thing of all," she announced.

"What?"

"I cannot believe what I saw out in the studio. Is it really you?"

"Yeah."

"The work is absolutely marvelous, Elli. Fascinating. Why have you not mentioned it before? Where did it come from? You never expressed any interest in painting, and now you have made some work that is downright spiritual. Layers of . . .of . . ." She waved her hands, searching for the word.

"Thanks, Mom. I'll tell you tomorrow, I promise."

"All right. Elli, I'm very impressed, and proud." She gazed down at me, swaying ever so slightly and shaking her head. "Tomorrow," she said.

"Tomorrow." I had to work at eight, but after. I made a mental note to buy ingredients for cornbread on the way home, then fell abruptly to sleep.

My mother was still in bed when I crept out the next morning, and again missing when I returned home from work, and when I went down to the dock for my daily swim I saw that the boat was gone. I scanned the water expecting to spot her nearby, but she was nowhere to be found. After a couple of hours passed without any sign of her I began to worry. I knew she was good with the boat and familiar with the bay's currents, but I'd also learned that even in summer they could be stronger than expected, that all kinds of little mishaps were possible. She'd been living in a city for a long time, and maybe had forgotten. I distracted myself by making a pan of cornbread, but checked the water every fifteen minutes. The tide was almost all the way out by then, revealing the grasses where quahogs were collected, and indeed a couple of people were wading around the area, but my mother wasn't one of them. By seven I was getting jumpy, partly because I had no way to go and find her, since she had the boat. I had just decided to walk to Moony's place to see if I could enlist his help, and had climbed down to the shore to go that way when I heard a car in the driveway. I ran back up the hill to see her bending over the bed of a beat-up truck, lifting out a big flat package. Theo stood by the door, his arms full of grocery bags. He smiled when he saw me, and said something to my mother, who yelled hello.

I let them inside in a whirlwind of elation, hilarity and another trip out to the truck for more stuff. "Oh, Elli. Theo took me to Provincetown!" She beamed at him while he piled bags on the kitchen counter. "I haven't been there in so long. What a difference! But it's still the same." She and Theo looked at each other and burst out laughing. "That's for you," she said, pointing to the package from the truck bed. "You need it. Now, I got stuff for supper. Ready made from Cookie's, the best Portuguese soup in the world!" She bustled around in the kitchen unpacking bags and setting the table. Theo and I stood around feeling useless until he suggested bringing the package out to the studio, where he said it belonged. He took it from me and I followed. As we walked the path he hesitated a couple of times, taking in the scenery. "Things have grown," he observed, then, "It used to be a sort of clubhouse for us." Did he mean my mother and himself? I didn't want to ask. When we got inside Theo set the package down. "Well. I have to get back," he said. "It was nice to see you again, Elli."

"You're not staying to eat?"

"No. I have plans, but thank you." We said goodbye and he walked back over to the house while I ripped paper off the package. Inside was a large wooden box full of tubes of oil paint. I rifled through them to see what colors my mother had picked. The basics: cadmium red, ultramarine blue, and cadmium yellow all in duplicate, burnt sienna and ochre, white, plus a huge tub of gesso. A fat bundle of assorted brushes lay in the box as well, and a roll of canvas. In the bottom were a dozen sheets of thick, handmade paper. I also found a box of charcoal sticks and more tiny tubes of watercolor.

"This other thing is a big roll of paper you can tape up on the walls for more drawing," my mother said from the doorway, pushing a long wrapped tube through the door. "And Moony can make stretcher frames for you. He used to do it for me." She stood outside looking in, nodding thoughtfully. "I think this place must be yours, now," she added. "You certainly are making good use of it." She stepped in and spun around, looking at everything on the walls, then at me in my nest of paper and art supplies in the middle of the floor.

"God, Mom, this is unbelievable!" I was already planning how to set up the space to store my supplies, and mentally reviving an easel design I figured I could make from some boards lying under the house. Was it real?

"I need some education, I think," I said spontaneously, since suddenly it seemed this thing was serious.

"Maybe. But maybe not. Let's go in. I heated up the soup and I'm glad to see you made cornbread."

"OK." I was starving, and very happy. I grabbed my mother as she turned to leave and gave her a bone-crushing hug. "Thanks, Mom."

She started down the steps to the path. I shut off the lights and followed.

"Your work deserves to be pursued," she said, picking her way through the ferns and poison ivy.

"So I've been told," I said. "Yesterday Martin bought one of my efforts."

"What? Martin Meyer? Mister Sipson's Island?"

"That one."

'Wow," said my mother, and whistled. "That's big." She made me tell her everything, from fooling around with my old paint set to buying the paper and tubes of real watercolor and my discovery of red-soaked paper, to finding the graphite crayon and abandoning color, to Martin seeing the work by accident and his comments, to the writing of the the check. I even talked about *To Ramona* and the orange light outlining everything that evening. As we ate I added more –about Martin's history, about Freya, the Calder and the entombment plan.

"Is it me or is that a little strange?" she asked.

The soup was delicious, pungent and full of beans, linguica and torn kale leaves. I was wondering how it would be with fish and suddenly remembered the missing boat. I said it to my mother.

"Oh yes, I forgot to mention. We took it to the landing. Moony is going to put a heftier transom on it so you can bolt a motor on there."

"What?" I couldn't handle any more riches. I had become used to my simple life, but I suppose my mother

258

would not have believed it, and maybe even felt a little guilty having left me to fend on my own.

"He says it's a good idea, and I think so too. I always had one when we lived here. Just a little thing, Elli. It's easy, and you'll love it. It will mean you can get back and forth to Sipson's to see your friends."

I was bowled over. In the space of two days I had money, art supplies and transportation, and only one more day of work. I thanked my mother for all her generous gifts. She hadn't once mentioned the fact of my dropping out of college, the wasted expense. I expected to go back; it was a vague yet persistent intention, but I had done nothing about it because of my other involvements. It didn't seem to be as important to her as it was to my father, and since she had not mentioned it and instead loaded me with the supplies I needed to occupy me until well into the next semester, I didn't bring it up. I thought I could stay until then, and start up again later.

"What about school?" she said, right on cue.

"I was thinking I could hold off for a semester, stay here and go when it's too cold."

"Honey, it'll be too cold in about two months." She suggested I come home for the winter, regroup and decide about school from a safe, warm place. "Here or there, but this time with more intention," she said, nodding in the direction of the studio. "You could help Christos. He needs it. And we can find a space for you to paint."

We left it there and moved on to other subjects, but a plan had been suggested that didn't sound at all bad, providing I could come back to Cape Cod for the summer.

Becca and I had a little ceremony after we finished the last load of laundry the next day. The motel had officially closed an hour before, as soon as the last guests left, and the owner came into the back to tally up and give us our final pay. He gave us each a fifty dollar bonus, which was generous and which he tried to use to extract from us a promise to come back again next year, but we left him with 'maybe,' then went down the street for ice cream sundaes. We walked with them along the railroad track a little way out of town and burned our uniforms in the shale with a stash of kerosene Becca brought from home. I was sad to part with her, but she was at the beginning of a new love affair and high on life so I tried not to cry when we hugged goodbye. Instead I told her I would see her soon, though I doubted we'd run into each other again. She hung around with a crowd of surfers who looked down their noses at anyone vaguely resembling a hippie, which I suppose I did then, purely because of my spartan lifestyle and my mother's old blouses.

When I got home I found my mother sitting on the bluff with Moony. They beckoned me over and pointed down to the dock, where the skiff was tied, bumping gently against one of the pilings. On the stern was a small, shiny red outboard motor. The rubber handle on the tiller had a pink ribbon tied to it.

"Happy early birthday," said my mother, beaming up at me.

"It's a ten horsepower, so it should get you over to Sipson's in about ten minutes," added Moony with a wink.

"If you go at full speed," said my mother.

"Which you will. It's not brand new, but it runs like it is." Moony smiled at her.

I ran down the steps to the dock to see it. A jazzy white stripe ran around its middle, with 'Johnson' spelled out above, and a sort of Spartan helmet detail on the top. I called up to them, "I need lessons!"

Moony came down to join me as I examined the thing. I was remembering the day I met Ray and Sylvie and the smoking, backfiring, rusty version clamped to their boat. It had seemed easy enough. Moony asked if I wanted to learn immediately. I nodded and hopped aboard. After half an hour we were zooming toward the narrows with me at the helm. Moony was right; it was easy. Starting was merely a matter of doing things in the right order, and the only other important thing was how to negotiate the wake of another boat. Revving the engine with a twist of my wrist was a thrill, and after nearly dumping us a couple of times with some reckless turns, we settled into a steady ride. After we passed my mother waving enthusiastically from the bluff and headed inland, I said, "I saw John Sipson again."

"Really? Where?"

I told him about the sighting in the turnip field the night Sandy drove me home from the Turk's Head. I also mentioned that because of her the skull had been returned, albeit in pieces.

"Oh, that's good." Moony nodded. "Very good."

As we turned and putted up into Meetinghouse Pond where his boat was pulled up on the shore, I described the Calder sculpture and Martin's plans for interring the skull underneath. I left out the part about Freya's bones.

"It'll be interesting to hear that report from John Sipson," said Moony, chuckling. "I hope I get to."

I maneuvered the boat over beside Moony's so he could check it. "So, what's your plan," he mumbled as he stomped the anchor deeper in the mud. "Going back to Paris?" He didn't look at me, but ran his hand along the gunwale of his boat, trying to be nonchalant.

"No, not yet," I said. "Not until it gets too cold."

He looked up, surprised. "Good. I'll bring some wood over, show you how to work the fireplace. You'll need it."

I conjured up the idyllic scene of me sitting in front of a fire wearing a pair of thick socks, a huge pad of paper on my knees and my crayon in hand. On the radio would be Leonard Cohen singing *So Long Marianne*.

"You can also show me where to find scallops." I added to the image a pan of them simmering in butter on hot hearth stones, or however one cooked in a fireplace.

Moony jumped back into the boat, grinning. "Yup."

We took off again in barely enough water for the propeller to function. A corkscrew of mud churned out behind until Moony lifted the shaft a few inches and held it that way until we hit a deeper channel. When we passed the place where John Sipson went to find whelk, we looked at each other in silent conspiracy, not having to say anything but both pleased we'd have continued opportunity to talk about him.

My mother was still standing on the bluff as I swung the skiff alongside the dock and cut the engine. I wasn't sure how much I would be using it to visit Sipson's Island, but it would be thrilling to be able to cruise around the bay not only with effortless speed, but facing forward. I felt a surge of affection for her as I ran up the steps, and at the top I slammed myself into her arms for another hug of gratitude that was more than for the engine or the art supplies, or the lack of judgment regarding my dropping out of college. It was for her trust in me —maybe originally a form of neglect given the circumstances, but I also recognized the bravery involved in letting go. If she hadn't, I might very well have been back in Paris never having driven a boat, caught a fish, baked cornbread, ridden my bike at night through a swarm of fireflies, let a tidal current pull me, collapsed a particle wave or seen a ghost.

Moony waited until we parted, looking out across the water at Hog Island, eyeing the tips of grass emerging as the tide dropped further.

"I'll see you two later," he said. "I might go and get some clams."

My mother kissed him lightly on the cheek. "Thanks, Moony. I'll see you on Wednesday, if not before." Her flight home was that night.

"I hope it'll be Monday, at the party," said Moony.

"Party?" She looked at me.

"Yeah, for Labor Day. Also a goodbye to a friend. I haven't had time to mention it to you yet. Over on Sipson's. Want to?"

"Oh yes. Absolutely." We could take the boat, I thought with satisfaction.

Labor Day Monday dawned in a late summer haze. It was dry but smelled of rain from the day before, when a steady drizzle had kept my mother and me inside for most of it, supposedly the northern end of a tropical cyclone that was threatening Florida. She helped me set up the studio in a more practical arrangement, and we dragged the boards from under the house for Moony to fix into an easel. We sat in the green chairs all Sunday afternoon talking about my father, about painting, about Cape Cod in their early years. She borrowed my drawing pad and dazzled me with some basic color theory, a little chart which still hangs over my desk.

I caught a whiff of something else as I lay in bed luxuriating about not having to be anywhere. It was the sweet, earthy scent of decaying wood, lichens in full ripeness, the tipover of the natural world into Fall. The bay is even more sublime at that time of year. In late September its waters take on a purplish tone from the sun's more oblique angle, and even seem to move a little sluggishly for a week or two before snapping to life for the crisp days ahead. Wild asters also bloom purple, and blend with deep yellow goldenrod, burgundy sumac leaves and the green-silver particular to dusty miller, to compose a striking fringe along the shore and lining the beach road. Out by the studio poison ivy leaves snaked their way up nearly every tree trunk and were already beginning to turn. I planned to do another series of red-stained paper drawings featuring their brilliant crimson against black pine bark.

Late in the morning I ventured into town for some food to bring to the party, but found everything except the liquor store closed. My mother had jotted down about ten items on a slip of paper, but I couldn't buy any of them, nor wine because of my age, which she had forgotten about. The town was deserted, and completely silent. It was an eerie sight after all the bustle of summer –the endless car honking, tourist chatter, slamming screen doors, and music from transistor radios. I coasted to a stop in the center of the crossroads and stood there, stunned. It was as if someone had pulled the plug not just on the clam shacks and souvenir shops but the whole town. It seemed deflated, emptied of all life.

"Elli, hey!" I turned to find Sandy standing in the doorway of the Foc'sle beckoning to me. I walked the bike over.

"I didn't know it would be this drastic," I said.

"Yup. Weird, huh?" She scanned up and down the road, yawning, which was unusual for her. Even the little fairy hanging in her cleavage was still, as if bored with the situation. Labor Day was certainly misnamed, I thought.

"I came to get some food for the party, but everything's closed."

"Oh well, help me for a sec here, will you? I have plenty, but I need to get it into the car."

She had three pans of stuffed clams, loaves of crusty bread, a bucket of the Foc'sle's famous chowder, and a cake. We wrestled a keg of beer into the passenger seat.

"How many people are you expecting?" I asked, eyeing it. I had the idea it would be just us, Moony and Joyce and a few others. Becca told me the restaurants all had their own season-end parties planned. She was going to one in Provincetown, which she said would probably go on for days.

"I don't know. Maybe a crowd." She seemed distracted, not at all her enthusiastic self, especially on a day for celebrating.

"Are you OK?" I asked her as we shoved the door closed on the keg.

"Yeah, mostly," she said, staring down at her toenails, which were painted pearly pink. She scuffed one foot against the other, scratching the perfect job. "To tell the truth I'm worried about what will happen when Sylvie's gone. I don't know how to cook, for one thing."

I knew they were used to some high-quality fare over on the island because of Sylvie's skills, but I had also observed Ray and Sal being pretty handy in the kitchen. "Don't worry," I said, draping my arm across her shoulders. "It will work itself out. It'll just be different at first."

"Mm-hm." She wasn't convinced. "I'm scared," she said. I saw a tear dribble down her cheek and gave her a reassuring squeeze. "Ray is talking about going with her, hiding out in the city rather than here. It's much more dangerous. And without Ray, Sal can't keep it together. I know him."

"They must be talking about it. It'll take a while, that's all."

She sighed. "What is Sal gonna do all day when I'm at work? In a month or so Martin will be gone, his house closed up, and Sal will be out there by himself. I don't like it." She let out an anguished moan and mopped her eyes with a rag she used for wiping off tables. I gave her a little speech about not jumping to conclusions, that it was a wait-and-see situation, that the war made everything difficult, and that Martin needed Sal and would surely make a provision for the new situation.

She blew a noseful into the rag, then looked at me over it. "You're right, Elli. I should be brave. Things will work out, won't they?"

"Yes." I wasn't sure about Ray and Sal getting away with dodging the draft, but for some reason I felt Sandy would be fine. Meanwhile, there was a party to get to, and I had to ride home and give my mother the news about the closed-up town. "I gotta go," I said.

"Don't worry about the food. We have plenty." Sandy skipped around to the driver's side of the car. "Shall I pick you up?"

I told her about the new engine on the boat.

"Cool," she said. She blew me a kiss. "Later."

Chapter Fourteen

We arrived at Sipson's Island that afternoon to find a dozen boats like ours already tied to the dock or pulled up onto the strip of sand alongside. I tied up to the nearest dinghy and we clambered laboriously over two others. I was balancing yet another pan of cornbread which miraculously made it to the beach in one piece. Joyce saw us and strolled over. When I introduced my mother she grabbed her hand.

"Pleased to meet you. We love Elli. How long are you staying?" My mother was led away while I found a spot to deposit the cornbread on the same long table I remembered from the clambake, the dogfight, and Leon's bit hand. So many things had happened that night. I stood gazing at the table for a few minutes, remembering. I hoped this party would not be so eventful, that my mother would not be too shocked when the joints were passed around. I scanned the crowd hoping to spot Theo, who would be a welcome companion for her among strangers, but he was not there. I saw several people I knew from the Turk's Head or other dinner parties, and spotted Moony sitting on a blanket with Joyce and my mother, pouring wine. At a honk from across the narrows, Sal jumped into a boat, started the engine and zoomed off to fetch more guests. I put the pan on the table and went over to sit. Moony winked at me as he made room on the blanket.

"This is marvelous," said my mother. "I never thought I'd see Sipson's alive with people." She glanced up the hill. "I hope I get the chance to see Mr. Meyer's house," she hinted, nudging me. "Especially the Motherwell. I can't imagine it." Behind her I watched Sandy and a few others fooling around in the water. They waded against the incoming tide for a hundred feet or so, then let the current carry them back to where they started. Whooping with laughter, they assumed various comical floating positions while trying to hold cigarettes, joints, or beer cans above the water.

"No party at the coffeehouse?" I asked Joyce.

"Nah, everyone's here. I don't feel like it, anyhow. The season is over, thank god." She slung an arm over Moony's shoulders, which made him glance around to see if anyone was looking. I wondered how recently their affair had begun, and if Moony told her John Sipson stories. Joyce swept her sphinx eyes over the scene on the beach while Moony and my mother started a long conversation about Parisian fish markets; what was available and how it was presented. I watched a beautiful old dory approach and then head to the north side of the island, where I knew Martin had a private dock. I could just make out Theo sitting in the

268

stern with Min perched on the bow seat as the boat disappeared behind the trees. I snuck a peek at my mother to see if she'd noticed, but she was deep into fish talk with Moony. Ray appeared on the beach arm in arm with Sylvie who held a big, golden-crusted pie against her chest, balanced on the cast, which was now painted all over with red hearts. They strolled down to the table, stopping to talk with people along the way. I wanted to go and say hello but stayed where I was, partially hidden behind Joyce, savoring the scene and and the wine and feeling a contentedness I hadn't experienced since I was a small child and allowed to sit on my father's lap after supper, watching the antics of grownups. The sand was warm and the music was sweet, some country thing I didn't know but liked. I asked Moony.

"Hank Williams," he said, then turned back to my mother. One couple started to dance in the sand, a sort of sloppy waltz to Hank's sharp guitar chords and clear tenor. Others joined in, and several of the ever-present posse of dogs chased each other around legs to the loopy violin refrain. Sandy and her group came running out of the water still laughing, shivering and spraying droplets, boogying along to the music with the others. The song ended and another began, Hank singing '*I'll Never Get Out of This World Alive.*' Moony mouthed the words in an undertone. Joyce kicked off her slippers, stood up and swayed in her long skirt. I was surprised to hear this music, stuff that at Bard I was told was the sound of the enemy, the red-neck hippie haters. A gust of wind sprayed sand into the crowd, briefly interrupting the dance. I looked south to see the tops of pines shimmying along too, then the wind died as quickly as it came up.

I wondered if Martin would appear. I hadn't yet taken his check to the bank because I liked the look of it lying there on my work table amid the detritus of the job. I wanted to thank Martin again, tell him about my plan to stay, about my mother's gift of painting supplies. I was looking forward to sitting in the green chairs with him discussing what makes a work of art. I wanted to tell him about my bountifully magic hand. I wanted to ask about his experience with the painting he bought from me.

The music changed and everyone wandered over to the food table, surrounding it to fill up paper plates. Joyce and Moony got up too, leaving me and my mother.

"You aren't hungry?" I said.

"Come with me. I'm shy," she said, which surprised me. Another first, I thought. Just then Theo came up behind us, followed by Min holding a platter of sliced cheese and salami. My mother gave Theo a big hug and stuck her hand out as Theo introduced Min, who held it briefly, smiled, then took off for the table. Theo spread out a blanket next to ours and sat down.

"Well, this is funny," he said to my mother.

"Us on Sipson's again," she answered.

"Older, yes, but wiser?"

"Absolutely not."

I looked back and forth during this exchange, trying to picture the two of them together, and failing. They giggled to some private joke while I watched Min carefully load up a plate and return. She put it on the blanket and we all grabbed pieces of cheese, a cherry, half a brownie.

Theo held one up. "Are these . . .?"

"I don't think so," said Min, smiling. "But why don't we find out?"

He stared at her, wide-eyed, then took a bite of brownie and handed her the rest, which she stuffed into her mouth. Much to my surprise my mother grabbed one too, bit into it

270

and held out the other half to me which I, with a small zing of apprehension about doing drugs with my mother, placed on my tongue, then chewed with gusto. It was delicious, soft and thickly chocolate. Joyce picked one up, broke it in half and fed a piece to Moony. A look of fear flickered in his eyes for a second, but he joined in.

"Is Martin coming down?" I said, as we all tried to be casual about the novelty of getting high together. Meanwhile down on the beach it was clear we were the only people not already there.

"Martin is, uh, sitting for a bit," said Min. She glanced at Theo. "Then he'll be here, he said to say."

"Meditating. He's been at it all day, practically," said Theo. "Apparently something's happened." He gave me what I took to be a conspiratorial look, a lifting of one eyebrow while nodding slightly. What was it supposed to mean, I wondered. Just then another gust of breeze wafted through our little group, carrying a moment's chill with the scent of yesterday's rain. Again I looked to the southern sky, and there the leading points of wispy mare's tails were just appearing over the tree line. Rain coming, which was too bad, but I knew from that formation we had hours yet. I made a mental note to get us back home in the boat before it began. The moon would be only half full later, so not much light. When Min, my mother and Joyce all started talking about Paris and the abundance of beautiful woven fabric from Morocco, like the blanket we were sitting on, I took the opportunity to question Theo.

"What's going on?" I asked Theo in a low voice.

"Not sure exactly, but I think she's around." He used his fingers to make quotes around the last word.

"What." I glanced at the others. "Freya?"

"Yes." Obviously.

271

"Did he put up the Calder?" It sounded impossible.

"No, no. Nothing like that." Theo sighed, motioned with a finger that we should take a stroll. We got up, barely noticed by the others except for Moony, who watched us go, curious. We walked several feet away to watch the current beginning to surge through the narrows. High tide was coming in fast. The swimmers had left cigarette butts stuck in the sand along the edge. Rushing water swirled through them and they fell apart, the filters floating away before I could catch them.

"I'm not sure, but it sounds as if she might have, uh, gotten through." Theo said the words, wanting to confide in me but not sounding convinced. When he turned to me he looked like he'd tasted something sour. His lips contracted, and he swallowed hard. I touched his arm to calm him, old hand that I was at paranormal events. "Otherwise, he seems fine. Same as ever, only more excited. Maybe a little *too* excited," he added.

"Should I go up there, do you think?" I didn't want to, especially having maybe just eaten a dope brownie, but Theo seemed distressed beyond what he was saying. I knew he didn't take Martin's quest seriously, but he was clearly concerned for his friend.

"I was hoping you would. Min is fed up with him. He spent yesterday traipsing back and forth in the rain from the house to the site, where he buried that skull in this hole he dug. Where the plinth for the Calder will go."

"I saw it."

"OK, so you know?"

"Yeah, he told me about his plan –the mingling of the bones."

"Exactly. Now, I don't know what I think about it but it's none of my business, so generally I stay silent." Theo rubbed his eyes, then looked up behind us, to the woods where the hole was. "Because of all that rain yesterday the site is a big mud pile. Martin went up there this morning early and found footprints in it. He says he knows beyond a doubt they're Freya's."

"What?"

"Uh huh."

"How does he know they're hers?"

"Oh, something about her missing the tip of the middle toe on her left foot." He shrugged and gave me an apologetic look.

I stifled a laugh, trying holding my face still. I didn't fool Theo, though. He smiled at me.

"I know," he said. "But Martin came back into the house this morning whooping with joy. He woke us up, then had Min cook hardboiled eggs, make sandwiches. She put them and half a dozen apples, cheese and some other food in a picnic basket while Martin took the blanket off his bed and got a sleeping bag out of the closet. He ran that stuff up to the site and came back for a pad of paper and I don't know what else. The pad's the one we use for our fourth dimension figuring. I tried to engage him, talk about what he'd seen, but he looked at me as if he didn't know me anymore. He was in a frenzy, intent on moving himself up the hill for some kind of stakeout. He was running around the house stuffing things in a paper bag. He said he was going up there to sit and that he'd be down eventually, then ran off."

"Wow."

"Yeah."

Another swipe of wind shot through our legs and ran up the beach. I heard some female squeals as it slapped into the dancers, spraying sand. The water coursing through the narrows reached our feet, and we stepped backwards onto the smooth rocks lining the beach. The boats tied together around the dock began to sway and knock against each other. I checked mine, to see if the prop on the new engine was still out of the water, but not close enough to scratch another boat. I felt a momentary surge of love for its bright red newness.

"All right, I'll go up," I said. "But I don't want to disturb him. Maybe I'll just take a peek and if he's just sitting there calmly, I'll come back."

"OK." I could tell Theo wanted me to do more, but he nodded and headed back to the blanket.

I walked along the shore to where a path cut up to the top of the island. I knew it led to a small clearing where Ray and Sal had constructed a platform which would eventually hold the batteries for a solar power station they hoped would run the island. A friend of theirs, a graduate student from MIT called Chuck, was working to design it. I'd met him once or twice, a huge man with wooly hair and beard who spoke constantly, a steady stream of technical information, raunchy jokes, political diatribe and recipes for wild-caught meat, usually squirrels. The station had started out as a grill, using an early camping device called a Sundiner, a big parabolic mirror made of fold-out mylar panels that heated up a surface for cooking hot dogs. The thing had grown by several mirrors and now housed a tangle of wire, car batteries and a pile of other stuff for the invention process. I reached it quickly and ran past along the path, crossed through the trees to other side of the island where Martin's hole was, then slowed down to tiptoe, carefully picking my way though the undergrowth. I heard Martin before I saw him, and ducked quickly behind a patch of milkweed. There he sat, back to me, on the edge of the hole with his legs dangling into it, looking out to sea and singing to himself. I couldn't hear the words, but the melody was sweet, a wistful lament which he sang twice in a high, tender voice, then stopped. He swung around, looked right at the spot where I crouched, blinked, then turned back. He watched the sky for a long time, sniffing the air as he scanned the coastline, humming pieces of the song again. Out beyond the barrier beach the surf was minimal, the usual long swells running at an angle to the shore and flattening along their length as they reached the sand. The wispy clouds I'd seen earlier had moved to hover over them, slender, feathery ribbons against the blue. I got comfortable and watched for a bit longer. Martin seemed all right to me, not jazzed-up or behaving in any crazy way, but waiting as I'd seen him do in the woods under the elm: patient, alert, calmly dedicated. I turned and began to make my way back to the beach, crawling on all fours through the grass, ferns and bushes. I noticed how fragrant the grass was in late summer, dry as it was and top-heavy with seed, and I stopped to savor its delicate scent. Or was it the fern I smelled? I went from leaf to leaf, inhaling, testing, crawling through the sandy-bottomed woods for ten yards or so, until I realized I was experiencing the heightened-sensory effect of marijuana and began to giggle at my behavior. I thought of John Sipson on the day I spotted him clamming with Moony. My approach had been similar, advancing toward them while crouched behind the marsh grass, hoping to catch him unawares. Perhaps he was watching me now, I thought, and looked around, but saw only fluttering leaves accompanied by the swishing sound of cedar branches in the wind, and the occasional cricket chirp. I stood up and walked the rest of the way to the shore to join the others, thoroughly enjoying my mild high, the beautiful day and the peace of mind about Martin which I would be happy to convey to Theo and Min.

An hour later he showed up on the beach, just as the sun was beginning to set. Its low light made everything glow with a purplish tint, just the edges of things lit up pink. Martin had changed into white linen pants and a light blue shirt which, against his deeply tanned skin, looked illuminated from within. His hair and teeth blazed extra white in the unusual light, and he smiled at everyone as he made his way around. My mother sat up straight, watching. We had long since finished off the thermos of sangria Joyce brought and I very much wanted more, but I was trying to be careful not to drink too much so I could ferry my mother safely home. I figured we had another hour or so to go before darkness and the wind, which had picked up quite a bit, would make it unsafe for me to cross the mile of water to Barley Neck. Since I got back from checking on Martin, Joyce had been dancing with Sylvie and Ray among a large group of people and Moony was over at the food table, sampling, munching, and yakking with anyone doing the same. Min, Theo and my mother were in deep conversation about the good old days in P'town. I was lost in a memory of being in a play back in school. I'd been bored with my role, which was minor and involved standing around a lot, waiting for my cue to get off stage. When Martin came strolling through the crowd I noticed how everything changed, as if an unspoken stage direction was suddenly put into motion and all the guests were the actors. I began to write in my head:

'A party: Evening on a sliver of beach, sun setting, infusing the action with the color of fairytale magic; pink, purple, sparkly. Downstage left, a dock with a dozen dinghies tied; on the right, a river flows past. Between them

276

a long cloth-covered table, heaped with the leavings of a feast. The table's legs are inches away from the high tide line. Behind the table, center stage, a crowd of hippies undulate to the music of James Brown singing, *Say It Loud, I'm Black and I'm Proud.* No black people are on the beach. Presently MARTIN enters from upstage, crosses to downstage center.

MARTIN: Where are you, Sylvie?

SYLVIE (detaches herself from the throng of dancers) I'm here! Where have you been? Come dance with us.

MARTIN: No, thank you. I wanted to know if you're pleased with your party. Are you having a good time?

SYLVIE: Of course, can't you see? She twirls around in front of him, then wraps her arms around his waist. She stretches up to kiss him, but MARTIN ducks away, holds her at arms length. SYLVIE does a backwards James Brown camel walk into the crowd of dancers and disappears. MARTIN pours himself a glass of wine from a bottle on the table and gazes offstage.'

I shook my head, releasing this inanity into the void, and looked around for something to eat. I was starving. I hadn't moved from the blanket since going up the hill to visit Martin, and to my knowledge my mother hadn't left it at all.

"C'mon, Mom," I said, tugging at her pantleg. "Let's get something more to eat before it's all gone."

She looked at me, slightly annoyed at having been interrupted, but went along.

"All right," she said. "I am hungry." We got up and skirted the dancers flinging their arms out and kicking up sand. When we arrived at the table Martin's face lit up with surprise.

"Oh, perfect. You're here," he said more to my mother than me, but leaned over to kiss my cheek.

"Mr. Meyer," My mother said rather formally, as she shook his hand. "Thank you for the party, and thank you for your interest in my daughter's artwork. It's impressive, isn't it?"

"Indeed." They sounded like they were in my play. They stood there being formal and uncomfortable, talking about Paris weather and remarking about the cheap, grapey wine as if it were a vintage Bordeaux. I had to say something to make it stop.

"I told Mom about seeing the Motherwell, my confusion over the water stain," I said, chuckling to Martin. "Remember?"

"Yes. It was the first time we met, wasn't it?" It hadn't been, but no matter.

"Elli loved that little postcard when she was just a kid," said my mother. "She called it 'Two Apartments Talking.' It's such a coincidence that the real thing is here in Pleasant Bay, of all places. A place very dear to my heart." She looked across the water to Barley Neck.

"Would you like to see it?" Martin gestured toward the path up the hill. My mother immediately put down her glass.

"Lead the way," she said, smiling.

We passed Ray and Sal assembling rocks into a circle around a small fire in the sand. Twisted pine branches were heaped nearby. As the wind picked up, a chill scudded over the sand. The heat would be good later, for when things calmed down. If anything the music was louder, the dancing more frenetic. The crowd appeared to have an insatiable, expansive, slightly out-of-control energy. Several people had stripped down to their underwear and

278

were piggy-backing on each other, spinning and falling, landing underfoot, continuing to dance on their backs. Sylvie was a mad conductor, yelling for the music to be louder, instigating chain dances then abandoning them to gyrate against someone new.

I watched her for a while, happy for her gratified, joyful mood. She would do well at the radio station, and thrive in that world, I thought. She shimmied sideways past Ray, giving him a little ass-pat as she went, and there behind Ray I saw, sitting in archetypal cross-legged comfort and sinking his teeth into an ear of corn was someone who looked an awful lot like John Sipson. I moved to one side for a better view. Sure enough, it was him. He chewed distractedly, mesmerized by the gyrations of Sandy and the others. Drips of butter glistened on his chest. But, I reasoned, if that were so it couldn't be him because the butter, and for that matter the corn, were touching his ghost-body which was not a solid thing. Also, how could the buttered corn be in one century and he in another? I took a step toward him. He looked up and smiled, waved the finished cob at me, then tossed it on the fire. Ray sidled around the firepit, blocking my view. By the time I got close enough John Sipson was gone but there, hissing in the fire, was the corncob. I stood watching the otherworldly teeth marks shrivel and darken, then poked it with the toe of my sandal. It disappeared as well.

"Elli, get your foot out of the fire," Ray said, elbowing me away.

I was still trying to work out the melted butter/chest thing as I sped up the hill after Martin and my mother, who had paused under the willow to look at the wall of windows.

"Oh, my goodness," said my mother. "It's dazzling." And in that perfect light it was. We three stood, our reflections slightly askew, assembled from broken pieces and tessellated into the blue background. As I had when I first encountered the effect, my mother clowned a bit, toying with the separation of limbs and head, or standing side-to, shrinking her width to nothing. I watched, gratified to see the childlike behavior.

"Please, come in," said Martin, waiting at the door.

Martin busied himself in the kitchen finding glasses and pulling the cork from a bottle of port, then he settled himself on one of the stools at the counter while I showed my mother around like a museum guide. She was hugely impressed by the Motherwell, stunned into silence as she stood mesmerized by its size, its light-swallowing black shapes. She looked over at Martin and slowly shook her head, bowled over by the fact of the painting's presence in such an unusual place. He made a small humming sound of affinity, and held out a glass.

"Port?"

"Thank you," she said, still looking around. We sat in the white chairs while Martin dug out some snacks. "Do you think the party is getting out of hand?" he said, gazing into the depths of the fridge.

"It's Sylvie's night," I said. "I guess it should be a blowout."

"Mm," he concurred, distracted. "I suppose so."

He came over and set down a plate with some dates and cut-up figs, then went over to the cabinet where he kept his photo collection, fished through and selected one. I was sure he was going to show my mother his picture of 'A Swim at Pochet'.

"Have you ever seen this?" When he handed it to her she held it about two feet away from her face to focus. She was more far-sighted than I remembered.

"Is it Hofmann?" She squinted, peering closer. "Yes. I see. It's the barn on Miller Hill, isn't it?" She turned to me, excited. "It's the art school I attended in Provincetown. Look." She held the picture in front of me. Mounted on cardboard, the black-and-white showed a group of about twenty young people crowded around an older man who was gesticulating, explaining something to them.

Martin hovered over her and pointed to a figure in the photo, a girl leaning with crossed arms on a rough wooden loft railing, looking down on the scene. She had dark bangs like my mother's. "Could that be you, Ria?"

My mother examined the image again. "It may very well be," she said. "Wow. Where did you find this?"

"Philadelphia Library. In a magazine. I'm ashamed to say I ripped it out, because they were closing." Martin picked up a fig, examined it, then popped it in his mouth. "I was looking at reproductions of Hofmann's paintings and ran across it. I just had to have it, I wasn't sure why at the time. Because of Hofmann, I supposed. Years later, after I bought your painting in Paris, I read that you'd been there and I've always wondered if this was another –ah – synchronistic event in my life." Martin winked at me, shielded his mouth with his hand and stage-whispered a singsongy "*Quan-tum entangle-ment, ta-da.*" My mother didn't react. She was absorbed in the image, lost in the past, concentrating on recognizing some of the other students without the help of glasses.

I smiled, humoring him. I wasn't about to get into that discussion again. I was simply glad that he seemed calm and coherent given what Theo had told me.

"I'm flattered that you like my work so much," said my mother, handing back the photo. "It really was exciting to be part of that scene. I was so very young, barely understanding what Mr. Hofmann was talking about, you know? Then I met Elli's father, who encouraged me. He really got what I was trying to do, and supported me – literally, as it turned out– in my career. He was so . . ."

I watched, mortified, as a tear dropped from her eye to the collar of her blouse, darkening its gray silk to black. Martin got up and headed toward the kitchen for a tissue as I put my arm around her shoulders. I felt like weeping myself, not sure whether from embarrassment or the mention of my father. "So sorry," my mother mumbled, making her side-of-thumb wiping gesture.

"Here you go, dear," said Martin, as he crossed the room with a box of kleenex.

"The thing is," my mother said as she got up to meet him. "About that painting you bought in Paris, '*A Swim at Pochet.*' Remember?"

"Oh yes. Of course I do," said Martin, glancing at me. "That painting . . ."

"Don't tell me." My mother interrupted him. She held up one hand in front of his face while the other snatched a tissue from the box. She took a long time blowing her nose into it, longer than needed to clear any cry-begotten clog. She was breathing into that tissue, in and out, holding it in place as if it were a life-giving piece of Scuba gear, while Martin and I waited. Finally, she dropped the hand holding back his words and gestured at the chairs. "Let's sit down. I have something to tell you about that painting."

Martin tilted his head like a dog does when it hears an unfamiliar sound, and sank into the chair my mother had just vacated, while I recrossed my legs and leaned forward, my heartbeat ratcheting up a notch.

She began. "The painting. I told you about that day, didn't I, Elli? When you phoned me." I nodded and looked at my fingertip, the finger I'd touched the green paint with after Martin's studio visit. After he re-painted the damn thing with his gestures.

I said to Martin, "She told me she was watching my father swimming freely in the water, while she was stuck at home with the baby –me."

"Yes, that's right," my mother went on. "But what I didn't tell you was that he wasn't alone. I walked over to the bluff with you to calm you down so you'd fall asleep. I was pacing back and forth, humming. And then I saw them." She stopped talking and began her tissue-breathing again.

"Who?" said Martin. I think he knew by then.

"He was with Freya," she said. "It was dead-low tide, and they were snuggled into the marsh grass, naked, kissing. That, and much more. I watched them until the baby fell asleep, then I went into the studio and just flailed away." She started to cry again, but calmly, without embarrassment. "It should have been called '*A Fuck at Pochet*.'" She stared at Martin, trying to read his face for reaction. I sat there with my mouth hanging open, struggling to comprehend the fact of their decades-old former connection.

"I had no idea," Martin said quietly. "She never . . ."

"She spent quite a bit of time here back then. Her family had a summer cottage, right? So, I'd see her at parties. She was so beautiful, everyone had a crush on her, and she liked to flirt. I didn't get to know her, but apparently my husband did. This was before you were married, I take it?"

"Yes. We met in 1950." Martin looked down at his hands. His fingers played *here is the church, here is the steeple* in his lap.

My mother added, "I don't know if it lasted, and then we were gone a year or two later." She giggled, a twitter with a bit of hysteria in it. "Theo was the one who told me just the other day, when we were reminiscing about old times, that she'd been your wife. I'm sorry you lost her, I truly am, but now, to hear that you, of all people, bought that piece. It's an extraordinary coincidence, don't you think?"

Martin nodded slowly. "Yes, and no." He glanced at me again, raising his eyebrows.

My mother went on. "There's something ironic in it, too. *'A Swim at Pochet'* is the work that launched my career in Paris. But how I hated that painting!" She chuckled, blew her nose again. "Don't you think it's all kind of funny?"

No one said anything for a minute until I piped up. "I'm not sure about 'funny', Mom. Sounds quite sad to me, actually," I said stiffly. I was not enjoying the mental picture of my father, naked, writhing around in the grass out there in the bay, the same grass I'd waded through collecting cherrystones, or watching horseshoe crabs, or trying to hide from the ghost of John Sipson. I took my mother's hand and she squeezed it.

"I don't know why I felt I had to tell that story. I suppose it would have been better if I'd kept it to myself." She looked from me to Martin and back. "Sorry," she added. We never should have eaten those brownies, I thought.

"It's part of the painting's history," said Martin. "Its origin. I'm glad to know it." He grabbed the bottle. "Now, who would like a little more?"

I wanted to leave immediately, to go back to the cottage and curl up in my bed and fall asleep so I would not have to think about my father, whom I loathed at that moment. It was time to head home if we were going to take the boat. I turned to my mother to say so, and I remember feeling a little annoyed when she held out her glass for a refill. Martin was reaching across the table with the bottle when suddenly he stopped and said, "Oh my god. She's there." He stared out the glass wall, a look of shock frozen on his face. Then he got up, crossed swiftly to the door, whipped it open and left. I saw him run full-tilt across the lawn and disappear into a dark gap in the trees. The dropped bottle tumbled, trickling an arc of its dark red contents across the yellow grass .

"Oh no. I'm so sorry." My mother said again. "Did I –?" She looked quizzically up at me.

"No, don't worry," I said. "I think Martin saw someone he knows."

She pulled another tissue from the box and wiped her face, then looked at the photo again before putting it aside. "Should we wait, or go back?"

"We might as well go down to the beach," I said. I was sure Martin would be gone for a long time even if it was only a willow frond he'd seen billowing loose, or the smoldering blaze of his Freya-longing fanned to new heat by my mother. I didn't think we'd see Martin again but we gave it another half hour just to be polite, and stood watching out the glass wall for his return. We did not talk about my father and Freya. My mother looked sideways at me a couple of times, gauging my level of upset-ness, but I kept my face still, my eyes on the trees, even though I wanted to run screaming away from her, that place, everything and everyone. I thought of myself sitting on the bluff in my father's threadbare suit and moldy hat, and snorted derisively. *Putain de batard!*

The sky above the tree line was a strange shade of pink —not a sunset tone, but one tinged with a weird gray-green, we watched the treetops whipping and swaying toward the ocean, no longer in gentle evening gusts, but a steady, insistent rush.

My mother put her arm around my shoulder "Maybe we should get back home," my mother said, watching. "It'll be dark soon, anyhow."

We left Martin a note thanking him for the interlude and the wine, and left. As we walked downhill I realized that the music wasn't playing any longer, and at Ray and Sal's place there were no people sitting on the deck playing guitars and beating on overturned flower pots. Things were strangely silent, all party sounds gone; only the nervous twitter of a wren hopping along a low branch told us there was still life on the island. We stepped out of the woods onto the beach to find the dogs lined up there in the shelter of the trees, sitting quietly for a change and watching the party crowd, who stood together on the shore gazing at the sky. My mother and I looked up too. There, in a mile-long swath from south to north as far as I could see, was an immense cloud. Shaped like a rolled up carpet, it rotated backwards on itself, shooting off bands of pinkish-gray froth as it advanced steadily across the bay toward the ocean. The tube-shaped monster took up half the sky, and as it came closer we felt a sharp drop in temperature and saw, lurking behind it, dark gray fog and a wall of rain. Several people ran for cover under the trees while others shouted for everyone to stay out in the open. One man stood like Jesus with his arms out, hair spilling down his back and a look of bliss on his face, chanting "Come. I am ready." I saw Ray heaping sand onto the newly-built fire, and Sal zigzagging through the crowd after Bobby, who squawked and ran flapping in crazy circles underfoot. Boats seesawed in the chop, banging against each other at the dock and straining at lines. I saw Theo trying to make order of them, coiling ropes tighter, pulling dinghies closer together. The long black cloud was enormous, nearly as wide as the island and roiling, slowly spinning in reverse toward the outer beach, where there were several hunting shacks and camps, all of them occupied for the holiday weekend, boats pulled up on the shore with kids' rafts floating around in between.

"Everyone, get in the house!" Ray ran around commanding. He held the case with the turntable to his chest. Rollo and Roxie trailed him, jumping up and pawing him anxiously. People stood in twos and threes under blankets, still dry, watching the phenomenon as it rose overhead, bringing the rain which we could now hear drumming on the roofs of cars parked on the other side of the narrows. The tide was at its highest, not running any longer, but buffeting the shore, creating wide rivers in the packed sand. "C'mon! It's not safe out here, goddammit! Follow me!" Ray ran down to the shore and like a sheepdog herded the stoned, stupefied party guests over to the path to his house as we felt the first drops of rain and the sky turned a sickly green, then dark gray and the wind whipped sand into everyone's eyes.

Suddenly Moony was there in front of us, panting and grabbing my mother by the arm. "You and Elli go up to one of the houses. This might be bad. I've never seen anything like it." He shoved at me to get going, snapping me out of my shock. I yanked my mother's hand and we ran back up the hill. The rain was now almost directly overhead and coming down at an angle. The noise of water hitting leaves was deafening –a crackling, slapping din punctuated by the muffled pop of breaking branches. The wind pushed steadily at our backs and made bushes whip back and forth, spraying water. We came to a stop behind a group of blanket-covered people waiting to get through the door of Ray and Sal's place. They were shoving and screaming, climbing over the railing. Hanging on its lower hinge, the screen door had been trampled and shoved aside but was still blocking the entrance. My mother and I looked on in disbelief as the Jesus guy grabbed it, twisted the frame into a pile of sticks, and heaved it off the deck. Then he slammed into the crowd and pushed through.

"C'mon, you two!" Min ran by, beckoning us. "We'll go to Martin's." She ran ahead up the hill and we followed, climbing over downed branches and sloshing through the wet leaves and beaten-down undergrowth. In the clearing the willow tree branches swung wildly, slinging jets of water. I could just barely make out the contours of the huge, serpentine cloud, which had already passed to the other side of the island and was headed, still revolving, toward the outer beach. Min fought to keep the door open against the lashing torrent and we bustled through, stumbling against each other to a halt inside.

"Oh my god!" my mother cried. "What the hell!"

"Take off your things." Min was already taking charge. "I'll bring some towels." She ducked around us and headed for the bathroom while my mother and I stood dripping, wringing our shirt tails and kicking off mud-encrusted shoes. In a few minutes we were sitting in the big white chairs, my mother in a plush blue bathrobe and I wrapped up in the spread from the guest room. Min took an elaborate candelabra off a shelf above the desk, lit it, and set it down on the coffee table, then walked around with a flashlight, checking the rest of the house. She came down from upstairs, a big smile on her face and a finger to her lips.

"Thank goodness," she whispered. "He's up there sound asleep, though I don't know how he could possibly manage in this." Yet even as she said it, the rain seemed to be letting up a little, the roar of it less intense.

Theo arrived in a gush of wet. Right away he asked, "Is Martin here?"

Min pointed at the ceiling. "Asleep, believe it or not," she said, still whispering. She went and got more towels and pressed them into Theo's arms saying, "Can I make anyone a cup of tea?" We all thought that sounded wonderful, and I got up to help her make up a tray. The dish of figs and dates was still on the coffee table. My mother picked a date and bit it in half, staring off into the middle distance. When the tea was ready we sat around trying not to get the upholstery wet and listening to the storm as it wound down. Theo wondered if anyone had seen a cloud like that, ever. "If you could call it that," he added, picking up a fig. "At first I thought it was the effect of that brownie."

"Me too!" said Min and my mother in unison as I rolled my eyes inwardly.

Theo told us the story of what happened to the Bay, to Cape Cod, the coast of Connecticut and Rhode Island and further north during the great hurricane of '38. "It was the worst storm ever to hit this place, maybe the whole country, I'm not sure. Back then we didn't have the warning systems we have now. We watched the sky and saw how animals behaved, and usually it was enough to tell us something was coming, but this storm caught everyone by surprise. It happened right around this time of year, too."

"The wind that shook the world," said Ria. "Isn't that what they called it?"

"Yup. Fishermen in Narraganset Bay said when they first saw it, they thought it was a fog bank, but it turned out to be a wall of water," Theo glanced outside, where the rain on the roof had gone from a steady battering to intermittent lashings of spray. "Here in the bay we lost almost every boat and many, many trees, but it was much worse inland. I read somewhere that for the following nine years, New England paper mills used the downed wood exclusively."

He went on to tell us about the hundreds of lives lost, the thousands of buildings destroyed, houses washed right off their foundations, uprooted orchards, flooded graveyards and other horrors. Thankfully, his account was interrupted by a knock on the door, and Min went to open. The candles guttered in the sudden breeze, spattering wax droplets on the table and threatening to go out. My mother and I cupped our hands around the flames as Moony stepped inside, shy and uncomfortable and soaking wet. He insisted on staying by the door even though Min invited him to join us.

"I only came up to say that things seem calm enough out there to leave and Joyce is dying to go, so I thought we'd row across to the car, see if we can get out."

My mother looked at me and said, "What do you think? Let's get a ride home. We can leave the boat, come back for it in the morning, OK?"

"Sure." I was worried about my new outboard, but more than ready to go home and change into dry clothes.

"Is everything all right down at Ray's?" Min asked.

"Uh, slightly out of control, but fine. Crowded."

"Let's go, then," I said. I had just turned to thank Min when there was a muffled crash from above, the tinkle of broken glass. We all froze for a second, then Min dashed up the stairs. We heard running footfalls, a pause, then "Oh no!" She appeared at the top of the steps.

"It was just the glass door, but . . . oh god. Martin's not here. It was a blanket. I thought . . ."

"What?" I started up the steps. "What do you mean?" Martin's bedroom was spare and pristine, except for the swinging door to the balcony, the wet floor beneath it strewn with glass from two broken panes. I looked at his bed. There, the black mohair blanket had been tousled, twisted up with a pillow or something, and pushed into a lump that did indeed resemble a sleeping form. I went over and poked it, just to be sure Martin wasn't underneath. "Shit. This means –"

"This means he's out there still," said Min, her chin quivering.

Theo and Moony wanted me to stay behind but I pointed out that I was the only one of us who had been to the site, even though Theo said he knew all the islands well and Moony said a girl shouldn't be out in a storm. I just grabbed Min's flashlight and barged ahead of them across the lawn and into the woods.

We shouted for Martin along the way as we clambered over downed limbs and pushed through the scrubby underbrush. The path was difficult to locate in the dark but we headed in the general direction, around the garden at the center of the island, which was flooded and cut through with deep channels where the deluge had rushed downhill. The track along the narrows was closer to the edge now, because a chunk of the bluff had given way near the path leading up to Chuck's solar project. We stepped carefully and kept going, angling back across to the other side of the island, holding branches aside for each other and calling out Martin's name. Theo had a flashlight run by a dynamo which he squeezed periodically. It made a wheezy, keening noise that added to the anxiety of our mission. The rain had all but stopped by then and I looked up. The sky was almost clear, just a few trailing threads of the behemoth cloud that had brought such damage. A few stars glowed weakly. I couldn't spot the moon. I caught up with Theo and Moony, who were waiting for me at the headland.

"Which way?" said Theo. I pointed. I could see the gap in the tree line where Ray and Sal had cleared the pines, and we made our way over to it. I was shouting for Martin and shoving through the bushes when suddenly Moony grabbed me from behind, pulling me toward him. I'd almost stepped into a newly created cleft in the floor of the woods, a long gash which, when we played our flashlights along it, led to what had been Martin's sculpture site.

The storm had dumped such a volume of water on the cleared ground that it had created a mini landslide, which left behind a wide, sandy slope studded with rocks and roots and ended in a pile of mud at the bottom. The tide had receded somewhat, and little waves were already beginning the process of turning the heap of collapsed soil into a new beach. Theo jumped down onto the slope, plunging knee-deep into the sandy soil, and stumbled out of sight.

"Theo!" I yelled. "Are you all right?" I couldn't see his flashlight any longer. I slid down the sand on my ass until I found some footing, then stood up and shone my light around until I located him, lying in a heap at the bottom, whacking his flashlight against his thigh to get it going again. "Let me have yours," he called up to me. "I think I saw something." I made my way to where he was struggling to sit up. Moony followed me, angling down in little hops. Theo took my light and we watched as he found what he'd glimpsed on the way down. I gasped when I saw what it was.

There, lying on one side, half-buried in the slope, lined and checked with age but with hair still yellow in spots, with one shoulder and breast exposed, was an old wooden ship's figurehead. Moony plodded over to it, heaving himself forward on his knees through the mud. He ran his hand over the face.

"Hey! This must be–" he started to say, then looked at me, widening his eyes pointedly, beckoning me with his head. I slogged over to him.

"God, Moony. It's Tom Sipson's," I whispered. "The one he –" Moony stopped me with a sharp nudge. It would have been hard to explain to Theo how I knew that. I cleared my throat instead and said, "Wow, this must have been buried for ages."

Theo arrived beside us. "What the hell?" He wiped dirt from the figurehead's shoulder and along the arm, which disappeared into the mud behind her back. He knocked on it, a dull thump. "Wonder what ship it came from. It's got to be at least a hundred years old."

Moony and I looked knowingly at each other. "Probably more," he said. Then he saw something over my shoulder and pointed his light at it. "Over there," he said, already scrabbling toward it.

Theo aimed his flashlight. "Oh no," he whispered.

Twenty feet away, partway up the slope, Martin lay on his back with his legs buried in the sand, arms extended overhead as though he were hanging out of the newly made hill. We groped our way over to him. The mud made a sucking sound every time I pulled out a leg to move forward and made going agonizingly slow. As we neared I saw that his head lay against a little plowed-up mound as comfortably as if he'd had it fluffed for a nap. Trapped by the weight of the sand, his shirt was stretched tight over his chest and gathered in packed folds, straining the buttons. I sat next to him, put my hand on his shoulder, and started to cry in a panicky, stuttering whimper. He was clearly dead. In all that mess Martin's face was clean, washed completely by the rain. Wide-open eyes stared lifelessly. His mouth was half open, pulled into a smile by the inverted position, showing his upper teeth. With his hair fanned out like a radiant halo in the light he looked almost rapturous, happy to be resting peacefully and looking at the sky.

We sat for a few minutes, letting shock turn into reality and listening to little wavelets slush over the mud, pulling it away. Moony turned off his light and gazed out at the ocean, now almost calm after the ruckus. The last remnants of the monster cloud had passed over the barrier beach, unveiling a sea of stars, the moon rising from the treetops.

Theo looked over at the figurehead, then back at Martin. "I guess he finally found Freya," he mumbled.

Chapter Fifteen

It took a couple of weeks for the news to die down around Orleans. Sandy told me that it was almost unbearable for her to go to work at the The Foc'sle and listen to people talking about it, making up stories about the island's eccentric owner and his band of drugged-up hippies partying out in the middle of Pleasant Bay. Ray and Sal left the island that very night ahead of the police, who had somehow been alerted. The cops sorted out the hungover party guests and sent them home after they sat through questioning, but it was pretty clear that the cloud, which was the other big topic in the bar, had caused Martin's death and nothing else.

It didn't take long for my mother to convince me to fly home with her two days later. I was so shaken by the night's events I felt that every ounce of desire for independent living had evaporated and I just wanted to go home and sit in our kitchen eating chocolate bars with my sister. And more practically, since I had no intention of cashing Martin's check, I didn't have the means to stay on and pursue painting. So we packed up, and Moony drove us to Boston. I sat next my mother holding her hand and we fell asleep almost as soon as the plane took off.

When I got back to Paris I spent a lot of time in my room, mostly sitting on the bed staring out at a pharmacy sign down the street. Its neon cross glowed, blurry yet steadfast in the rain, and made me feel safe. Returning home I saw that I'd been changed, though it took some time before the shock wore off. Enlightened by what had happened to me, I began to understand life in a new way. After a few days I let my hand –which I was happy to find was still affected by its thrilling ability– draw the sign, a beacon of aid and recovery, over and over with a fountain pen I filled with green ink. My mother would look in on me periodically, but I think she knew I needed to process my experiences in the trancelike peace of picture-making. A week or two passed, my drawing pad filled, and eventually I ventured out into the rest of the apartment. My father's collection was still everywhere but now there were gaps in the familiar landscape of *objets* and very often I would find Christos, his partner, sitting in the middle of a nest of file folders, sorting through paper, searching for a certificate of authenticity or assembling the chain of provenance that would allow him to sell a piece of Anatolian pottery or Byzantine glass. He often asked me for help. "Just filing!" he'd wail. "I will pay you well." But it took me longer to accept my father's dalliance with Martin's wife than the death of Martin himself, and in my mind, for a few months anyway, my father's belongings were as tainted as he.

Sandy kept me updated all that fall via butterfly- and flower-decorated letters, her upbeat personality shining from every one. From them I learned that Ray was squirreled away in an apartment in Cambridge, cooking for Sylvie and writing a novel about living off the land on Sipson's. Sandy said she and Sal listened every morning to Sylvie's show on WBCN from our cottage on Barley Neck, where they stayed until they took off for Vermont. I haven't heard from her since then.

It's spring in Paris, and as beautiful as all the songs declare it to be. I take giant sniffs of fragrant city air, enough to last me for a while. I've sent some things on ahead, mostly art supplies and some records, but also a few boxes of my beloved Blédine cereal and other French staples. This time I have the right clothes, and a proper bathing suit. Also a wad of cash I earned from helping Christos sort out my father's labyrinthine bookkeeping, not to mention the sale of an ancient Greek Tetradrachm coin I found slotted into the stuffing of a doll he gave me when I was six. I have forgiven him, and gone back to loving him, though not in exactly the same way. I consider myself lucky to have had such a grand character for a father.

Yes, I'm going back to Barley Neck. Moony will collect me from the bus station in two days' time, and take me there. It won't be the same without the clan on Sipson's, but I'm sure I'll find some new friends. I will especially miss Martin, but you never know, I might see him again.

I would like to thank the handful of people who generously gave their time to paint a picture of Sipson's Island as it was in those days and in the years after. Although this is a work of fiction and Elli et al. are all imagined characters, a few tidbits of the real lives of these friends have been incorporated into the story, because some gems you just can't make up. Deborah Ullman sat with me in a coffeeshop for hours talking about her life in the sixties; Jay Harrington and Joanne Burns told me about life on the bay back then, and Mary Kay Hartley painted a vivid picture of the town's atmosphere at the time. I thank Irèn Handschuh for her description of growing up in Paris, thus revealing that she ate Blédine cereal for dinner. I am fortunate to have the excellent writer and teacher George Foy as a long-time friend, and even luckier to have had his thoughts, edits, and corrected French improve this book. And, always, I thank my wonderful husband Bob Dibble for his ongoing encouragement and assistance.

K N

CPSIA information can be obtained
at www.ICGtesting.com
Printed in the USA
BVHW031759300820
587657BV00001B/111